David's mark

By:
DeWayne Watts

To Marge:
Read Chapter 7 with the lights on

DeWayne Watts
May 30, 2014

This book is a work of fiction. Names, characters, places and incidents either are products of the author's imagination or are used fictitiously. Any resemblance to actual persons, places or events wither living or dead is purely at the extrapolation of the reader and is entirely coincidental.

Copyright 2014 GDW – **Tasana** ~ Tennessee USA

Acknowledgments:

First and foremost, to my wife; for her loving kindness toward me; as she listens to me while I read her my books.

Second to William Gordon; for taking the time to proof read the manuscript to find my many spelling errors and typos.

Shai, my eldest son for correcting my Spanish.

Forward

The story line itself is fictional; any similarity to persons living or dead is purely by the extrapolation of the reader. The story itself is told in first person as if the events did in fact take place as presented. Although I have relied on some events of my past to help with the story line, each event in some way has been fictionalized. When an event that is drawn upon is fictionalized the names of people have been changed or altered, as well as names of towns and places.

Introduction

How does one tell the story of one's life that is so unbelievable as to make it believable? I'm sure that throughout the world in the plethora of bookstores there are many books on lives of people, many perhaps full of exaggerations and hyperboles, written by those who just wanted to add some color to their lives even if it meant getting outside the lines. You almost can't blame them, because with just as many exaggerated stories that line the shelves, there are those that are fact, in fact so factual that they seem to be works of fiction.

That is where this story belongs. I lived my life and still have trouble believing what I lived, in fact without the evidence that I was able to gather I wondered if I had lived a dream. But alas, it was I that traveled the long dark and at times foreboding path called my life, and it was I that sat and watched the events of my life unfold. The story I'm about to share with you is but a small portion of my life and it is true, as to the best that my memory can recall. Events in my life that seemed to be beyond belief I was able to confirm with photos, police reports, and letters from the period, interviews, school records and hospital records. I spent about seven years collecting the information, the quest was started more to prove my memories as false but in fact just the opposite occurred, not only did I confirm my memories, but I learned more about myself than I wanted. As hard as it may be to believe my earliest memories are from about age two, and I do intend to include as many details as I can, I am after all sharing a portion my life for good reason.

So how do I prepare you, the reader? I cannot say. How do you prepare someone for a walk of truth down a path so dark and hateful that my Post Traumatic Stress (PTS) may become yours? Hollywood has made more movies than can ever be watched in a lifetime that fall into horror or thriller. But in those movies we watch for the most part they are all works of pure fiction; but when we watch a horror movie based on a true story the effect runs much deeper into our emotions, because we know it really happened to someone, somewhere; and that someone could have been the boy next door. This story may have that effect on you as I tell it. Your emotions may be drawn in, you will see this in your mind's eye as you drive down the road, you will try to make sense of these events as you hear them, it may, just may invade your dreams at night causing you to wake up screaming in a cold sweat.

However this affects you as I tell it keep in mind, it happened to one little boy living in America in the nineteen seventies. At times he may have been your next door neighbor, a fellow Cub Scout or Boy Scout. You may have sat next to him in church or at school. I say this because in my life we moved on average three times a month for the first nine years of my childhood. As I tell you this be thoughtful of where you were, when I was, you might just remember a little blond boy with hazel eyes now long dead.

It's not possible to tell the entire story of my life in the amount of time I have, however there was a friend that I had made that became the closest friend I ever had in my life, his name was David. This is the story of David's mark; a mark that he had to bare because of me. I will start with my birth in nineteen sixty seven, and take you through to the first day of January nineteen seventy seven. It's necessary to start at nineteen sixty seven, to better understand the person of my dad, and what shaped my thinking up to that point in time. It was the person of my dad that my life joined with David's and it was also the person of my dad that so many other people's lives crossed, and when crossing paths with my dad, the outcome was never good for anyone. So although it may appear to be a single life story with a lot of detailed information about me and my family, this background information is laying the groundwork to better understand the events that led up to my meeting and befriending David and what followed in December nineteen seventy six. Without this background understanding of myself and my dad, much of the events about David could not be understood. So keep in mind as I tell this, although I have to tell my story this is really the story of David's mark.

Chapter 1

Mom's Perfect Family

Her daddy had told her to be careful when kissing a boy; you could get pregnant that way, but if truth be told I suspect my mother did more than kiss on the dates she had as a teen. When she finally met the man that would become my dad I suppose like any young woman in the early nineteen sixties her mind had been filled with ideas of the perfect family from shows like "Leave it to Beaver", "Father Knows Best" and the many other perfect family shows that were still running on black and white television in the nineteen sixties. It's apparent from the photos of pre-nineteen seventy three that my mom endeavored to be the ideal mother from the late fifties early sixties and attempted to squeeze my dad into the role of Danny Thomas from "Make Room for Daddy" television show. But my dad would not and did not squeeze.

My parents married prior to nineteen sixty five, due to the date of my older sister's birth, but as to when, mom either can't remember or just does not want to. But that may be understandable; she was never without a man around her, and men were coming and going from the house all the time. It was in nineteen sixty five that my older sister Holly was born; she was a large baby and stayed a large girl and kept large into her adult life. She was not overweight; dad said she was just big boned.

At the time of her birth my dad was attempting to get his break into the sporting world, at just about any sport he could. He was a semi-pro golfer, dragged raced at a speedway and played minor league baseball. It was the last sport that he got his break in. As he told the story and my mom added to it, just prior to the knowing of my conception dad did get his break into the majors, he was set to play professional baseball; which was his lifelong dream.

He once told me on a hunting trip, that when he was in high school (a single room school, just high school years) he started playing baseball and he turned out to be a natural. As he told it, he carried the school team, and the school sponsored him with a scholarship and later a talent scout pulled him into the minors. His dream was becoming a reality, and when he got his break into the majors he started to live his dream. The way it was told to me, mom agreed to the majors since they only had one child at the time, but it did not take long before his dream became my nightmare. My mom got pregnant with her second child; me and she offered my dad an ultimatum.

My mom was not about to raise two children on her own while my dad hopped around the country most of the year batting at balls, so a line was drawn. Dad had to give up his offer to enter the majors and make the family work, or she would divorce him. It was not long after that mom filed for divorce, but there was a huge problem, it was nineteen sixty six.

In nineteen sixty six women did not divorce their husbands and my mother's mom, Grandma Williams, made sure my mother understood that. My mom however was going to stand her ground. But as days turned into weeks the tension between my parents and my mom's family grew worse. My mom does not remember exactly how long she and dad were 'divorced' but when weeks rolled over into months the family pressure on my mom grew worse, then something snapped in my dad, and this is where everyone differs on the details of the events.

Before I explain just what snapped in my dad I need to fill in an event that may help explain the snap. I was born before dad's return into the family. Although he was still a part of my mom's life and present at hospital for my birth, my mom and dad were still living apart. I don't know if dad spent any time at our house on Garrison Street after I was born, but my mom told me that at the time he was living elsewhere. It was during the early months of my life that my mom got an unexpected look into the darker side of my dad's life.

In her account of the event; my dad had showed up at the house one evening in a state of near panic. He pounded on the door to be let in and then sat down on the couch and started "crying like a little baby" to quote my mom. He explained to my mom that he had gotten into some trouble and did not know what to do. He had borrowed some money from a guy and was not able to pay it back, and now he found himself being chased by two men, wanting to get the money back for the guy. It was after dad's explanation that she and dad heard a pounding at the front door. After a few minutes the pounding stopped and then one of the two men kicked in the door; one grabbed her knocking her to the ground, while the other took hold of dad. After some discussion about the money, the one holding dad took off his belt and placed it around dad's neck, he would tighten it until dad was choking, then he loosened it to allow him to catch his breath. He did this several times, while my mom lay pinned, by the other guy, on the floor. The tightening and loosing of the belt caused dad to pass out a few times and he needed to be awakened so the guy could do it again. No matter how many times dad was choked he would never give the guy what he wanted, the money. At this point as my mom was telling me the account her voice got quiet and her tone changed and she said that it was then that the man holding her...she stopped her story and after a long pause she continued, after they were done, Doc agreed to what they wanted. She said that all this was happening with me and Holly in the other room.

My mom then went on to describe the men to me, one of the men, I believe I was to later know as Clifford; and she said the other man's name was John. That was the extent of her story. If this Clifford is the same that became dad's lifelong friend and the man she referred to as John is the same as the John Graves that became his friend, then this was dad's entry into a darker side of doing business.

Dad did not accept the baseball offer and when he approached mom for her to stop the proceedings of the divorce she refused. It was at this point that Grandma Williams forced my mom to stop the divorce and to add to the pressure dad sat in a bathtub, presumable at Grandma's, with a snub-nosed .38 in his mouth until my mom agreed to stop the divorce. The only detail everyone does not agree on is how the .38 was used, and where dad aimed it, he says he never put it into his mouth, but did not deny using one, and my mom and her family are firm that he held the gun in his mouth while sitting in a bathtub.

From combining the tales from both my mom and dad they got back together shortly after the event with the two men. In early photos of our house on Garrison Street in Walnut Oklahoma dad is holding me with Holly standing to his side, in another my mom replaces dad. We appeared to be a happy family at that time in those photos. My mom never gave me a reason but around this same time they studied with the Mormons, perhaps in an attempt to fix their marriage problems, or get out of the life dad had stepped into, whatever the reason the study did not last long and the Mormons fall out of the family photos, but in a figurative sense and in a literal sense, my mom took a lot of photos of our perfect family days.

Shortly after the encounter with the two men, John and Clifford, my mom became pregnant again with Beth, my little sister. Beth was to be labeled the makeup baby for the rest of her life, and she never lived down that moniker until her death. It was never known who really fathered Beth.

    Not long after Beth's birth my mom and dad went into debt for a newly built home in a brand new sub-division on what was then the outskirts of Walnut. To fill this brand new home; according to my dad; my mom went on a shopping spree at Sears, new kitchen appliances, television, console stereo, new furniture, dishes, she filled the whole house with new everything. My mom now had her perfect family, a working husband, new home, new furniture throughout, three kids and even the preverbal dog, or in the case of my dad, dogs. Dad was an avid hunter, and he had several hunting dogs, in fact aside from playing baseball or golf, my dad spent all his free time hunting. We also had our personal family dog Snowball, a huge dog that I remember was mostly white fur.

    I don't want to overlook a few memories that I have prior to our move to the new home in Walnut. For my second Christmas I got a pull dog that squeaked when you pulled it behind you. My dad's mom, Grandma Smith, had a house in Oaktown Oklahoma that each room was connected via a door. You could start from the living room, enter the dining room, cross through two bedrooms and end up back in the living room. This setup was perfect for a boy of two and a half to run the track while pulling a squeaking little dog toy. Of course it played on the nerves of my Grandma. I have many fond and cherished memories of my Grandma Smith, which I'll recount as the story unfolds.

    Prior to moving to the New House in Walnut in nineteen seventy, from my viewpoint there was nothing that stands out in my memories that is worthy of recall, my little life was perfect, but from nineteen seventy forward it seems as if a video recorder started in some recess of my mind and a vivid recording of my life started. So it is from September nineteen seventy forward that the memories of my life started to be recorded in a manner that haunts me to this day. I have been asked many times why I dwell on my past, but in truth I do not. I live in the here and now, but I also have around me what one could only call a holographic projector, this projector replays events in my life constantly. Without any prompting, or deliberate thought from me, I'm subjected to a replay of any given event of my life as if it were taking place in my present life. The past is in constant overlay with the present. In fact I spend a great deal of mental energy attempting to keep the projection off.

Life in Walnut was great, as far as I was concerned, mom was trying hard to create a "Leave it to Beaver" perfect family life for me and my sisters, she had decked my room out in a cowboy and Indian motif, my bedspread and sheets were blue and brown with all sorts of cowboy and Indian decals randomly spaced throughout, and I had the curtains to match.

As you entered our house you found yourself in the living room that was open to the dining room with a sliding glass door to the backyard. To the left was the garage door and off the dining room was the utility room. To the right of the dining room was a breakfast bar that opened up to the kitchen. The kitchen exited into the hallway, as well as the living room. The first room, as you walked down the hallway, to the right was my room, then my parents; on the left was the bathroom across from my room to be followed by my sister's room. A linen closet stood at the end of the hall. I have some very fond memories here, ones that when looked back upon are happy, although under the surface the darkness was waiting.

By the time we had settled in Walnut we had already moved several times and lived in several states. We started off on Garrison Street in Walnut Oklahoma; in nineteen sixty eight we went to Des Moines Iowa for Christmas but got snowed in so we 'lived' there with my aunt and her family for a short time. In nineteen sixty nine dad moved the entire family to Gallup New Mexico, the only thing I can remember about New Mexico is the pair of cowboy boots I got. They were my first pair of cowboy boots and I was walking tall, they were black with white etching and I never wanted to take them off. That was when I had just turned two, but for some reason those boots are forever impressed upon my memory.

In late nineteen sixty nine dad moved the family to Mesa Arizona. Of course at the time I had no idea that the evil in my dad had started to ooze out, but later mom told me some unsettling details about our move to Mesa. Dad had lost his job and was unable to support the family, he was already an alcoholic at this time, which explains the constant moving and looking for jobs. He moved the family to Mesa, to live with his sister and brother-in-law. I don't think we ever unpacked, in the photos I have of this time me and my sisters are standing in what was our family living area with the walls packed high with boxes, but it was what dad made my mom do that was unsettling. My Uncle James had a requirement for dad and my family to stay there, dad pimped out my mom to my Uncle James, she referred to it as 'James was always groping her'. She told my dad, but he never defended my mom, he felt she was doing her part to help the family.

From Mesa we moved back to Oaktown Oklahoma and stayed a bit with my Grandma Smith until dad could find a job and get us into a place, which was in Terlton, that was in early nineteen seventy, it was in September that we moved to Walnut. Dad was a welder, and a good one. However welding required a steady hand and if creating a seam for an oil pipe or gas line, a perfect weld. When dad drank he had neither a steady hand nor a perfect weld. So he was fired from many good jobs. In all this time however he kept close ties to Clifford, as to John I cannot say much about him yet, but I will later.

December twenty fifth nineteen seventy was an important Christmas; it was the first one we spent as a perfect family in the Walnut House. My life was looking like it was going to be a cookie cutter perfect life, school, girlfriends, plays, band, sports, college and on to the perfect American Dream, life was going to be great. For the next two years from my little view of the world, life was just getting sweeter and sweeter every day, my life was a box of chocolates.

My mom was teaching me to dance to Credence Clearwater Revival, I had a best friend named Little Nate, and I was even allowed to spend the night with him at his house, and he had the second most perfect mom and dad, Jan and Nate. In nineteen seventy two I was enrolled in Head Start and was even allowed to walk to school with my sister Holly. In May nineteen seventy two I had my fifth birthday and I got everything I had asked for. I had asked for a Coke-a-Cola truck big enough for me to ride on, which I did down the length of our driveway. I had also asked for a Ken doll, which I also got, nothing I asked for was ever refused. In the summer of nineteen seventy two our neighbor's daughter died of cancer, death was explained to me as if she was just asleep, I asked why she could not be woken up, and was told she was in heaven, of course hell was never brought up.

The Fullman's were not our next door neighbors, but lived a few houses down. Sharon was mom's friend and was also our god-mother, she had two girls and one son, Phillip, and it was her oldest daughter Kelly that had died. I spent a lot of time with Phillip, even though he was much older. He was someone that brings up fond rich memories, like an older brother whose only goal in life was to protect you. I was at their house during one violent spring storm when a tornado warning was announced on the radio. He and I were in the garage digging through old stored stuff when we heard the flash, and he being a curious boy lead me over to the garage door raised it a few inches and we lay on the concrete floor peering upward. Our intent was to watch the tornado as it passed over, but all we saw were some angry clouds.

During a different tornado warning I found myself at home with my mom and sisters. We had no storm shelter or basement, our home was built on a concrete slab so my mom took my sisters' twin beds and pushed them close together and then turned the mattresses sideways and we took shelter under a homemade fort. Again the storm passed over without ever removing a blade of grass, but this time my fear was heightened, a tornado warning at night, in the darkness is by far more fearful then one in the daylight.

Saturday mornings and cartoons were the life of a child, but you had to have a bowl of Apple Jacks with your dose of weekly cartoons. One Saturday morning dad and mom slept in and no Apple Jacks were forth coming, so Beth and I came up with a great idea, breakfast in bed. We started removing the food from the cupboards and the fridge and taking it into my room and placing it on my bed, we took all we could carry and thought we needed., Once we had all we needed we sat across from each other on each end of my bed and draped a sheet over us, we then commenced to preparing the perfect breakfast in bed. Without thought we started to randomly mix different items together, trying to figure out what was needed to be mixed with what. The clanging of the dishes woke up dad and mom and they came into my room and removed our tent, we were exposed.

After a few choice words which I don't remember because I was more worried about what was going to happen after the talking stopped, mom and dad took all items back into the kitchen. When that task was completed mom took Beth into the other room to spank her, and dad stayed with me in my room. He had me bend over his knees and pulled down my shorts and gave me a couple of swats on my bare bottom, I don't recall every crying, or it hurting. Beth and I never attempted to cook on our own again.

This is the only spanking I can remember my dad ever giving me. It was year's later dad told me that he was never involved in physically abusing or hitting me. Although later he would strike me and allow others to hurt me, he himself never spanked me or was personally involved in any abuse that was done to me.

It was also that same summer that Little Nate and I had a very deep and philosophical discussion about knee caps. We were both sitting on the top of one of my dad's dog houses with only a pair of shorts on, our knees bent. We moved our caps around and were in a deep discussion as to what they could possibly be. After what seemed like hours but was most likely minutes we came to the only logical conclusion we could, they were cooked eggs, we had solved a great mystery.

Leroy was a boy that lived directly across the street, and he was my personal nemesis. Leroy was not just mean he looked mean, jet black hair, huge ears that held your attention and a stocky build for a little boy, he took his meanness out on me. I suppose his parents just did not get him the toys that he wanted so in his hate he either had to have mine or destroy them, this was my first look at envy, I was to see the darkest side of it in just a few short years. Leroy was intent to just take what was mine at any cost, he wanted to ride my Coke truck even though he knew he was too heavy, but it was Ken that he wanted the most. One day while I had Ken behind the wheel of a large truck Leroy came over and plopped his mass across from me while I was playing in the driveway. He asked if he could play and I told him no, Leroy did not play with people he controlled them, so I learned to just say no to Leroy. But on this occasion I should have said yes, in less time than it takes to think it through he reach over to my truck, grabbed Ken and ripped his head off, then while laughing he ran back across the street to his house. I picked up Ken's dead lifeless body and his head and ran into the house. With tears in my eyes I handed him to mom hoping she could save him, but alas at that time it was hopeless, there was no way to reattach his head. Ken's final resting place was the trash can. Mom did however make a solemn promise to me, that for Christmas of nineteen seventy two she would get me a new Ken doll, and that was the upcoming Christmas. It was enough to dry my tears.

    I have many other great memories of our house in Walnut, even ones of other tornados, my first day of Head Start and asking mom which sock goes on which foot, summer days with friends and just spending time with my mom. But for the most of my time at the house in Walnut dad was seldom in the picture. He told me he was working most of the time; mom says he was out playing golf, baseball, hunting or out drinking. Later I learned it was mom who was correct; my dad was out hunting most of the time, and drunk while doing so. I spent many evenings looking out the window wondering when my dad was going to be home, so in the end to spend time with him I asked mom to wake me up at five in the morning to eat breakfast with him. Most mornings it was gravy, biscuits and bacon, but I got to spend time with my dad, always after he left for work I was carried off to bed. I suppose those early morning breakfast times are the only really good memories I have of my dad, he never played sports with me, tossed a ball or taught me to ride a bike. He never took time to show me how to swim or even let me get to know his bird dogs. I now know that my dad kept his world separate from mine, I was never allowed in his world and he would only cross into mine when a darkness fell.

September nineteen seventy two, just two years after it started, my perfect life in Walnut was over. Without any explanation the three of us kids were taken to my Grandma Smith's house in Oaktown and dropped off. We were told we would have to stay with my Grandma for a few days. My Uncle Mike, my dad's brother, lived with her but he would be with my mom and dad.

Over the course of several days dad, mom and Uncle Mike would arrive at Grandma's with a load of our stuff and unload it. One day dad and Uncle Mike showed up with our swing set, and stacked it in parts against the side of the house, where it died of rust years later, only one lone swing survived, it was nailed to the branch of a pecan tree out behind Grandma's house. My mom had bought me and my sisters that red and white swing set when we first moved to the house in Walnut. Me, my sisters and kids from all around the neighborhood spent countless hours playing on it, that swing set had become a symbol of my childhood, and now it was dead, eaten up with rust. I had no idea what was going on, but things in my life started to change fast like someone switching the channel on a television, never stopping long enough for me to get any idea of what was on.

Then as quickly as it started all the chaos ended, dad and mom arrived at Grandma's one day to take me home. Of course I thought I was going home to our house in Walnut, but we pulled into a strange driveway, and to a strange house that was not my home. Later I learned that we lost the house in Walnut and most of our stuff. According to my Dad, he had put the Walnut House in his name as well as the Sears account, and it was now all lost. Later dad explained that they, or he, had filed for bankruptcy because that 'mother of mine' never stopped spending and he was unable to pay the bills. Although no accounts were in my mom's name dad said that she bought so much stuff on credit that he was unable to pay even the house payment. I do remember seeing a big Sears truck in the yard at Walnut loading up our appliances, but I failed to make a connection until dad explained to me what I just said. However we did lose our house, appliances, and some other items, but we were still a family. I was hoping that moving here would allow our family to start all over, but we could not, the thread in the tapestry had been pulled.

The bankruptcy account, as I said, was dad's version of why we moved out of the house in Walnut, mom's account is less dramatic. When I relayed this account to my mom she told me that dad sold the Walnut house for no apparent reason and we bought the house on Kern Street. The bankruptcy part she could not confirm or deny. She did say that:

'Doc may have filed for bankruptcy'.

Because of this I include her version and dad's since I do not believe it possible to know the entire truth. It's remotely possible that we lost the house in Walnut due to dad's involvement with Clifford and John. From the time of their first appearance at the Garrison Street house, both of them started to become a fixture in our lives.

So we now have two versions of the same story, neither of which fits the exact facts. So what is the settlement? I suppose there is truth in both stories, a truth which will never be fully known. Perhaps mom did spend too much and dad sold the house as punishment, or because he felt at the rate of spending he would not be able to keep up with the payment? Mom says she was not a spender of the money, he controlled it all, and I find that to hold deep truth as well. My mom later told me that she was raised and accepted that the husband is always right and he is to never be questioned. So in her marriage to dad, she never contended with him, just agreed with all that he told her to do. So what's the real story to losing the house in Walnut and the move to Kern Street? I think the answer lies decaying in a grave just at the border of Oaktown and Smith Counties in Oklahoma and somewhere in the marshes off of Avenue J in Texas. In this case the truth will never be known.

Our new house was located on Kern Street in Oaktown Oklahoma, we called it the Kern Street house, it was in fact at this point that I started to give the houses we lived in names. The Kern Street house was an older home, and over the years the foundation had settled so there were cracks and downhill runs throughout the house. It was a house falling down around me, a fitting symbol of my own life.

The Kern Street house was laid out different than the Walnut house, of course you entered the living room and it too opened to the dining/kitchen area. The bathroom was off the kitchen on a raised platform, it was as if the kitchen and bathroom were an afterthought that someone added. From the living room to the right was a doorway, entering that doorway was a small hallway that had three doors within a few steps. Directly ahead became my room, to the right Holly and Beth and to the left became my parent's room. Turning to the left in the living room there was a door that led to the garage. This house was small and tight. It sat on a corner lot and had a huge yard, but the yard slopped and then pooled so when it rained it was mush and useless to play in. Dad fenced in a small part of the back area and built pens for his bird dogs, and the grass seldom got mowed. I had no friends to speak of; my life had become empty and lonely.

Mom enrolled me into kindergarten and Carl Sandburg was my teacher. I was in a play that year, I think as a bush or tree, it was not important what I was, I was in the play. Mom noted in my baby book that...

"You are on top of the world and are proud to go to school."

I was already aware that I had a thirst for learning, and I wanted to know everything about the world around me.

Although we had a different house I was sure it would become our home. And I think mom wanted to make our family work this time as well. I could tell this time she was going to give it her all. In photos from our time at the Walnut house she had bruises all over her arms where dad was already beating her, but he kept making promises that he would stop, and she believed him. His love for her was displayed by physical abuse, and that was what she was beginning to understand and believe that love was. Dad had never beaten mom in front of me up to this point, so as far as I knew I had perfect parents.

Dad's thinking on physical abuse was difficult for me to figure out. He would beat mom and leave marks and bruising, but he never hit me, save twice, and was almost afraid to leave a mark on me, until that night in December nineteen seventy six, then he of course changed. Even to this day I can come up with ideas that seem plausible, but in the context of the time they simply don't make any sense.

That winter was a harsh winter, times got lean and eating became a daily hunt for my mom. Mom had noted in a letter to her sister that we could not even afford to buy meat. Dad had started a new job and after his trial time was up he got a raise to about $3.25 an hour. In that same letter to my aunt my mom expressed that after his raise they could now buy a freezer and stock up on some meat and other canned foods. In early spring mom got the family involved with The Town and Country Christian Church. My mom was desperate to make the family work, even at the cost of being beat by dad, and she felt that somehow God had to be a part of that process.

My Ken doll was not under the tree for Christmas of nineteen seventy two, but my mom had prepared me for the loss; she had explained that she and dad were having trouble putting food on the table and they had to provide for us first. Of course I asked about Santa Clause bringing it, although I don't remember her answer, I do remember this being the first slip of my faith in the jolly old man. She did however reaffirm her promise that Ken would be under the tree next Christmas which would be December twenty fifth nineteen seventy three. She added an 'I swear' to her promise this time, and this time I put my entire faith, trust and hope in those words of my mother.

On the evening of March eighteenth nineteen seventy three which fell on a Saturday, my mom and dad had invited some friends over for supper and at the last minute they had canceled. My mom and dad sat at the table trying to figure out what to do about the meal before them when a knock came at the door. When mom opened the door they got their answer; there stood the preacher with his wife and kids from The Town and Country Christian Church. Dad and mom invited them in and dad put on his other personality, the one for persons outside of the family, as the adults sat around and talked Bible we kids played. My mom noted in a letter dated March twenty second to her sister,

"All the kids were yelling and we just acted like it was every day to us."

It was not long before the preacher said a prayer and we broke bread. In that letter to her sister my mom's fondness for the preacher is easily seen.

March was mild in the year of nineteen seventy three and it carried over into April and April turned into a beautiful May, we continued to go to The Town and Country Christian Church and dad continued to be home only sometimes. My life on Kern Street had become a shadow of my life in Walnut.

On May twenty forth nineteen seventh three I passed what should have been remembered as a milestone in any child's life, I graduated kindergarten. However this most significant event in a child's life was to be over shadowed by the storm building between my parents. Although not known to me, on the horizon a massive storm was moving into my life, one that would forever destroy all that had been built up to this point, and with this storm, recovery would become just a passing thought.

May twenty fifth nineteen seventy three, I turned six. We celebrated my birthday at home on Kern Street, this was the last entry my mom made in my baby book regarding birthdays, and she noted that I had several friends over, Windy (who was Holly's friend), Jane and Kathryn who were red headed sisters that lived across the street and were the daughters of my baby sitter. She also noted that Sharon came over and helped dad put in a window AC, and that I got my first bike. I just wonder where my boyhood friends were, I can only suppose that I did not have any, a conclusion I must arrive at because I have no memory of having any at this time.

My birthday fell on a Friday that year and the following Sunday May twenty seventy nineteen seventy three the family went to church as we did every Sunday. The preacher gave his sermon and being a small church we had no Sunday School. After the sermon my mom ushered all the kids into the kitchen, and another party was given in my honor. The church kitchen was small, it had a brown refrigerator and I remember my mom was pouring orange soda when she was called out of the kitchen.

Dad told me later that my mom was having an affair; he said it was with the preacher of The Town and Country Christian Church, Steve. I remember a hand drawn, shoulder up portrait of my mom hanging in the living room after March nineteen seventy three; she only said that Steve had done it. On this Sunday May twenty seventh nineteen seventy three, during my sixth birthday party that affair exploded at church. My mom never revealed to me if Steve was in fact the preacher of the church, but it is the only logical conclusion. Mom never said much about Steve except to say he was the most decent man she ever knew. The fight at the church had reached such a crescendo that all of us kids were taken outside, but even there we could hear the yelling. When we left, we left with my mom alone.

    I didn't see dad the rest of the day, from what I now know of him I suppose he drank until he saw the bottom of several bottles of whisky, for the rest of that day I can't recall a single event, it's just lost to time. It was not until the next day that I finally saw my dad again, Monday the twenty eighth, when he came home for supper. No words were exchanged between mom and dad, but in private they were discussing divorce, the hang up, my dad did not want my mom to have me and my sisters, I don't think he wanted us either, but he was going to ensure she did not get us at any cost.

    As the days of that last week in May passed the tension between my parents grew. I could feel it and I could tell something was wrong, but at six years old I could never have anticipated what was about to be unleashed. During the brief times dad was home, there were whispers in the dark and icy looks between my parents.

    Thursday May thirty first nineteen seventy three, in order to cope with my mom's affair dad turned to drugs. In a bar that he spent a great deal of his time in, in the city of Walnut he had explained his sad miserable life to a stranger who then gave him some pills; he took them without asking any questions. He popped them in his mouth and chased them down with Wild

Turkey and Pepsi, for the moment his problems had been washed away.

June second nineteen seventy three fell on the Saturday following my birthday, I don't remember dad being home at all. Mom's anxiety had increased, she was never one to yell at me or tell me to get out of the way, but this weekend was different, for the first time the television became what she sent me to. We did not go to church Sunday June third for the first time in a long time and I would never enter another church by choice for the rest of my life. Sunday night dad came home and the storm clouds grew darker, the noise from the clapping thunder was ear shattering, the lighting from the words was blinding, when this storm unleashed its full fury there were to be no survivors, only remains of people that once made up a family.

Monday June forth nineteen seventy three, dad was gone when I got up, my mom made me and my sisters play outside most of the day. I seem to be able to recall every minute of this day, as if time hung still. I didn't at this time understand the connection between time and space made by Einstein, however this point in time has been forever frozen around me, the entire day is stuck and unmoving. My mom seemed different, sure of herself, confident as one would be when coming to the conclusion of a long thought out choice. She was both light on her feet and heavy in her emotions. Outside, in the small fenced in area, I played B-I-N-G-O with my sisters, and then we sang 'This Old Man' over and over. I did whatever I could to attempt to move time forward. I knew I was waiting, but for what I was waiting for I had no idea. Had I known what I was waiting for, I would have found a way to stop waiting.

For years in my adult life I would lie in bed dreaming of time travel and going back to the week of my birthday and kidnapping myself and saving myself from Monday June fourth nineteen seventy three. As I look back in time I realize that all the events of my life that mutated into the nightmare it had become branched out from my sixth birthday. If I were somehow able to return to that point and save myself before the person I was at that time had been murdered, and another person survived in my body, I felt I would have had a better life. I studied time and time travel for almost two years and learned that the laws of physics forbid time travel, so I resigned any hope of going back in time to save myself. However had I been able to go back in time it would not have been me I saved but some other boy. We are the sum total of our life's experiences, both good and bad, had I removed me in the past, I would not be me in the present. It is a paradox that is without any answers or hope of understanding.

    It was around four that Monday evening of June fourth nineteen seventy three that mom asked me and my sisters if we wanted to help make supper. We of course jumped at the chance, we were never allowed in the kitchen while mom cooked, and the stove was the forbidden zone. My mom intended to make dad's favorite meal; she had figured it might just soften the blow of what she had to tell him. I was asked to prepare the water in which to boil the potatoes for mashing, Holly peeled and carefully diced the potatoes. Mom set the dishes out on the table and let Beth place them in proper arrangement, and the frying of the chicken was of course left in her skilled hands. Once everything was set about and it was times' turn to work on the food and I directed my attention to other matters and quickly lost track of time.

    It was not long before my mom called me and my sisters back into the kitchen; we took our places at the table, and waited. Dad was always home no later than five o'clock in the evening, but the big hand of time passed the five and continued on its journey around times' face; I became transfixed on that clock. The clock face was white with bold black numbers and a transparent plastic cover, on its outside was a black plastic geometric curved design that came to a curved peak at its top. I studied every curve and watched as the second hand clicked my future into my past. My mom had noticed my locked gaze on the clock and explained that time would pass more quickly if I did not watch the clock, so I redirected my attention. Around the table sat my sisters in their assigned places, the food had been set out in an array that was pleasing to the eye, dad's seat was empty and my mom paced the floor. It was approaching six o'clock and dad was still not home, I learned later he was drinking up his courage; the storm was building in intensity.

    I didn't notice the clock or the time when the front door opened and dad stood there in silhouette, it was then that I felt it, his pausing in the doorway, right hand still on the doorknob left hand holding his dinner bucket, it felt as if all time and space had stopped and was bent around him, he had become a force of gravity so powerful that all attention was lost forever when directed his way. His body language, his chemistry, his attitude, whatever he brought home with him that day was shared with the entire family the second the door opened, the air was thick and heavy with it, it lingered and stunk with cheap whiskey and cigarettes, but his words and the feeling behind them were crisp and clear. He dropped his dinner bucket on the couch, and with the next clap of thunder the storm unleashed all it fury.

    "Susan." Came a voice out of my dad so dark and evil that I sat motionless at the kitchen table afraid to even take a deep breath.

    "I want to see you in the bedroom, NOW!"

    Mom's face contorted into one of terror. She had been hit by dad before and she felt she knew what he was capable of, but nothing in their past could have ever prepared her for what was about to happen. I watched as she vanished out of sight and around the corner of the hallway door. Had I known that that would be the last time I would see my mom as I knew her I would have hugged my mom goodbye. Before she took that dreadful turn into a lifetime of darkness she was the best mom in the world, I was the most important person in her life, and I came first. I was never in her way, I was her dancing partner, and I was free to hug her when I felt scared, she was my mama, but that day, that Monday June fourth nineteen seventy three, my mama died and someone else moved in to her mind.

After my mom turned the corner dad followed closely behind, and the silence was deafening, I heard nothing, not even whispers. Holly, with a raised voice, turned her head from her seat toward the hall and told my mom and dad that supper was getting cold, when in fact it already had gotten cold, and it would be the last supper in the Smith home and forever remain uneaten. The silence was suddenly and without warning broken by sounds that I had never heard, screams that when they reached my ears caused me to at first freeze as my mind attempted to process exactly what the sound was and then attempt to reject what I was hearing. It had the same effect on my sisters, Holly and I locked eyes, neither one of us knowing what to do. It was the next sound, an unexplainable sound that set my small body into motion, Holly and Beth followed closely behind me. I rounded the door to the hall and just stopped in my mom's doorway, Holly and Beth nearly tumbling behind me due to my unexpected stop.

Dad had mom back into the corner, his fist was repeatedly crashing down onto her face, with each connection came a smack and crunch, and red blood splattering across both walls and dripping from his clinched fist. He grabbed the sides of her head and pounded my mother into the wall, then still holding her by the head he thrust and pivoted my mom around, picked her up and threw her onto her back on the bed, in a flash he was on top of her, hands around her neck, removing the very life out of her. My mom's eyes were dying, she was going to lose, I had to do something, I had to save my mama.

"Dad! Dad! You're hurting her! Stop!" Was the only thing I could think of, but it was enough to draw his attention away from her.

He turned to look at me, what I saw was not my dad, this was a demon, the monster that lives under every child's bed, the creature that lives in the closet that you have your dad check for before you go to sleep, my dad was the monster that I feared the most, my dad was the horror of every child's nightmares.

"Get out of here!" The monster said back in a growl that seemed to reverberate in the air and carried a deep dark tone.

As his voice released those words his hands lost their grip, and my mom broke free. Under the fear of a torturous death the human body is able to do things that seem to defy the laws of physics, in that single moment, time slowed down enough for my mom to act. As she turned her body my mom appeared to rise and fly, coming to stand on the bed and yet never touching the bed, in a single leap she cleared the headboard and pierced the screen covering the window, and in that same frozen moment she gave me instructions.

"Go call your Uncle Mike." And she was gone.

I turned to run with my sisters following closely behind. I understood my mom clearly, we did not have a phone but our neighbor across the street, Mrs. McCall, did. The three of us bolted out of the front door and ran to Mrs. McCall's house. Holly in a breath explained what had happened and gave Mrs. McCall Uncle Mike's number; Mrs. McCall called my Uncle Mike and after hanging up made another call to the police. Within minutes my

Uncle Mike showed up, and soon after that several police cars was parked outside of my house.

In nineteen seventy three there were no laws that saw a wife or kids as having rights, a wife and children were the property of the husband. No laws existed that allowed the police to just take dad off to jail, my mom had to ask the police to take dad and in nineteen seventy three the law would favor him in this instance. So the police acted as a barrier between my mom and dad, until the situation between the two changed. I and my sisters stood in Mrs. McCall's doorway watching, her large body blocking my only means home. Holly however was determined to escape, and she did. I watched as she bolted back across the street, and I attempted to follow Holly, only to be hauled back by the large mass of Mrs. McCall. Holly made it to our front porch, where my mom was sitting and Holly dropped in beside her. From what I was able to see, dad was removing his clothes from the house and placing them in his green Maverick. Uncle Mike loaded dad's guns into his own car, and the police stood by and watched as my family was destroyed. When I saw dad get into his car and start it there was no force in nature that could hold me back, not even Mrs. McCall, I bolted out of Mrs. McCall's door coming to a dead stop in the middle of the street, grasped the door through the rolled down window with my little hands and peered into my dad's driver's window.

(I want to note before I tell you the following conversation, I remember it verbatim. I can't explain how I can remember these events as clearly as I do, and more so the exchange of words between my dad and me, nevertheless I do remember.)

"Where're you going?" I asked my dad sitting behind the driver's wheel, the monster I saw earlier was now gone.

"I have to leave."

"Whenya' coming back?" I asked.

"I won't be coming back."

"Why, what'd I do?" I was sure that dad's leaving had something to do with my birthday party since that's the first time I had heard my mom and dad fight.

"Nothing, you did nothing, but I can't come back."

I let out a yell and started to cry, through my tears and mucus I started to plead and bargain with my dad. I would be willing to never have another birthday, I would be a good boy from now on, I would mind dad and do whatever I had to, and anything he asked of me I would do, just please don't go.

"What did you do to that boy?" Came my mother's voice from the front porch.

"Nothing Susan, I just told him I won't be coming back."

"You got that right, and don't think you're ever coming back."

My dad patted my hands twice and then I took two steps back, I turned to watch his car as it drove off toward Walnut. I focused my eyes on the horse decaled gas cap in the center of the back of his green Maverick. I watched until my dad was gone, and then I remained in the middle of the street crying, I knew this was somehow my fault, I should never have had my birthday party, I destroyed my family, and I was a bad boy.

An arm came around my shoulder, it was a police officer and he guided me back to the porch where my mom still sat, my mom embraced me in her arms, stroking my blond hair as she pulled my face into her chest. The hurt ran deep, so deep that I thought all my insides were twisted in knots. I saw the images of the monster, the red of the blood, and the face of my dad going away. Nothing I replayed in my mind made any sense; everything I thought I knew about my dad was all mixed up in my mind. I wanted to throw up, but there was nothing, my family never ate its last supper, and for some reason I was not hungry, but I was cold, alone and now afraid. I turned my head to look down the direction that took my dad to see if perhaps he would reappear, nothing but Holly sitting next to mom. No one ate that evening, and sleep was hard, but this was an easy day when compared to what was to happen over the next three years, although this day set into motion all the other days, the other days to come would be far darker days, evil had moved in when the monster came out from under the bed.

"June 5th 1973 Tuesday

Mary;

I haven't forgotten you, it's just so much has happened here. Doc is living in Walnut now. We are in the process of a divorce. He beat me up and I told him to leave. He said if I let him come back he wouldn't hurt me anymore. I told him it just wouldn't work. When he does come here I always stand or sit near an outside door. Before, he had me cornered and I couldn't get away. He messed my face up for several weeks...

The men in the Smith family all have records of beating their wives. I'm pretty sure Doc's father did. One thing for sure I want no part of it. He had been drinking or I don't think he would have hit me so many times and so hard. Even now I am scared of him. He told me a week ago that some guy in a bar gave him some pills and they made him feel real good. I don't know if he is still taking them or not. If he tries anything else I guess I'll have to sell the house and move. That stupid dope can make people do things they wouldn't normally do. If he was to ever kill me, I just hope the kids don't see it and that he wouldn't kill them as well. Don't think I'm crazy for saying that. My neck carried bruises where he almost chocked me to death. He did all that in front of the kids. They were screaming and crying and he still wouldn't stop hitting me. I jumped out the bedroom window. The screen has a hole in it where my foot went through it.

Love Ya; Susan E"

My mom wrote that letter the day after dad nearly killed her. Dad had in fact moved to a storage room with a single cot in the back of a bar in Walnut; at least this way he was close to what he loved the most. My life started to change direction that day, and I had to grow up, the boy of six that was once innocent and viewed the world with wonder could no longer exist, someone else had to take his place, someone much older.

"June fourth nineteen seventy three, today Brian D. Smith age six was found dead in his sleep. It is believed that the monster that lives in every boy's closet and under his bed somehow was able to gobble him up. His remains have yet to be found."

Chapter 2
Innocence Lost

"To Brian,
You are our only son, so you are very dear to us. Always carry your name with pride because you belong to a family with lots of love in it. As each day passes and you get older you leave us fond memories to remember and look back on. You have a lot of love in you so give it freely. There will always be love for you in my heart and a very special place. Never be afraid to show love, it's always needed. Always remember me when you are in trouble. Two can work out a problem better than one.
My love for you, Your Mother; Susan E. Smith"
Written circa: nineteen sixty seven.

I'm sure that when my mother wrote that in my baby book her words were true, at least at that time. But life and time changes people, even mothers. From June fifth nineteen seventy three forward not one of those words I just told you held truth in any way. Although not a lie when my mom wrote them, they became a lie when I needed them most.

After dad moved out, time of life started to move quickly for me, my mom had to go to work and took a job as a car hop at Sonic; and she was still seeing Steve. She would load us kids up and take the car to Otasco. She had me and my sisters wonder the auto parts store while she left with Steve then to return hours later or as I remember. This went on for a few weeks, and then suddenly it ended. Looking back it became apparent that my mom was in a wonderland wanting the relationship with Steve to became her new life, but whatever life Steve had, he wanted to hold on to it. And hold on to it is just what he did.

I personally have only one memory of Steve ever having any direct interaction with me. It was after dad left and he took my mom, me and my sisters to a very nice Mexican restaurant called "Casa Bonita". Inside were waterfalls, caves, and tunnels and it was a very beautiful place. As we were walking in I realized that I had forgotten to wear shoes, I never liked to wear anything on my feet so I never gave it a second thought when we left the house. Steve did not miss a beat; he put his arm around my shoulder and pulled me forward and to him and simply said...

"Don't worry about it, just stick close to me."

That was it and we were in. I do remember in vivid detail the inside of the restaurant, but I don't remember the trip home so I'm assuming I fell asleep. It would be a long time before I would see Steve again, but I would see him again, I just don't remember him being there as often as my mom remembers.

When my mom had to work she left me and my sisters with Mrs. McCall across the street. I remember the first time me and my sisters were left there, I had never been left with anyone for any reason outside of family members before and I was scared. Even though I knew the McCall's, I was now being babysat, so all the rules were now unknown to me. Mrs. McCall was a very large, short, round woman, and far from jolly, she was bitter and hateful. Her hair was fire red and she had the temper to match. She had two daughters, Jane the oldest, whose hair was also fire red, but long and stringy. Then there was Kathryn, she was about Beth's age, she also had red hair, but cut short.

On my first stay there I was given the grand tour of their house, it was a basic layout for a farming town in Oklahoma, and there was nothing about the house that gave it its own personality. It was also drab inside, cold and deathlike, lifeless. After the tour Jane asked me to play house with her out in the backyard, I started to follow her out the door as did my sisters when Jane stopped and turned around to face my sisters.

"Hey Holly, why don't you and Beth stay inside and play with Kathryn."

The statement caught my sisters off guard so the two stayed behind. Jane then took my hand and led me out back behind her house. I had never been in their backyard and I had also never seen a stand of bamboo. It was a large stand and Jane had made some trails through them and took me deep inside. The trail was long and winding and after a few turns we came to a clearing, turning back I could see we were out of sight of my sisters and Jane's house. Jane then told me to take off my cloths but I refused, so she explained that we were playing house and I was to be the baby and she was to be the mama and she had to dress me like a baby. Since I had never played this version of house I assumed it was the rule so I took off all my cloths.

It just after I turned six in June the summer of nineteen seventy three that I was abused in this manner for first time, and since it was presented as a game it tore away all the natural safety protocols, so for many years I had become an open target for abusers. It was as if I stood as a target, and Jane had planted a bull's eye on my personality. But I want to be clear, my telling you this story of my life is not about this manner of abuse, it happened and it was what defined me for the next several years, but I wanted to mention this account because of the personality changes it made in me, which will help in later parts of my story. Suffice it to say that for several more years I had encountered many more of these types of abusers and because she took away my natural defenses, I never really resisted. This will prove very important when I speak of David later, as you will see.

Before the end of summer the McCall's moved across town and the games with Jane ended, but they left a deep scar that I would carry the rest of my life. A scar that would never really heal, and would be reopened by the one man I should have been able to love and trust the most, but would come to fear more than anything else in my life, my dad.

After the McCall's moved my mom no longer had a free baby sitter, so we were left home alone when my mom left, to fend for ourselves and many times it meant being creative to come up with food to eat. Holly was the oldest being seven in mid-nineteen seventy three so naturally she took charge of me and Beth. There were many days that she was unable to find food in the house to put in our bellies, so she did the only thing she could, she had us walk to Grandma Smith's house across town. Although my mom did work, looking back now there was no way considering all the time she was gone that she was working, the three of us found ourselves home alone nearly every sun up hour of the day.

Grandma Smith lived with my Uncle Mike across town as I mentioned earlier, just over two miles from the Kern Street house; it was a straight walk more or less. If I stayed on Kern Street for about two miles and then turned left when I got to Sixteenth Street I had only two blocks to go. Grandma lived on Sixteenth Street and Dogwalk. But getting there was not easy.

The first hurdle was the house just down and across the street; I called it the Haunted Chicken House. The front of the house had a fence that was overgrown with vines and bushes, and peeking through the fence you could see there was no grass in the yard, but it was full of large birds and chickens. The house itself was small, with a crowded low front porch that was scattered with items that were surely used for human torture or so my imagination dreamed up. Giving the house that final touch of hauntedness was the fact that it was dark; it was covered with grey and black tar paper for siding. I made a point to stay on my side of the street when passing and I always kept my eye on the house, just in case something were to suddenly try to snatch me away.

The next and greatest hurdle was Beth, she was far too young to walk that far without giving out easy, so Holly and I took turns carrying her, when we both just gave out and were too tired to carry Beth, we would stop and rest. It may seem hard to believe that a seven year old, six year old and four year old would take on this type crossing, but hunger is a powerful driving force, and it drove me and my sisters to walk across town. Also in two thousand twelve if anyone saw three kids this young walking about the police would be called and the parents put in jail before the kids reached the end of the first block, but not so in nineteen seventy three, the world was a much different place back then.

When I did make it to Grandma's she always took me and my sisters in and fed us, and from time to time she would give me and my sisters a .50 cent piece and we would walk to Tote-a-Polk two blocks away to get a soda, ice cream, candy bar and some penny candy. Penny candy was not .01 cent each, but I got three pieces for a penny, and I loaded up on the junk.

Since Jane had abused me in the manner that she did, my thinking on certain matters had already altered, I started to run around in my underwear and even nude, Grandma would chase me with the fly swatter, but I would just run outside, it was after all just a game. One day while I was sitting with her in the big rocker, we were looking at a National Geographic magazine when we came across a photo of some nude natives. I'm unsure exactly what happened, but Grandma said I was going to be a nasty boy, a trait that was growing deeper inside me and one that my dad would later take advantage of.

For my sixth birthday, like I said, I had gotten a bike, but of course dad was not around to teach me to ride it, so it sat for some time until life took on a more normal pattern for me.

Sometime in late June my mom did start to work with me to teach me to ride the bike. In the driveway of the Kern Street house she would hold it up while I attempted to peddle off, I earned many scrapes and bruises, but they are good memories that I have of my mom, and some of the last good memories I have with her. I did finally get the hang of it, but not to the level that I had wished to, I would never considered myself among those thrill bike riders, and my bike just became a point A to B bike.

     June eighth nineteen seventy three, I was spending more and more of my time at my Grandma's and Uncle Mike's house, in fact some weekends I would just stay the entire time. But this was the first Friday after the fight between my mom and dad, and my mom or grandma felt that some time was needed away from home. Uncle Mike had his shows that he watched, 'The Carol Burnett Show', 'Hogan's Heroes', and the like, but that Friday as he was turning the dial I found a new family. He passed the channel the show was on and kept turning, but my words, jumping, and excitement caused him to turn the channel back just as quickly. There on the screen in the center seat was the man that replaced my dad, Captain James T. Kirk.

     This was the first time I had ever seen Star Trek or heard of it, and it was a deep fall at first glimpse. Within a short period of time I had formed a new family alliance, Kirk was my father who had an affair with Spock's mother and so Spock and I were brothers and Dr. McCoy was my Uncle. The rest of the crew took up their family positions and in the span of the summer of nineteen seventy three I had a whole new family, unreal of course. Star Trek was to become the stabilizing force in my life for the foreseeable future, from the adventures the crew encountered I learned the values and morals that shaped my life and character. But it would take something else to unseat this fantasy life, something that would test the character of any person. I did not know it at six years old, but I was on a path that would lead me to a world of darkness and foreboding fear. But as William Shatner once said in a Saturday Night Live spoof, I had to 'get a life'. And in December nineteen seventy six a life would be taken and I was forced to 'get a life'.

    I had obtained an old cassette tape recorder and attached a strap to it and draped it over my shoulder, I now had a tricorder. I had some old toy image blocks that were about the size of a modern day cell phone and now I had a communicator. Since I had nothing that looked like a phaser I used my hand. Grandma's back porch became the bridge of the Enterprise, and the back yard was all the strange new worlds that I got to visit. I would spend hours playing Star Trek from Grandma's back porch, it was a large open porch with a hand railing all around the edge and a set of steps in the exact middle facing out into the backyard. Grandma would not let me set any chairs on the porch so I had to improvise, I would stand in a frozen position when I was supposed to be sitting. I must have look like a young crazy boy on that back porch, standing in one position talking and giving orders to a crew that only existed in my mind. Sometimes I would walk up to Spock's station or another crew members' station to give orders always making sure I took that step to the upper decking. The transporter room was another matter altogether, on many occasions it proved very dangerous to transport to the planet or backyard. The top most step going down to the backyard was the transporter platform, I would stand on it and make the transporter noise with my mouth and then jump from the step to the ground. Sad to say in my world of Star Trek Scotty was not the best transporter chief. Many times I had a hard landing, as the porch was high off the ground, but it was the best transporter I had, and Scotty was still the best transporter chief to be had. Reflecting back I wonder what went through my Grandma's mind as she watched me out of the kitchen window or the neighbors as they watched from their yards and houses, but at the time I did not care, I was in a safe world and safe environment, playing Star Trek in Grandma's back yard that transported me away from the reality of my life.

Bobbie; my mom had befriended her at a bar and as it turned out she lived in a trailer about two blocks down Kern. She was a single mother of an only son named Josh. Josh was twelve years old to my six years old, and he would enter my life with such a force as to never be forgotten, and re-enter it yet again and again. At twelve years of age Josh was someone I took to, at first, but then later I dreaded even being in the same room with him. It was in late June that mom had befriended Bobbie and the two would remain friends for only a very short period of time, but it was enough to introduce Josh into my life.

He was like any normal looking growing boy that you might see and never notice; in fact you would never be able to see him as a predator. He had sandy brown hair, and I could not tell you what color his eyes were as I never looked into them. He was a rough boy of sorts, I suppose his own guilt of the acts that he committed upon me and my body did not allow him to act in a kind manner toward me. Josh was coming-of-age and he was struggling with feelings that he had no comprehension of. Looking back it's only logical to conclude that he too had been abused in the manner that I was, why else would a twelve year old abuse me in such a harsh physical manner? I guess it was more physical abuse in the form of beatings and kicking around after he was finished than anything else, therefore I guess it was the heavy guilt he felt that caused him to act so harshly toward me. Jane was the first female and Josh was the first male, but given their ages, Jane was just a girl and Josh just a boy, I don't hold either one of them accountable for what they did, they would never have done what they did to me had it not been done to them. They were simply acting out and repeating what they had learned. But what they did to me opened up my personality that much more so that many years later it would cost me more than my own life.

      Josh, bike riding, Grandma's, Tote-a-Polk, Star Trek and just plain fun were to settle into a normal pattern for the next few months of summer, if you can call that mixture anywhere near normal.

      The first time that I kissed a girl of my own choosing was with a girl named Lisa. Her grandparents lived a few blocks past the Haunted Chicken House, as I walked to Grandmas. I had seen her out playing and stopped to talk to her and over a period of a few weeks Holly befriended her. I thought Lisa was pretty, I suppose I had started to look at people in a new way given the events of the past weeks with Jane and Josh.

      Lisa had long blond hair and blue eyes, and just a spattering of freckles across her nose; she was someone that if you sat next to long enough, time lost all meaning. She had somehow learned that I wanted to steal a kiss and no doubt it was my sister Holly who told her, so it was arranged one day. While we were playing hide and seek I was the seeker and Lisa and my sisters were the hiders. I sought out Lisa first and with little effort, found her. She was hiding in the garage and had faked fainting on her grandparents riding lawn mower, so I quietly walked over to her and stole my first chosen girl kiss, it electrified me. Even though I had already engaged in acts with Jane and Josh, this was my choice, this was my kiss, it was more than I could have ever anticipated; this was what a coming-of-age experience should be like. I never did kiss Lisa again and we did not become girlfriend-boyfriend, but we did remain friends and we did keep playing together.

For the remainder of June and July, and into August my new normal life took deep root, Josh paid me regular attention and when he was not around I did what all boys did on summer vacation from school, I enjoyed the summer sun. I don't remember being enrolled into the first grade, but it happened in late August, so here I was six going on seven years of age, a young boy without a father around and a mother who would rather leave her children home alone while she picked up men in the bars around Oaktown.

My mom and her new girlfriend Bobbie were the players, they would pick up men and keep them long enough to milk them for what they wanted. It was not always money or a relationship they wanted, they would also get the men to buy them gifts, clothes, shoes, purses whatever my mom and Bobbie needed at the time from the man they had on their hooks.

I don't remember that anything ever happened at school that late summer that stands out, I remember we did have an art assignment; we had to draw a picture and then color it. I drew a picture of a farm house with the barn in the background that sat along a dusty dirt road. I had a box of crayons and in it was about forty eight different colors; I managed to use all of them in my picture. I won first place for the most colorful picture and for being the most creative, the prize a Zero candy bar. That was my first taste of a Zero candy bar, and later I learned it was my mom's favorite candy bar.

All three of us kids were now in school and it allowed my mom more free time to skip about in her newly discovered life. I believe that since the divorce from my dad she felt liberated in a way. As I mentioned earlier, when she was married she thought that she had no voice in her marriage and that she had to agree with everything my dad told her to do. Since Steve broke things off she had become a wild child, thus her meeting Bobbie and having many new boyfriends. In September nineteen seventy three while at the Little Dixie Bar she found the new love of her life that would create another fork in my life and introduce me to a whole new routine, but I will get to that later.

      Throughout the entire summer I never saw my dad, my mom told me he was no longer living in the store room of that bar in Walnut and she had no idea where he went, he just seemed to drop out of my life. Since my birthday back in May, three months prior, I had started to miss my dad. Although the memory of what I saw him do to my mom was still vivid in my mind, my heart wanted to let him back in and I wanted my dad around, someone that I could look up to and call daddy. My mom never did remarry after the divorce, and what she brought around the house was not even worthy to call a human, mostly drunks and freeloaders. But like all the events in my short life up this point, things had a way of changing very fast, and another change was approaching very quickly, one that would later play right into the hands of my dad. I had become desperate for someone to step in the place of my dad, someone that could emulate my dad, and what my mom brought home from the Little Dixie Bar saw that desire in me and took advantage of it.

Chapter 3
"There is no Santa Clause and God Does not Care for Little Boys."

I don't remember the entry period in my life for Charles; it seems he was just there one day, apparently from nowhere. I can only suspect that mom brought him home from the Little Dixie Bar one night. My mom apparently felt that Charles was the next best thing to a perfect man and I believe it was her intent to marry him. She felt that Charles would be just what she needed; she transferred her feeling of need to me and my sisters.

Within days of Charles coming into my life he got to work on converting the garage into a new master bedroom for him and my mom, after all he was moving in and he did not want his and my mom's bedroom right next to mine, the reason for which I'll make apparent later. The remodel went quickly, much of the transformation took place while I was at school and then one day it was done as if the garage had been a bedroom the entire time. Charles and my mom moved into their new master bedroom, sharing the same bed my mom had shared with my dad; Holly then took my mom and dad's old bedroom next to mine.

Charles entered into my life in late August or early September nineteen seventy three, it seems as best I can remember to be more in favor of September. And it did not take long before his true intentions became apparent, he liked me a lot, I'll explain later. While living at the Kern Street house Charles took a series of photos of me, I call them "The Kern Street Series", because he took other series of photos of me. But this was the first time I was photographed in this manner, but it would not be the last, to this day I do not know what happened to all those photos.

Since June fourth nineteen seventy three my life had changed so much and so fast that I could not remember the person that I used to be. It was now September and I was someone that I did not even know anymore. It was only three months ago that I was looking forward to my sixth birthday and excited about going in the first grade, I still worried if I was dressing myself correctly, and I was the brother of two sisters that I loved and cared about. But now I was a small scared little boy who did what others told me to do without question, and allowed others to do things to me that I did not understand the need for.

Charles was having a profound effect on the way my mother viewed me and my sisters, and the change in my mom was dramatic toward me and my sisters. I'll just tell you an example; we were eating supper one night, me and Beth on one side of the table, Holly across, Charles at one end and my mom at the other. My mom had made a salad this particular night and Beth hated tomatoes, so under the table she was passing her tomatoes to me, but Charles noticed her passing them to me. In the beginning of the conversation to follow it was apparent that my mom did not feel it was an issue, she was willing to allow Beth to give her tomatoes to me, but Beth would have to eat more lettuce, and my sister gave no resistance to that idea, but Charles did. Charles felt that if Beth was not made to eat her tomatoes she was getting her way, in effect Beth was defying my mom's authority, my mom's attitude quickly changed.

I sat next to my little sister and watched her. She put forth the greatest effort to swallow each bite of the tomatoes. I continued to watch as tears started to stream down from her eyes, while she begged my mom to just let her eat more lettuce, she even offered to eat more vegetables. But the pressure was on mom to be the one in control, no compromise no yielding. Beth started to gag and choke, coming near to throwing up, in the end she just could not get a single bite of tomato down. My mom offered her another chance, but Charles demanded that my mom exert her parent-ship. Beth was ordered to the bathroom, with my mom following her. Looking back as I tell you this I think the guilt of what Charles was doing to me was carried over into his control of my mom and my sisters; he was changing rapidly day by day, and his changing was effecting change in my mom.

As an older brother I felt I should have done something, anything. I should have protected my little sister, I should have offered some kind of settlement of peace, but I didn't even try. My mom had never been abusive to me and my sisters; she had never done anything to any one of us to give me thought about what she was about to do to Beth.

I sat there looking at my supper plate in silence when without warning the screaming started. A spanking should never have brought on those kinds of screams, not like the kind we heard from my mom just months earlier, and they seemed to continue and continue, without letup. I started to cry, I cried for my little sister, I cried for myself and I cried for my future. I cried because no one else would cry for me or Beth or Holly, I cried for a little boy I once knew named Brian.

When my mom came out of the bathroom I noticed that she tossed a switch into her room. Now before you ask I need to explain what a switch is. A switch is long limb but small in diameter that is cut from a tree. Some abusive parents use it to hit little children. A peach switch was preferred by my mom and later by Doug, as it had a whip effect. I had never seen a switch or had even conceived of the idea of my mom using one to hurt me and my sisters before that night. Then as quickly as the screams started, all went silent, and the bathroom door flung open. My mom exited the bathroom, closing the door behind her and then sat down at her place at the table, she then looked up and Holly and me.

"Go clean up your sister."

Her words were said without any feeling or remorse, and Beth was not her daughter but me and Holly's sister. We both got up from the table and went to the bathroom door, Holly entered first, and after I entered Holly motioned for me to shut the door.

I was not a doctor, and Holly had only played doctor with me and Beth, neither one of us had any real knowledge of what to do with what we encountered. My mom had stripped Beth nude and from her mid-back and down her legs she was covered in bloody whelps, some were open with blood still flowing freely. Holly took a wash cloth and wet it with warm water and started to clean the red blood from Beth's bottom. On the more serious cuts Holly had me place band aids, me and Holly then helped Beth on with her panties. Her back and legs were worse as this seems to be where my mom was aiming, and with each touch of the wash cloth Beth let out a small whimper, there was just no life within her to cry out anymore. Me and Holly did the best we could for Beth, but we both knew it was not enough. I started cleaning the blood from around the toilet on which mom had Beth bent over, as well as the drops of blood on the floor. Holly then helped Beth to her room so she could put her to bed. I watched from the bathroom door as my sisters passed through the dining room and into the living room to disappear into Beth's room, the entire time my mom never looked up from the table. The event was never spoken of by anyone else ever again in the family, it just was one of those things that happened, right or wrong, it happened and from that day forward I never left a bite of food on my plate.

I don't know the why, or what circumstances lead to what I did, but I did what I did, and the why remains unknown. September had rolled into October and the world was screaming as it was dying around me, older boys and men were doing things to me I thought not possible, my mom was no longer my mom, and somehow it was all my fault because of my sixth birthday party, my life had become Dante's Inferno.

Charles had been gone for over a week, I was never told where he had gone or for what reason, but he did manage to call every night. The month was October, toward the last week, the day I don't know, the reason escapes me, but what I did I can see as if I'm doing it all over again today. My sister Beth was for some reason sitting on the kitchen floor, between the chair, which was pushed against the table, and the kitchen sink. What she was doing I don't know, why she was on the floor I could not venture a guess, where the Phillips screwdriver came from and how it got into my hand I cannot recall, nevertheless all these unknown elements came together that day and at that moment. I do remember that I approached Beth from behind with the screwdriver in my right hand, I was on the tip of my toes, just quietly creeping along, when I saw the screwdriver being raised into the air, but still in my hand and then it came thrusting down toward her back. Somehow the screwdriver made contact with her back, tearing through her shirt and then craving a path through her skin and between her ribs and just to the left of her spine and to the right of her shoulder blade. As the screwdriver penetrated her back the forward movement of my body carried me forward with it and the screwdriver continued on its path into her back as far as the handle would allow. In seconds blood covered my right hand, as it started to pour from the wound I had just made in her body. At the same time that the screwdriver was making its way into her body she let out a scream that caught my mother's attention, but my mom's arrival in the kitchen would be too late. I released the screwdriver from my hand and watched my sister as she collapsed to the floor, struggling as she reached back to try and pull the screwdriver free, all the while blood pouring out of her body and covering the kitchen flood in its dark red coloring, the smell of iron started to fill the room. My mom rushed to Beth and as she reached her she reached out and punched me in the chest knocking me back and away from my sister. My mom turned Beth over and cradled her in her arms while sitting crouched on the floor, in less than a minute my sister bled out. I stood by and watched as my little sister died in my mother's arms, and at my hand, on the kitchen floor of the house on Kern Street. Only months earlier I had saved my mom from the death grip of my dad, and now I killed my baby sister in the very same house.

    My mom ordered Holly to go across the street and call the police, but before she went my mom told us both she would do the explaining of what happened to the police.

    "Listen and listen good you two and especially you Brian."

    I gave my mom my full and undivided attention.

    "I'll do all the talking when the police get here; you're to say not a word, nothing! Got it?"

    I nodded my head up and down, telling my mom yes.

    "You got it Holly?"

    Holly did the same as I did, saying nothing.

    "Now go Holly, go across the street and have the neighbor's call the police, but don't tell them why, I want you back over here this time and not to be kept trapped."

    Holly bolted for the door, and it seemed that she had returned just as quickly.

    When the police and ambulance arrived my mother was still on the floor cradling my dead baby sister, tears streaming from her eyes. When the emergency personal reached my sister there was nothing they could do, all the life had drained from her body and onto the kitchen floor. The police did question my mother and she explained that Beth was sitting in the kitchen floor playing when she, my mom, asked me to run and get a screwdriver to tighten the handle on a cooking pot. As I was making my return to the kitchen I was running through the house with the screwdriver when I tripped and fell forward and toward my sister, and in the process of trying to break my fall the screwdriver penetrated my sister in the back. What my mother told the police shocked me and my sister Holly, but we kept our mouths shut as instructed.

    The police accepted the explanation my mom gave without asking too many more questions, after all everything my mother explained fit with the murder scene perfectly, even though what my mother told the police was completely false it fit perfectly with the visible evidence. It would be years later in my adult life that I realized why my baby sister bled out so quickly, the screwdriver had entered deep enough that it cut into her Aortic Arch, all the blood exiting her heart was now spilling out through the cut the screwdriver had made. I stood by my bedroom door and watched as my sister's body was placed in a plastic bag and zipped closed, then she was placed on a gurney and wheeled outside and placed in the ambulance, that was to be the last time I would ever see Beth, my mom had chosen a closed casket funeral. After the police left and the ambulance drove off with my sister's body, my mom cleaned up what remained of my sister from off the kitchen floor, then nothing.

    Nothing else, no yelling, no being sent to my room, no nothing, and the memory of the event just stops, as if the tape broke and the reel kept spinning flapping the broken end of the tape around over and over. I'm sure that something happened, after all it was my mom who screamed and punched me, but there's simply nothing on the recorder but white noise, just nothing. The following weekend we buried my sister, my mom did attempt to find my dad and let him know, but like I said earlier he had exited our lives and my mom did not know where he was. We had gone from a real family of five to a family of four and now to a family of three.

We never spoke of the event with Beth again and my mom gave Charles the same story that she did to the police, she did not add to or take away from the given account, but she had rehearsed it over and over, and in each telling she made sure to alter a single piece of information just enough to give the appearance of memory latency. She was never called out on the facts by anyone she told the account to.

October gave way to November and Thanksgiving was quickly approaching, and for the first time our family had no Thanksgiving plans. Each year we had spent Thanksgiving with Grandma Williams or Grandma Smith, but this year mom said we would stay at home. With Charles living off what little we had I could tell we had too little for a Thanksgiving meal, we had no turkey or even the trimmings; I did not see how we could have a Thanksgiving dinner.

The Haunted Chicken House down the road, the one my sisters and I avoided when we walked to Grandma's, held the answer to our Thanksgiving dilemma. I had seen chickens before and they did indeed have many chickens running around in their yard, but those bigger birds, I had never seen one before and did not know what they were called. One November evening, in fact close to Thanksgiving one of those bigger birds suddenly got loose and found its way into our backyard, it was a turkey. As I tell this I do give thought to the improbability that after living next to the Haunted Chicken House all that time, that suddenly on a day close to Thanksgiving and for the first time a turkey gets loose and finds its way into our backyard. It is more likely that Charles stole one and somehow dropped it in our backyard, nevertheless that turkey wanted to keep its freedom and its head, and perhaps it knew its fate with the fight it gave. Charles was chasing the turkey around the backyard and into the kitchen, as he had left the back door open. In describing a grown man chasing a wild turkey inside and outside of a house it may seem funny, but it had a sense of macabre to it.

    The chase for the turkey continued until it made one indecisive move, it had attempted to turn and run out of the house again when it paused in the doorway, as if trying to choose the safest direction to run in, that's when Charles saw his opportunity, he slammed the door closed as hard as he could, catching the turkey about the head and neck. When the wood of the door made contact with the head of the turkey a crushing sound was felt throughout the kitchen, and the air left me, I stood and watched the violent death of a frightened bird. Its death was not quick, as it fluttered and flopped around the kitchen, wings flapping as if it were trying to fly away and feathers thickened the air. Charles sped up its demise however by picking up a large carving knife and killing it dead, and was then that we had our Thanksgiving dinner, the first one without Beth and my dad.

    After that most horrid Thanksgiving meal my mom moved me and my sister to Walnut, to live at Charles' house. Throughout the first of December we packed and moved our family things to Walnut one load at a time. Charles had a big house, which he inherited from his parents. Mom had locked up the Kern Street house, she refused to sell it or take it out of her name. She always felt after what my dad did to her that if any other man tried it she would need a home to run to, but it will reenter the story at a future time.

    Charles was a decent man and he kept himself clean, which is surprising considering most of the men that my mom had brought home; he had brown hair with a slight reddish tint that although it hung just above his shoulders he still needed it cut. His eyes were blue and surprisingly warm and inviting. He carried a stocky build and his entire body was covered in hair. Charles was a fun man, when others were present, but like my dad he had two clear and distinct personalities, one for the world, the other for home and then one for me, so I guess he really had three personalities.

Walking into the House of Charles you found yourself standing in the living room and to your left was a big stone fireplace, and just beyond that a half wall that led into the dining room which gave way to a kitchen door. Beyond the kitchen was the back porch which had been converted into a bedroom, and it became Holly's room. Off the living room and to the right was a doorway to my bedroom, and from my bedroom you could pass through another door to a small hallway which gave way to a door to the left which led you back into the dining room and one to the right that led into the bathroom, and going straight you entered Charles and my mom's room. This proximity places Charles in a direct path to my room, only a few foot falls away.

Charles was the first father figure to enter my life since dad exited, and if you remember I had told you earlier that I was desperate to find a father figure to replace my dad. Charles picked up on that desire from the first time he met me, and I played right into his hands. So it was Charles as the figure of a man that I should have copied before age six. I think had Charles been different, I mean a true man, he would have made a great dad and my mom would have had a great husband. My mom later told me that he was just too immature. I pressed her for more details and she confessed that Charles was just eighteen when she met him, keep in mind my mom was about twenty eight, a ten year age difference. Not a huge jump, but considering that Charles was basically still in the latter half of puberty and adolescent, that had a huge impact on their relationship and what he felt was appropriate to do with me. It could be that Charles had not grown up yet and did not understand his place as an adult, but I guess I could be making excuses for him.

    Right after we moved into Charles' house in Walnut my life and routine changed again. Although some of these events he had started at the Kern Street house, he kept himself at a distance. But here in his house Charles had taken to making nightly visits to my room, and as I said his eyes were warm and inviting, he never 'hurt' me like Josh had. Of all the people that did this manner of abuse to me, Charles came across as the most kind and gentle. He made what he did seem as if it were an act of love, and he even called it love, which added to my confusion and more importantly lowered my natural defenses that much more. I was starting to lose all understanding of what reality was with people like Charles. But regardless of how he presented what he did after he left my room each night I felt dirty and empty inside and I wanted my life to end.

    Something in me crawled and itched to escape, it told me what Charles was doing was bad and wrong, but he was also the grownup, so he had to be right about what he was doing to me, or so I figured at six years of age, but he was also my first grownup and not to be the last. Jane and Josh were closer to my age, Charles was eighteen, and men his age were not supposed to do these things to little boys. Although Charles presented what he did as an act of love, and was kind about it, he also had to ensure that I kept quiet like Josh did. I had seen what my dad almost did to my mom, I had seen my dad nearly kill my mom, I could not watch as another man did kill her, and Charles promised me he would finish what my dad had started, so I choose once again to keep quiet, and once again I gave up my right as a victim.

Charles took another series of photos of me here, I've never seen these photos or the negatives, but I do however remember them being taken. Most were taken in the back yard, and were of me with other kids, whom I have no memory of. I do feel somewhat bad that I don't remember the other kids in the photos. I feel as if I should remember them, but years later things would be so complex in my life that I could care less about remembering anything.

We had an awesome snowfall just before Christmas of that year, which I got out and played in with Charles. As a child it's easy to get distracted when you see something as pure as a layer of snow hiding all the ugly underneath. I had fallen into thinking that it would be better for me to be covered over, like the white snow that covered the ground, and then one day I would hope to be pure again. My thoughts started to become filled and preoccupied with the concept of death, and of having never been born; I needed and wanted to die.

That Christmas of nineteen seventy three was much on my mind, even with all the badness that had entered my life. Regardless of the things Jane and Josh did, and disregarding the nightly visits from Charles, my mom had made a solemn promise to me last Christmas when she told me that Ken would be here this Christmas. She swore by her promise and I had placed a solid faith in that promise, my Ken would be under the tree this Christmas of nineteen seventy three.

I awoke early the morning of December twenty fifth eager to rip open my Christmas packages, my over anticipation was killing me; Ken was waiting to be a truck driver again. With my overzealous commotion it was not long before everyone was up. With a fury, bright colored paper went flying and gasps and oohs were expressed, along with a few sighs when clothes were opened. I eagerly held out my arms for each package wondering which one held my friend Ken, perhaps it was the next one, nope, well it had to be the next one as the pile of presents was getting smaller and smaller, my hope was fading, nope, nope, nope. When all the pretty little wrapped gifts had been handed out and opened, I saw that Ken my friend was nowhere to be found. I looked up at mom and the look of heartache on my face left the question unspoken, but it was Charles' voice that I heard, "Little boys don't play with girl dolls."

Here the man that visits me every night was telling me that I can't play with Ken. The rest of the day I walked about somber, in deep thought, contemplating what a promise was and what truth was. How could my mama break her word, how could she lie to me, how could she believe Charles, a man who prefers to be with me over her? My mom was nothing but a liar. I learned the word, 'mope' that day, as well as the phrase 'be a man' 'it's time to grow up' 'don't be a sissy' and understood what it meant to be a liar, Ken was not a sissy he was a truck driver, my truck driver.

Every Christmas forward I reminded my mom about her breaking her promise and asked her about my Ken doll, until she died. This was the first of many promises that my mom would break. I don't know why, but the promise of Ken was a promise I've never let go of. I suspect that the breaking of that promise represents a great deal more to me then I realized, after all it was the first promise with a lie that my mom told.

The day dragged on until its end and I continued dejected. Just before I went to bed I went in my room and put "The Chipmunks" Christmas album on and stood by the stereo listening to the funny little voices.

"*Christmas, Christmas time is here, time for boys and girls to cheer, me I want a....*" Ken doll.

After a few more of my favorite Chipmunk songs I sat down on the edge of my bed and waited.

When Charles left my room I put my head toward the living room door which was the foot of my bed so I could see the lights mom left on on the Christmas tree. I watched as red, blue and green winked at me over and over, their light blurred from my tears. I tried to talk to God, I wanted to talk to God, but like everyone else He was out or busy and not listening to me, the lights on the tree continued to wink at me. I must have watched most of the night, until the last fading of my awareness they continued to wink at me. Before drifting off to sleep on that faithful night of December twenty fifth nineteen seventh three I had arrived at a sound conclusion, one that I would carry for the next fourteen years, perhaps it is still lingering in the deepest recesses of my mind,

"There is no Santa Clause and God does not care for little boys."

When I awoke the next morning the red, green and blue winks were gone, I was now someone no one cared about.

There's really only one other event that has a place in my memory that involves my time with Charles and in his house. The timing of this event took place after the Christmas tree came down, so I will just put it in the first week January nineteen seventy four, if nineteen seventy three was a fast year, nineteen seventy four would be a wink in time.

The last memory I have with Charles is the mouse. My mom had set out several mouse traps, as we did have many mice, and every morning Charles made the trap rounds to clean them out. The trap behind the fridge was clear so he moved on, but while he was inspecting other traps the one behind the fridge spring shut with a loud snap, Charles did not hear it, but I did. I went to inspect it myself and a poor little mouse was caught by one tiny little foot. I sat down next to the fridge and as gently as I could I pulled the trap toward me. I started to stroke the mouse on his back in an attempt to calm him. I could tell he was scared, his entire body was heaving so quickly that I thought he would explode. I told the little mouse to settle down and that I was going to free him. I explained to the mouse that I too knew what it was like to be scared and afraid and trapped, I kept stroking his tiny back as I spoke trying to calm him down. After a few more seconds I reached to steady the back of the wooden trap so I could pull up the clasp, when suddenly from above me came a foot crashing down. Charles had found me and the mouse and in one smashing drop of his foot the mouse was crushed, it's little red blood and guts splattered on my legs and hands. I looked up at Charles and yelled at him for killing my friend, he just laughed at me, my mom scolded me for attempting to let a filthy mouse live. Charles walked off laughing and calling me names, I turned back to see the mouse I was just talking to and reassuring that all was well, now dead and lifeless. I took the trap out the back door and dropped the dead mouse to the ground; I now realized that I didn't have a chance in life, I was just a mouse, caught in a trap.

 Not long after the death of the mouse my mom had discovered Charles with me. She had gotten up to use the bathroom one night and heard some noise in my bedroom and walked in on him. She never reported him to the police, and never talked to me about what Charles was doing. After she caught him with me mom left Charles in early nineteen seventy four and for a short time we moved back into the Kern Street house.

 My mom catching Charles with me changed her and for some reason she started to hate me; she even started to view me with disgust, as if I wanted to be a part of what Charles was doing. Even though I was still six years old to my mom I had become some dirty disgusting filthy boy. It was this change in thinking that also played a key role in what my future had in store with my dad. Had my mom seen me in a different way, as a little boy that needed to be protected from someone like Charles instead of someone that wanted to be a part of what he was doing, maybe my life would have worked out differently, even without her in it, her loving me could have altered my thinking enough to make me love myself. Nevertheless when she caught Charles with me, it affected her view of me and that night the last of any love she had for me faded from her heart.

Chapter 4
A New Hope

Nineteen seventy four and nineteen seventy five are going to be the toughest years to attempt to put structure to. During these two years I moved so often and so many changes occurred in my life that in every interview with family and friends about these two years they all told me..."you just can't do it"...meaning that there was no way to put time and events in any logical order. So I shall attempt to do what is considered by my surviving family members to be impossible. One methodology that I will employ is logical order of events that should have happened. Although I knew where I was at a fixed point in time, how I got there and how I ended up at other points is unknown to me. In some cases I have employed a pivotal event, something that happened in public that made the news, that I can clearly remember the event and where I was to extrapolate the date and place. So with what I do know I will use simple conjecture to connect the dots to missing times and locations. So as I tell you these two years it should be kept in mind that not all the events are in chronological order, or some members of my family may have been elsewhere, there's just no way to get these two years in correct order.

After my mom found Charles with me that night, as I mentioned earlier, she left him. It was sometime in the early part of the second week of January, the exact date is left in the purview of the teller of those events and I have yet to get the same answer from two tellers, so I will choose the beginning of the second week of January. When mom left Charles we had only one place to go and that was to return to the Kern Street house, the home she owned. However time and events moved so fast with so much crammed into every fraction of time that getting each person, place and event correct is just not going to happen.

Once we returned to Kern Street, Josh reentered my life. Holly believed that he had befriended her; she was fully unaware that it was me he had befriended. When we returned to Kern Street Josh noticed that I had changed, grown up mentally. Prior to our move to Walnut to live with Charles I was timid, shy and reluctant, now I was bold, open, outspoken and determined to be the one in the center seat, and I hated everyone. Josh took his abuse of me to a new level, he equalized it. He was no longer mean and hurtful as he once was, so it meant being a bit more open about our friendship and letting Holly fall to the side.

Josh made arrangements for me to start spending some weekends with him, since his mom and my mom were always out bar hopping, so it would afford us time to be completely alone. My mom agreed to this because she felt it would be good for me to hang out with an older boy since I did not have my dad around; by now Josh was about thirteen and was starting to change. If my mom knew what Josh was really doing to me she may have reconsidered my staying with him so much; well, on second thought she may still have agreed.

I won't recount every event at Josh's as it's not necessary, but I revisit Josh at this point because it will help to understand later in my life why I was so open to what my dad did with me. Without this background information it would prove too difficult to understand why I had to go along with what my dad did. But again as I mentioned earlier, this story is not about this manner of abuse, it's simply being included to help understand events that I will recount later in this story. Josh reentering my life over and over is also important in that it allows you to understand why my resistance failed. The repetition of his reentry and as often as it occurred laid the foundation for what my dad did to me in Texas in nineteen seventy six. Without Josh reentering my life over and over and repeating what he did over and over I think it might have been a different outcome in Texas, but I'll never know, I can't travel back in time and change anything.

It was about the middle of March nineteen seventy four and the weather was starting to turn into spring when Josh had learned I was back, and as I said he renewed our friendship. Josh was a strange boy; he was quick witted, but had a non-feminine girlish way about him, his personality is really hard to capture. He looked like an all American boy, and even got rough at times, in a football sort of way, but he had his girlish side about him. Since it was now late March I was nearing my seventh birthday and had gained an enormous amount of experience in my relationships with people and understanding them, even at age six going on seven I wanted to control the events that I was involved in, I wanted to be in control of my life. Josh and I never did become real friends in any manner of the word, but I was just someone that he took advantage of in his life as he made his way through his life.

Sometime in early April nineteen seventy four my mother found another boyfriend, I don't remember him at all, just that we moved across town into his house with him. Holly told me his name was Mike, but I have no memories of Mike whatsoever. What I do remember is moving across town into a white house that was long and narrow, something like a trailer but it was a wood framed house. What was nice about moving here was the reprieve from Josh, someone I would never have to deal with again in my life. Mike, whom I have no memories of, never touched me or took an interest in me, so I finally got the chance to settle down into boyhood that spring of nineteen seventy four.

That spring of nineteen seventy four I got to watch a Monarch butterfly break free of its cocoon; I got stung on the foot by a honey bee, and learned that I was mildly allergic to bee and wasp stings and I shared many memorable starry nights with my mom under a pecan tree while she strummed out folk songs on her guitar and sung with me. This was the mom I remember, and this was what a six year old boy was supposed to be doing. For this brief moment in time it seemed as if my mother loved me again, as if she did not see me with disgust because of Charles, and it was as if I had never stabbed my little sister. When I think back on these moments I'm filled with good warm feelings.

I never questioned the absence of my dad, after all he did say he would not be back, but one day my mom told me that she was taking me and my sister to Grandma's because dad was there and wanted to see us. This would be the first time since the death of my little sister that my mom would be able to talk to my dad, and he was still unaware of Beth's death. It was late April when mom dropped me and Holly off at Grandma Smith' house, I ran inside as fast as I could to see my dad, and then I jumped into his arms giving him a huge hug, my dad was back.

My dad had come back to me and he was going to make up with my mom and then we could all sit under the pecan tree singing folk songs, I was going to get my life back, and maybe even my Ken doll. A little boy's six year old fantasy, of a life to never be, all planned out in his hopes. But when I got inside Grandma's house my fantasy came crashing down around me.

Dad had moved to a small town outside Galveston Texas and was working in the ship yards. While there, in a bar, he met a woman named Donna and they were to be married later in the month. Dad had come back to take me and my sister to Texas for the wedding. But I wanted no part of it, no one could replace my mom except mom and therefore no one could marry my dad except my mom, Donna was a traitor, someone that needed to go away. But nothing I said was going to convince dad that what he was doing was wrong, that he was making a mistake, he was intent to marry Donna.

Donna had just exited a divorce of her own, and from that marriage she had a daughter named Kris. Kris was about three years old and by looks could pass for a blood sister of mine. Donna was a barrel racer for the rodeo circuit throughout Texas and she was training Kris to ride as well. Donna had in fact come from a family that raised, bred and used horses in rodeos.

My mom took me and Holly inside Grandma's house, and once the initial greetings were over, dad asked where Beth was, now came the explanation. My mom took dad into Grandma's bedroom and shut both doors, it did not take long before we all heard dad crying. Later my mom told me that she gave dad the exact same explanation of the events surrounding Beth's death that she told to the police and Charles. Once again my mom saved me from certain death. My mom never told me why she told the police what she did or why she repeated the same story to Charles and my dad, but it is still the story told to this day, well until I just told you what really happened. Dad did not take it so well and later it would add to his reasoning of why he did what he did to me. Every event of my life that affected my dad from May twenty fifth nineteen sixty seven until the time my mom told him about Beth just added to his hatred toward me. My fate was sealed at birth and there was nothing that I could do that would allow me to avoid the clash that was only a couple of years away.

While dad was visiting it just so happened that the Budweiser Clydesdale horse team was at the Gibson store. Dad got my mom's permission; and took me and Holly to see the team of horses pulling an old fashioned Budweiser wagon. I remember the horse's huge hooves, and watched them closely as dad took photos of me and Holly standing in front of the team. I was worried that they might step on me; I was after all very small and skinny for my age.

Dad wanted me, Holly and Kris to be at the wedding, all three of his children, but I wanted no part of his marrying Donna and made my feelings known to all. Dad did not want me at his wedding as a beloved son, but more as a trophy to show off to his new in-laws and friends. When he and Donna left, Holly returned with him to Texas to attend the wedding. Although I did not attend the wedding, I did see the photos and hear the stories. Dad and Donna got married on horseback, against her parents' wishes, but it was dad who pushed it by them. From that encounter Donna's mom and dad saw what my dad was and attempted to warn Donna, but Donna did not have her glasses on, she could not see clearly what she was getting into with my dad. When they first arrived in Texas they moved into a small trailer near Bandera Texas. While in Texas dad had renewed his friendship with Clifford and John, the two had somehow ended up in Texas together. Clifford had formed a large company that catered to the rich and powerful, and John was his second in command. Through the company Clifford had made connections with government agencies and congressmen as well as some of the most powerful people in Houston. I'm going to refrain from naming the company or what type of company it was. Because my dad reconnected with Clifford and John, dad had set the stage for the most dangerous bend in his life, a bend that I would get caught in.

Back in Oklahoma I was now alone with mom and was looking forward to my seventh birthday in a few weeks. It had been a long hard year and at last my life was settling down and I was for the time feeling safe. My mom still lived with Mike, whom I have no memory of as I mentioned, but it was just the three of us now. I had gotten good at riding my bike and was allowed to go off on adventures. On that side of Oaktown the city had made huge drainage tunnels, big enough to ride a bike in. I had made friends with several other local boys and we would ride the tunnels together, although I now realize that riding in sewer tunnels was nasty, at the time it was an adventure. The next few weeks were perfect. I explored a path along a wooded edge that led to nowhere, and someone new entered my life, someone who would play a most important role in saving me, I met a boy who never was.

This little boy never got to exist, he was someone that was just there one day, from nowhere, and he told me he was there for me. I asked him where he came from and he said a place called Tasana.

"What is Tasana?" I asked the boy who never was.

"It is the place in your mind from where I'm from."

The boy who never was continued to explain over the course of some days what Tasana was, and today I fully understand. At some point during nineteen seventy three with everything I had been through I had created a safe place to go when being mistreated, the place was Tasana. As it turned out in my adult years I learned that Tasana is a real word and a real place. It has both Alaskan and Asian roots, so most likely the Asians carried the word to Alaska. However the meaning in Asian is uncertain, there are several ideas to its meaning, but in Alaskan it means "the seat on top of the mountain from which the river flows". In my world of Tasana it's a beautiful paradise, free of any persons that wanted to do harm to me, a place of complete safety.

I entered Tasana through the Gateway of Protection, only those pure of heart could enter. No monsters or people that hurt other people in any way could gain entry, so I never saw anyone else allowed entry, as I never knew anyone else pure in heart. I was always barefoot in Tasana, there were no shoes allowed. From the Gateway of Protection I walked across a vast field of meadow flowers, they would tickle as they brushed your ankles.

There were purple, yellow, blues of all shades and there were Bachelor Buttons everywhere. As far as the eye could see the flowers covered the ground, there fragrance filled the air with smells of hope and peace. In the distance a stand of trees grew and I would run through the meadow of flowers kicking up pollen and petals and scattering honey bees being disturbed as I ran toward the trees. I never got stung here. When I reached the stand of trees they were tall, strong and powerful, their tops creating a canopy above me. There are trees of all kinds and all heights, but within the forest there is no darkness, light reaches every point, and the shade of the leaves flutters in the gentle breeze. The deeper into the woods I went I came to a stream, so clear, so beautiful, and so fresh that you can feel its cleanliness without having to put your feet in. In the distance you could see the mountain that the stream flowed from, powerful and protecting. The sun danced off the water and made swirls of light that filled the air just above the stream. I put my feet in the water and lay back on the soft grass at the edge. I folded my arms behind my head and looked up into the canopy of trees through which an opening was created in the trees for me to see the deep blue sky and watch the white clouds go by. This is Tasana, this is my safe place and this is where a boy who never got to be lived.

"So why are you here now?" I asked the boy from Tasana.

"You need me, you can't be left alone."

"How did you know I was alone?"

"Everyone in Tasana knows you and we watch over you to protect you."

"But then why do people always hurt me?"

"We can't stop the hurt in the real world, we can only save YOU, we can only shelter and protect YOU." The boy from Tasana said tapping the side of his head.

After that first meeting and introduction he quickly vanished from my sight, but as the days and weeks past he would return again and again. It seemed to me that he returned when I was all alone or feeling down, I soon understood the meaning of what he said on that first encounter, that everyone in Tasana knew everything about me and when I needed help the most he was there. It was in early May that the boy made another appearance, one that allowed me to realize who he was, or would have been.

We walked about in the yard, by now I had gotten use to him suddenly appearing, but at times he still caused me to jump. He was my age and almost a reflection of me, but yet different. Sometimes his hair was darker, but always within a few shades of medium blond and his eyes was emerald green yet mine were hazel green, he was built like me, thin and light on his feet, and he was a great deal smarter than me. He knew things about people that I did not and he understood things about people that perplexed me, and more than that he knew me better than I knew me. I enjoyed talking to him, he had a deep intellect that I learned to trust and depend on. The boy from Tasana was the boy I so longed to be, the boy I would have been had my life taken a different path than it did on June fourth nineteen seventy three.

"So what do I call you?" I asked the boy from Tasana.

"What do you want to call me?"

We walked about a bit more as I was trying to think of a name, when he reached out and took my hand. He led me to the pecan tree that mom and I would sit under some starry nights while she had played her guitar and we sat down. I was still at a loss as to what to call him, I just could not figure out what name fit him. As I was thinking about a name I started to move dirt around with my finger, drawing letters attempting to write a name, all the time I was thinking about the boy from Tasana, how he would suddenly be there and then not, it was then that I had his name.

"How about Greg?"

"Greg?"

"Ya, Greg. You remind me of a friend I had in another time. He was there when I was little and now he is not here with me anymore."

"Then Greg I am."

Greg was an echo or shadow of who I could have been; as if on some parallel plane my mom's perfect family did stay together and we lived on to have a happy family life. Greg would remain with me throughout the rest of my life, at least to the point that I started to write this at age forty-five. However as I grew he did not. Greg never grew past age seven, but he remained far smarted then I was to ever achieve. As time went on he spoke less and less, but in December of nineteen seventy six he stopped speaking to me forever, although he still remains with me. I will speak more of the events of that December later, but that December was going to be the culmination of all the events that I had survived thus far and all that I would endure over the next two years, coming to a completion at the hands of my dad.

May twenty fifth nineteen seventy four, my seventh birthday had finally arrived. Dad, Donna, Kris and Holly had returned from Texas to Oklahoma for my birthday and my mom took me over to my Grandma's to visit them and celebrate my day. Greg had told me that dad and my mom were to never get back together so it was easier for me to accept Donna as a step-mom, but it was under protest that I went along with dad and Donna's marriage, but in my heart I wanted my mom and my dad back together.

Over that week in May of nineteen seventy four a lot of photos were taken of what remained of my family. I stayed the entire time at Grandma's and tried to make the best of this type of split up family, although I wanted my mom and dad back together, this was a larger family, and with the addition of Kris it was easier after the loss of Beth. Then it was over, the visit, everyone had to return to their lives. Dad, Donna and Kris returned to Texas and Holly decided to move back with me, my mom and Mike. When August rolled around it was time to enroll in school again, but my mom had a brilliant idea, no doubt at Mike's bidding.

    I asked my mom before she died where she got the idea and she refused to tell me details about any part of that August and early October nineteen seventy four. I told her the things I did remember and she told me that it is best that I didn't try and remember the rest. The only detail my mom willingly filled in was that it was dad who forced her to remove me from the school, and he never explained why. Since my mom was seeing Mike at the time I'm going to conjecture that Mike was the catalyst behind the entire idea. My mom and Mike's brilliant idea was to enroll me into a Catholic school for boys. It turned out to be a very very bad idea.

    I was taken to St. Andrews Catholic School for Boys, which was only a few blocks away from our house, and enrolled. I had not been to a church in over a year and the last one I was in was tiny, this church was massive. The school sat at the bottom of a hill and I had to walk up a set of steps to get to the church. To enter the sanctuary I had to walk down a long arched outside hallway, the door to the sanctuary was wooden, huge, heavy and dark. There was a sidewalk that went to the left of the sanctuary doors that led to the parish door, which was also made of wood, huge, heavy and dark. It was not until my early forties that the nightmares of St. Andrews finely stopped.

In the nightmares I was always floating just above the ground in the arched hallway, when I reached the massive doors they opened up to allow me in and I was sucked away into darkness. I always woke up at this point, soaked from sweat and sometimes I think I had wet myself as well. I would get up, clean myself up, put on clean clothes and lay a towel on the bed under me, always trying not to wake up my wife, sometimes she did wake up because she felt the wetness.

School there was harsh; nuns in a boy's Catholic school really were mean. I did get the ruler smacked across my palm and knuckles many times. The corner was a main stay for me and the other boys had no mercy on me. I don't remember asking for any of what they did to me, nevertheless I was the object of their bullying. I also had to go to the sanctuary every day for choir practice. All the boys had to sing in the choir, there was no getting out of it. Inside the church I remember it being dark, and mostly wood, and the feeling I got inside that church was cold and distant. But I loved to sing choir music. I remember being taken to the parish a lot, but once I went through the door all goes to darkness. At times I've had dreams about going through the door and being met by the priest and taken away, and I wake up cold, shivering and covered with sweat.

No matter what I asked my mom about St. Andrews she told me that some things are better never spoken of. I used to beg her to tell me and she always refused. I called St. Andrews when I turned forty and asked about the school records from the nineteen seventies, the nun asked me my name and then put me on hold. When she came back on the phone her explanation was difficult to believe.

"Mr. Smith?" She started off.

"I'm still here."

"All the records from nineteen seventy four were destroyed while they were being transported to the Diocese in Walnut."

"Excuse me?"

"The records from the year you were here were destroyed in transport to Walnut years ago." She explained again.

"I understand what you just said, but I never gave you the year I attended, I only gave you my name. So just from me giving you my name you were able to know what year I was there and that those records were destroyed? If those records were destroyed, how did you know what year I was there from just me giving you my name?" I reasoned out for her.

Click, she hung up the phone on me.

Since I can't recall the events clearly I'm not going to put anything down that I feel happened, false memories can happen that way. By early October I was removed from St. Andrews and placed in regular public school.

I'm unsure where I lived from late October to November. My mom and Mike had split up so I'm going to have to assume we moved back to the Kern Street House. The time reference here is just too shattered. But that Halloween my life took a haunted turn down a dark lane. If you took all the events that have happened to me up to this point and somehow squeezed them into a single fraction of time and had the fraction loop for time indefinite it would have been better than what I went through from October thirty first nineteen seventy four to January first nineteen seventy seven. All the fury of that Halloween was released that day, not all at once, the darkness and evil oozed out only a little at a time, black slime with smells of sulfur and the burning flesh of little boys being cut from their bones, ugly, dark, black, hateful, bleak, shadows everywhere, monsters under the bed and in the closets crawling about your bedroom and waiting for you to close your eyes, and at no time a safe place to hide from it all.

Chapter 5
"Kids; This is Doug!"

My mom had met a new friend, Kathy. I'm not sure how or when, but the two became friends quickly. It's funny how people somehow connect and reconnect and that is just what happened to me when my mom met Kathy. When my mom pulled me out of St. Andrews she enrolled me into Roosevelt School. Mrs. Tunley was my new teacher, and she was the first black person I can recall ever interacting with. I had no preprogramming as to races or color, so I never thought of her as any different as my other teachers; I never gave a second thought to races or color, to me people were people. She was a large round woman, but carried her weight well, and she was funniest teacher I ever had. She made learning fun and enjoyable, she made going to school something a kid wanted to do, something I wanted to do and she made it a welcome place of escape for me. I still consider her the best teacher I ever had.

I had a seat toward the back of the class, but a girl I liked sat toward the front, her name was Kim. Kim dressed in a very girlish manner, cute dresses, mostly red, pink, and white that puffed out at her waist; she had long dark hair, and a fantastic smile. I tried my best to get her to notice me, but I was less than a wall flower to her, so I did the unthinkable. During class one day I slipped from my chair and onto the floor. I crawled up the isle until I reached her desk, and then gave a tug on the hem of her red dress. When she turned down to look at me I asked her for a kiss, and she leaned over and planted a kiss right on my lips. As soon as our lips made contact all the kids in class either laughed, said "gross" or let out some other type of remark. Mrs. Tunley walked right up to me and grabbed me by the collar of my shirt and hauled me out to the hall. I was both elated and scared. Once in the hall she gave me a 'good boy' smile, then she sent me to the office. I was on my way to the office but my head must have been in the clouds because I don't remember what happened when I made it to the principal's office.

As Halloween nineteen seventy four rolled around Kathy learned of a haunted house across town near the old Indian cemetery and she and my mom thought it would be a great idea to take me and Holly along with Kim and her brother Jason. I wish they had reconsidered. The people who sponsored the event spared no cost when putting it together, the effects were very believable. The house it was held at was three stories, and sat on a hill with a high stone wall out front, something right out of a Steven King book or what you might see in the movie "Psycho". The house itself carried the part well and it was without a doubt the scariest place I had even been too. All of us were walking across the lawn toward the left side of the house when out of nowhere came a man with no head, where his neck should have been, blood oozed out with what I guess was supposed to be brain matter, it scared Holly and in her fright she started backing up.

All eyes were transfixed on the man; Holly was too scared to scream, but just kept backing up toward the wall, and at the base of that wall, a concrete sidewalk. As she approached the edge of the wall someone else noticed. My memory from this point on fragments, because the players of the haunted house did not stop the play and at the same time death was about to befall my sister, it was surreal, and it was haunting. All I can remember was a man reached his arm around Holly and it was stopped, the part of the play where Holly falls off the wall never happened. Who the man was is debated between my sister and me to this day, but she was saved at the last second. We then left the house;

and the Halloween of nineteen seventy four took on a never ending haunt.

I say the man who caught Holly was Doug, she remembers differently; nevertheless Doug entered our lives that November of nineteen seventy four. Kathy had introduced my mom to Doug and right away mom and Doug moved in together. This living together has proven to be one of the biggest factors causing confusion among me and my sister. For years I had thought that all these men my mom lived with were my dad's, that mom had married them. The concept of two people living together without marriage was unknown to me and therefore I always assumed that Doug entered our lives by marrying my mom. Not so. In my research for this book I came across an entry in the Smith family tree that noted

"Susan Smith was living in Santa Fe Oklahoma with Brian, Holly and Doug".

The entry was dated for late nineteen seventy four. This being the case my mom and Doug lived together but never married, well sort of, which confused me because I had always thought they did get married. The two of them living together explains why so much confusion has existed for so long in attempting to sort out a time line for nineteen seventy four. By back dating when Doug moved into my life from the family tree entry, even without a marriage, most events however fell into place.

When my mom and Doug first got together they rented a house across the baseball field beside Roosevelt school so getting to school was just a walk across the street and cutting through the baseball field. It's important to note at this point while living with Doug we moved nearly every three months. Reason being that Doug had multiple warrants out for his arrest throughout Oklahoma and a few other states. That being the case, putting the order of the homes we lived in at any given time is beyond any hope.

In all the time since my mom and dad divorced my mom never spanked me for wetting the bed, she figured it was because of what I went through, but Doug's approach was different. Before my sixth birthday I had not wet the bed, but it was only after my sixth birthday and after the mistreatment of me started that I started to wet the bed. However Doug figured I was too lazy to go to the bathroom and liked to wet my bed and I enjoyed laying in it. He convinced mom of this and in the beginning he allowed her to spank me, but slowly he started to administer the spanking every morning and my sister got the same. He held back however, he restrained himself until my mom was adjusted to his way of thinking.

I could easily see that Doug was going to be a bully and going to be strict so one night at the supper table he and I got into an argument. Since he had yet to adjust my mom's thinking properly to his, he kept his restraint, but I unleashed all my pent up frustration that had built up over the last year. In the end I decided to run away, and I did. Paul, a friend of mine from school, lived about two blocks away so I packed up what things of mine I could and walked to his house. I don't think Doug expected me to approach another house or that I knew someone around our house, because right after Paul's mom opened the door my mom was standing right behind me. My mom made some excuse as to why I was there while I tried to plead my case, and then my mom dragged me back to the car.

Mrs. Tunley was still my teacher and after Doug moved in she noticed a marked change in my behavior. I had started to wet myself during the day as well as soil myself. She would ask what had changed at home but I just couldn't tell her. One day she attempted to pry a little deeper. It was during recess time and I had been playing well with the other kids when I just quit playing. I walked over to the steps and sat down on the oversized concrete sidewalls along each side of the steps; I pulled my knees up to my chest and buried my head in the fold of my body. Mrs. Tunley approached me, sat down on the other sidewall and asked me what was wrong. I did not reply or acknowledge her but held my silence. I remember she then moved to the same side of the steps that I was on and she placed her arm around me. As soon as I felt her arm around my shoulders I looked up at her, and tears flooded my eyes and over flowed onto my cheeks. I explained that I had messed in my pants and if I went home to change I would get a spanking. She asked if I knew that I had to go to the bathroom and I told her that it just came out. She pulled me to her and told me I needed to change that I could not keep dirty clothes on. When I stood up to walk home I realized then just how kind of a person Mrs. Tunley was, because she too was crying.

  I slid off the side edge of the sidewall and walked across the baseball field toward my home. The walk I took was slow and I lingered as much as I could. When I walked into the house I was asked what I was doing home from school so early. I told my mom what happened and she told me to get cleaned up. After I came out of the bathroom from cleaning myself up Doug was waiting for me in my bedroom, switch in hand. I was not able to return to school that day or the next few days; I needed time to rest from Doug's switching. Mrs. Tunley did reach out to me and wanted to help more but after running away and Doug's switching I had learned what pain and fear was and also Doug and my mom reminded me and my sister of the dangers of talking about family business outside the family. My running away had been the catalyst that altered my mom and she adopted the same view of punishment that Doug already had. Doug beat me when I got home that night from running away, while my mom sat by and let him. It was then that I knew my mom was gone forever, and my relationship with her as her son was to be but a forgotten memory of a time long past.

This singular event opened the door to Doug's tending to my punishment for the remainder of the time that he was to be around. Not to confuse a spanking with a beating I need to be clear, Doug did not spank, he intended to break the will of a child, and it was my will he was intending to break.

Doug would use his leather belt, a switch or in some cases a piece of lumber. I think he enjoyed beating me nude and while I stripped he would just randomly hit me. He would not hold me down on whatever I was bent over, he could care less if I moved about or where he hit me. Although most blows did find my little bare butt, many found my legs, back, arms and sometimes my head. Doug also had no restrain, he beat until he got tired, so the old adage of forty minus one did not apply when he took to beating me. I would speculate that at times I got far more than forty strokes. But one of the worse strokes I got and for some reason I always did it, was when I turned my little body around to beg for mercy. In the act of turning I exposed my genitals and he continued to beat. So at times I took a few blows from the belt or switch to my genitals. This happened only a few times as I learned that no matter what, to resist the urge to turn around. And every time I got beat, in one way or another blood was drawn.

On two different occasions we had told Grandma Williams about Doug and my mom writing hot checks, and stealing, and for this we got beat. While attending Wilson Elementary School I had approached the principal once to explain and show him the results of Doug's abuse. Me and my sister stood in the principal's office telling him how Doug treated us, and I even took off my shirt to show him the bruises, whelps and also the marks on my back and legs. The principal seemed very sympatric and understanding and assured me that he would get me some help. That evening when the school bell rang at the end of the day the principal collected me and Holly and walked us both out the front door, what I saw caused me to freeze at the foot of the school steps. The principal had called Doug and told him the story of my lies; and there at the curb Doug was parked at the end of the sidewalk leaning against his car, waiting for me. When I got home I learned the painful way of the value of keeping what happens in the family, in the family.

  For a short time we moved to another house about two or three blocks away and spent out the rest of nineteen seventy four there. Dad, Donna and Kris came back to Grandma's for Christmas of nineteen seventy four and me and my sister spent Christmas at Grandma's house. Once again dad left and returned to his life with his new family in Texas. My mom and Doug moved around Oaktown for the next few months and then the unthinkable, Kathy had rented the Halloween Haunted House and offered my mom and Doug to move in and share the rent and living expenses.

  Kathy, Kim and Jason had already moved in when my mom, Doug, me, and Holly started to move in around March of nineteen seventy five. I had only encountered Jason briefly and never had the chance to get to know him, of course I had a crush on Kim, and this was the same Kim I had crawled on the floor in first grade to steal a kiss from, but by now she had forgotten who I was. As I got to know Jason it became apparent that he was insane. The word insane or crazy is tossed around a lot as a label, but as I unfold the events of the Halloween Haunted House it will become evident that Jason was truly insane. I fully believe that Jason was also abused, but I also believe that he suffered physical abuse at such intensity and at a young age that it did something to his mind. I believe that he lost any and all human compassion.

I want to tell you the layout of the Halloween Haunted House. Entering you entered the living room, and to your exact right was the master bedroom. Doug and my mom moved into it, I never went into their room, even when we first toured the house. From the living room you passed into the dining room, and to the left a door to the kitchen, here I'm confused because I seem to recall a small area off to the right of the kitchen that had red chairs and a small table, but it's hard to recall. To the far right of the dining room was a door that lead to another room with a fireplace, this could have at one time been a sitting room. The fireplace had a huge white mantle that was elegantly carved and had an old southern charm to it. If you turned around and stood facing the door you entered this room by, to the right was a door, and beyond was a very long narrow hall, room for only for a single person to get through at a time. At the end of the hall was a bathroom. Then looking back and to the left was a stair case to the second story, and across from it was a side door leading outside. Going upstairs from the top and to the right was a room, then to the left was what became the play room and turning to the left again became me and Jason's room. I'm sure there were more rooms and as for the third floor I don't remember ever going up there. To this day I still have dreams of this house, mostly centered on the long hall leading to the hidden bathroom, but there seems to be no substance to these dreams. The dreams appear to focus on this bathroom acting as a hiding place, a place of safety in this house.

While we were moving our stuff in Jason, who was the same age as me, was busy throwing a box of tomatoes against the wall in the sitting room. It's better not to try to understand why, he just did it. As Holly was carrying her doll house upstairs, which was made of sheet metal, she stumbled at the top and sliced the front of her leg clear to the bone and perhaps into the bone. I was at the bottom of the stairs when she turned around and I saw that her leg was covered in deep red blood. She was still unaware of what had happened, and when I saw the blood I screamed for my mom and my mom rushed her to hospital.

I was sure that the house was haunted. I heard music all the time when no radios were on, the playroom had the most interesting returning items, even though thrown out, and a barrage of constant strange sounds. One of the returning items in the playroom was a simple piece of wood with a nail in it. Holly had stepped on it first and it was tossed outside, then me, again it was tossed outside and I believe each of us kids stepped on it in turn, but the wood seemed to always return. The playroom itself held most of the feelings of being haunted, I can't explain what the feelings were, but it just felt that way to me. I managed to keep my sanity while living there, but as for Jason, he just flipped.

One day, perhaps in late March nineteen seventy five, Jason tossed all the furniture on the second floor out of the window, then he perched himself on the eve of the highest part of the roof, and there he sat. Doug tried everything he could to get Jason down, but he was unable to climb that step of a pitch, so Jason sat, crouched like a Gargoyle on the edge of an ancient church. Then suddenly and without any warning he launched himself off the roof of the third story house to land safely on one of the mattresses he tossed out of the window. Doug did give him a beating and then made him haul everything back up to the second floor by himself.

The street the house was on ended in a T intersection and at the end of the road was an old Indian cemetery. The first grave date was unknown, but some graves had dates going back to the seventeen hundred's and maybe even older. Some of the graves had been dug up for supposed hidden Indian treasures, and I often played there late into the night. Once I tripped into a dug up open grave, it was a frightful experience to be lying in an open grave and looking up into the night sky through the leaves of trees hundreds of years old. I spent an unusual amount of time in the cemetery, and there's no reason why. Although I found it to be extremely frightful, it was also somehow peaceful.

Before the month of March, we had moved several more times; one move took us to Drite Oklahoma. By now even though my mom and Doug had still not married, his beatings continued to grow in intensity. Living in Drite was my introduction into the real life with Doug. This is where he unleashed his full force on me and my sister. I was approaching my eighth birthday but I'm surprised to have survived to live to see it. Doug had had it with me and my sister getting our way all the time, what with wetting the bed, talking back, and not cleaning our dinner plates. He was now about to show us who he was, as my mom said earlier in November nineteen seventy four…'kids this is Doug'.

It just started one morning, no warning, no nothing, morning bed inspections. Holly and I had our own bedrooms that had a shared wall, Holly's inspection came first, and her screams sounded the alarm for me. The idea of spanking a child for wetting the bed is abuse, regardless of the reasoning of the parent, it's abuse, but what Doug did was…far worse.

I was jerked from a deep sound sleep by the sounds of Holly's screams and pleads for mercy. I didn't have any idea what was going on, but whatever Doug was doing to her I knew I was about to experience the same. Holly made every promise she could in an attempt to end the beating Doug was giving to her, and I believe she would have made a deal with the Devil himself if the beating would have stopped. The screaming continued on and on, there was no let up, then suddenly it died off to a whimper, and a deadly silence filled the air; I dare not move or breathe. I then heard a clinging sound; it was the sound of a belt buckle. Doug would rattle his belt buckle to let me know he was on his way. When Doug entered my bedroom he paused at the foot of my bed, and then with a quick snap the covers were pulled off me and the wetness I was lying in was fully exposed.

I had no time to process what was happening as it happened so fast, I felt his hand grab the back of my neck and the grip was strong enough for him to lift my entire body from off the bed. With his hand still gripping the back of my neck he thrust my face into my pee that covered my bed. He pushed my face into my pee cutting off all air which forced me to draw in a gasp of air through my mouth and at the same time drinking in my own pee. As he was pushing my face in my pee, he was shaking my head back and forth like he would do to a dog that he was rubbing its nose in its own excrement. When he was satisfied with the extent of pressing my face into my wet bed he picked me up by my right wrist, and then as he held me high in the air he started to beat me with his belt, not caring where it landed. I know I screamed pleaded and begged as well as twisted and fought with what little might I had. But nothing stopped the beating, I was being hit everywhere, and I was in pain, then he stopped and I was dropped to the floor. I managed to crawl to the corner of my bedroom and when I had made myself as small as I could I peered out to watch him, to ensure that he was done with me and I waited for him to leave my bedroom.

After a few weeks Doug started to get creative in his attempt to get me to stop wetting the bed, he wrote my name on my sheets with the notation that *"I pissed the bed at night"*. He would then hang them outside of my window for the neighbors to see and he would also tell me he was going to send me to military school. But what he did to my sister was far worse than hanging my sheets out of my window; he made Holly wear a sandwich sign to school which said on both sides *"I piss the bed at night."*

It's important to keep in mind that this was nineteen seventy five Oklahoma, teachers did not get involved in the home life of students, but they did what they could for my sister. The first day Holly wore the sign to school it was a surprise to the teachers. When they learned that Holly would be wearing it every day they helped her out as best as they could. As soon as Holly got to school a teacher took the sign off her neck and hid it in the office. After school they waited until most kids were gone and put it back on her neck as Holly and I left for home. The grueling part was that Holly had to walk to school and home every day wearing it. Seeing these things done to my sister taught me how to hate people, and I hated Doug, and at the time my mom for allowing him to do this to me and my sister.

Around the end of March to the first of April nineteen seventy five we had moved back to Santa Fe Oklahoma. I think the first house we lived in was the School House. Not that the house had been a school house, but there was a row of buildings behind the house that me and Holly played school in.

In order to avoid peeing the bed at night Doug had cut off all liquids after five o'clock in the evening and exactly one hour after I went to bed he would get me up to stand in front of the toilet until I peed. To this day I still go to the bathroom exactly after one hour after going to bed. Doug, like my real dad was an alcoholic and smoked cigarette's heavily; and to this day when I smell those two things together I have a dreaded sickening reaction.

Not long after we moved in the School House we moved again. Doug and mom moved us in a house at the foot of the elementary school on the crest of a large hill. So getting to school was just a short walk next door.

It had been a bad winter that year and in early April we had an unexpected huge snowfall. The snow was wet heavy and deep. In Oklahoma they seldom closed school when it snowed, and I did live next door so getting to school was never a problem. I was still wetting the bed every night and I believe Doug was getting worn out beating me every morning, so on this morning he changed his approach. He did not beat this morning, as he had been doing every morning, but he did have something new for me, and I learned what it was in a hurry. As every morning, I had my wet bed inspection, my covers were jerked off and an inspection for a piss spot and wet underwear was made. Of course I was wet as was the bed, but one morning things changed. Allen picked me up, (Allen was Doug's son from his other marriage, and he was in his twenties) carried me outside and tossed me off the front porch, the front porch was high and had a half rock wall around it. Allen tossed me over the rock wall and I landed in the deep snow. I was wearing only my pee wet underwear.

    I quickly ran back up the stairs and pounded on the locked front door. I was told I could not come back in until I quit pissing the bed, where is the logic in that statement. After I realized that all my pounding was fruitless I found a corner on the porch where no snow had fallen, it was a roofed porch, and I made myself into as small of a ball as I could and sat there waiting. I don't think I had to wait more than ten minutes, but I had no way to tell time. By the time my mom did let me back into the house I was freezing cold. I wonder if the only thing that prevented Doug and perhaps my mom from just letting me freeze to death or starve me to death was the fact that my death would have landed them in prison. It's impossible to know why they always intervened when they did.

    Doug had changed in many other ways as well; the first notable change was milk. I was no longer allowed to have any, and the same applied to my sister. The second was food. The general rule was I ate after my mom and Doug, and what I got to eat was not nearly enough or the same. When my mom and Doug had company over I was given the same food as everyone else, but seldom was I able to eat it all since I was not use to eating that much food at a time. My meals were also cut to two a day, however if for some reason a beating did not suffice for Doug's needs, I also got no supper and many nights I went to bed hungry. There were many days I ended up having only one meal. It was not long before Holly got desperate, she was growing and hungry, so she and I started digging through the trash and removing the bones left by my mom and Doug. Holly would sometimes work on breaking down chicken bones for days. Looking back at photos of me during this time, I had gotten smaller, much smaller. In fact in some photos from this period I look smaller than I was in previous years. Holly says I was emaciated, nineteen seventy five was turning out to be a bad year.

    I have some good memories with my sister here, so everything was not all that bad. We started to depend more and more on each other, and we developed a metaphorical way of talking to each other. We had learned that if we spoke in what appeared to be stupid stories, we avoided some conflict with Doug. I also spent more time outside and away from my mom and Doug. I had learned that the less they saw of me the fewer times I got hit. I often played out in the storage shed with my sister. We played school, house, and bank whatever we could think up to play to use up time.

    I don't want to forget Star Trek. It was still running on television and it was the one thing that my mom fought for me to watch. She had to have Doug's permission and how she obtained that I will never know, but I never missed it weekly, my mom made sure of that. I've never been able to understand my mom, although she despised me for what she believed was my being a willing partner with Charles and for killing my sister, she still fought for me to have some enjoyment in my life. Perhaps it was her way of keeping me in some type of control; I've just never been able to figure out her behavior.

    Doug had moved the family again, we stayed in the same town and we still lived close to the school. But now we lived across the street and on the next block over. The town water tower stood right next to our house and bordered our back yard.

Death, no seven year old boy should ever see his best school friend die, but I would see it happen more than once with my young eyes. While attending school in Santa Fe I had made at least one friend, and sad to his memory I can't pull up his name. I suppose this may in fact be good, as remembering his name would complete the memory, something I may not want to do. We had made rubber band guns and played cops and robbers and during recess at school we played cars in the dirt. We did boy things, and he was my friend, whose name I've now forgotten.

The school sat atop a large steep hill. If you were in a car you had to really give it the gas to make it up the hill. The top of the hill was in a blind spot for drivers, and it was also at the crest of that hill that they had painted the school crosswalk. Every day after school my friend and I had to cross the street to reach our homes. A teacher would stand watch at the cross walk and I would hold his hand as we crossed the street. This day in May toward the end of the school year proved different, and I've no idea why. We had been waiting a long time, when suddenly he dropped my hand and stepped into the street without getting an all clear from the teacher. As soon as he entered the street a large two tone brown station wagon appeared. The driver had to lay heavy on the gas to pull the massive full sized station wagon up the steep hill, and as he reached the top of the hill the full power of the motor took charge. The front passenger finder caught my friend in the side; he spun as if doing a final dance move and then fell in front of the tire. The driver realized what had happened and hit his brakes as the entire mass of the car passed over my friend's body. The car came to a rest with the lower half of my friend's body sticking out from just behind the front passenger tire; I did not wait around for what I already knew, my friend was dead. I ran across the street to the town water tower and sat there crying propped against the leg of the tower. I must have sat there for several hours before I noticed the twilight of evening approaching. My heart started to race, I knew what I faced when I got home. Slowly, as slow as I could, I walked home, why should I be in a hurry? Regardless of when I walked through the door now, the end was to be the same.

When I did finally walk through the door my mom and Doug were waiting for me, I don't know if they had heard about the accident at school, but if they did it did not matter to them. Doug ordered me to my room, and a few minutes later he followed me in, jingling the buckle on his belt as he came. By this time in my life I was not allowed to cry when being beat, if I cried or screamed it fed into Doug's fury and he would order me to shut up crying with a new hit to reinforce his meaning. And as he made contact with each new hit he would always say the same thing.

"You wanna cry? I'll give you something to cry about."

Then smack, another hit with the leather belt. So if I cried I got beat more and if I did not cry I got beat until I cried. I took the beating and after he was done I sat on my bed and did cry, for my friend and for me. As I said this was not to be the last time I would have to watch one of my friends die in front of me. It was to happen again.

By this time in my life with Doug he expected perfection out of me. When he told me to do something it had to be done right the first time, no mistakes, no excuses, no justification. If I did mess up a job or if I forgot to do something he had told me to do, a beating was in order, followed by my doing or redoing the task correctly. This sounds like a simple teaching lesson from a parent, but when I say that Doug expected perfection from me, he expected perfection. Since what he asked was impossible I got many beatings for just not being good enough. What surprises me is that to this day I now expect perfection out of myself, and I know for certain I can't live up to my own expectations.

May twenty fifth nineteen seventy five, my eighth birthday and it was looking to be a blast. Grandma Williams had a special surprise for me; she said it would be something I would never forget. My mom took me and my sister to Pawnee to celebrate my birthday and then later Grandma drove me and my sister to the

Pawnee Theater. Standing outside the theater she gave both of us a .50 cent piece to get popcorn and a drink, then I saw the poster on the movie house, "Star Wars", I couldn't contain my excitement. I found my seat toward the front middle and planted my butt. For the entire movie I neither took a breath nor moved from my seat, I was awe struck. Up to that time it was the most impressive display of Si-Fi I had ever seen, it was even better than Captain Kirk. When I left the movie house I could not stop talking about "Star Wars" for days, but it quickly became apparent that Holly wished I would stop talking about it.

    With my mom and Doug we moved so often that sometimes we never had the chance to unpacked. One time Doug moved us into a small trailer on the outskirts of Santa Fe. My mom had made homemade chocolate syrup and it was far better than store bought. Later I had asked her how to make it; she told me that the recipe is on the side of the coco can. It's just one of those funny little quirky memories. While living at the trailer I finally got to learn what Doug did for a living. He had asked me one evening if I would like to go with him to work the next day. He just wanted free labor, but I agreed and went with him to work, after all this could be a way to get on his good side. It turned out that Doug was in construction, he built houses, and I hated anything to do with construction. It was the last time I ever went with him to work.

    Just after my birthday in May around the thirtieth, Doug moved my mom, me and Holly to the outskirts of Augusta Georgia. Just in case you are not aware of where Augusta is, Augusta is somewhere between the Sun and hot. We took Interstate ten on the way to Georgia, and most of Interstate ten is a bridge over the swamps of Georgia and Louisiana. Doug told me if the car were to run off the bridge the alligators would eat us before help could reach us. I became afraid to drive over bridges after that trip and later while I was learning to drive I would close my eyes when going over bridges, sometimes I still close my eyes.

We lived in a trailer in Augusta Georgia, that I'm surprised had not been condemned. The back wall in the living room had a section missing, so you could see right through the wall and into a black berry patch that grew behind the trailer. In my room the closet floor was missing, so I guess I had an escape hatch of sorts if I were to ever need one. It was here that I got to watch my first episode of "The Mickey Mouse Club".

The only other kid to play with was my sister Holly so I did my best to put up with her; we played baseball a lot in the front dirt road. Once while I was pitching the ball to Holly she hit it back in a straight line at me, it landed dead square in my chest. I fell to the ground gasping for air; it had deflated my diaphragm and knocked the wind right out of me.

Taking my turn to do the dishes was one of the most dreaded chores I had to do. If Doug found one single speck of anything, even dust, every dish in the house got pulled and I had to do every single one. I learned to make sure the dishes were perfect on the first wash.

My mom and Doug had been living together for over a year and in early June of nineteen seventy five they decide to get married. It was in fact a sham wedding; if they were married Doug could claim me and Holly as dependents and file his tax returns as married, thus saving money in each year. My mom and Doug did a good job creating a sham wedding, it took place in a preacher's house; I sat on the couch with my sister and watched. When Doug got us home that day after the wedding he sat us on the couch and gave a short speech, we were to no longer call him Doug but dad. I spoke up.

"But you're not my dad." I said

"You have two dads now." My mom answered.

"You're to call me dad." His voice was demanding and threatening.

That ended the conversation. In truth Doug and my mom never were legally married, I'm not sure how they did it or what they did, but it was enough for them to save money on filing taxes each year. For years I had believed that my mom and Doug were in fact married.

Doug's abuse and beatings grew worse after the wedding; he must have gotten tired from beating me all the time because he developed methods of torture. One method was the nose in the circle. He drew a circle on the wall and I had to put my nose in it, the catch, the circle was at such a height that I had to be in a squatted position but on my tip toes, the result? After a couple of hours all I could do was roll over and let time stretch out my legs. I fear this is what may have contributed to the damage with my legs, causing me to be confined to a wheel chair after age thirty five. Other forms of punishments were sitting cross legged with hands folded, this was not too bad, but I hated it. If I got into a fight with Holly my mom had us get into the center of the living room and fist fight it out until one of us fell to the floor in exhaustion. My mom would also bite me as a form of punishment, I really never understood the logic of my mom biting me, and so the lesson she thought she was teaching me is forever lost. Groundings from *EVERYTHING* and for weeks were common with Doug, but for some reason it never applied to Star Trek. As odd as it may seem my mom and Doug allowed me to watch it and it was never used as a threat or punishment, maybe it had become a pacifier for me. I suppose I just need to stop trying to figure the Star Trek thing out. But the go-to punishment was always a beating, quick easy and it gave Doug the thrill he needed.

What my life had become living with Doug became the normal way of life for me. After all, this was now my life, daily beatings and punishments that amounted to torture, so I had adapted. He was also demanding about me eating all of the food on my plate, at this point my mom and Doug were still putting my food on my plate, mostly things that I found disgusting. If I did not eat everything, I had to remain at the table until I did, even if it meant all night. I did spend many nights at the table, and my food was still in front of me the next morning, and I always gave in and ate it. I shall stop at this point about what may or may not have happened after eating such food, as I don't trust my memory, but as I recall, if I threw it up, I had to eat it all over again, but I feel this is an un-trusted memory.

It was not long before Doug moved the family from Georgia back to Drite. To a certain degree things started to settle down to what had become for me a normal routine. Doug was still beating me in the mornings, food was given more as a reward or payment, and I was skinny and getting skinnier everyday but since the withholding of food was gradual my body was growing accustom to it.

We did not stay in Drite for too long, maybe a month or two at most, and then Doug moved the family to Oiltown sometime in July nineteen seventy five. It was here that Doug added a new element of punishment for me.

Our lives crossed again with Kathy, Jason, and Kim and Doug paid Jason a weekly allowance to beat me up on a regular basis. Doug also continued with my pet names, pussy, pansy, panty waist, sissy, faggot, and more. Each month the way Doug dealt with me changed, there was no consistency; I was always trying to figure out the rules to each change. With each change that Doug implemented the reason for the punishment also changed. So no matter what I did or how hard I tried to be good, it never mattered because I never knew the rules since they changed so often.

Bath time was once a week and me and my sister had to share the same bath water, if my cousins stayed all night the bath water went that much further. I don't think I ever got to take a bath first, and believe me when I say; everyone pees in the bath water. Oiltown holds a lot of strange memories for me, mostly what are called flashbulb memories. Most of my memories are vivid and detailed. But Oiltown is the only time in my life, that I can say my memories are flashbulb memories. Perhaps because so much happened in such a short period of time that I still can't piece it all together. Maybe I should not even try either. The only thing that I can remember clearly is that I was nearly starved to death while we lived in Oiltown, and not the way a kid might express starving, like I said I was getting at most one meal a day and that was usually oatmeal.

Not long after we moved back to Oiltown Doug got word that the state police had learned he was back in Oklahoma so again we moved and this time to Robstown Texas. Life in Robstown was hard; make no mistake Doug found a way to make it harder on me. I guess it was because I was getting older, and he viewed me more as a threat; I don't know. Doug and my mom expected far more from me and my sister than we were able to give, more than we should have ever been asked to do. We did our best to keep the flames of abuse down, even throwing surprise parties for my mom and Doug when we thought he was mad at us. He had also used the circle on the wall punishment more and for a longer period of time on me in Robstown. It was while living in Texas that I remember the pain in my legs getting worse. It's a pain I will never forget, because I now live with it every day, and am no longer able to walk. Also Doug started to make me eat things that he knew I hated, I spent many nights sleeping at the kitchen table. He told me if I were to throw up I would have to eat it, but as I mentioned before it is not necessary to expound on that thought.

My mom and Doug managed the "Silver Dollar Motel" and so many people came in and out of my life in the summer of nineteen seventy five. It was more or less a live in motel for many guests. One family that lived in the motel had two boys Dale and Vincent; and I hated both of those boys.

There is one outstanding event that is most likely the cause of some brain damage to my sister Holly. Doug and my mom had left me and Holly alone to watch the motel for an entire day. Normally nothing ever happen at the motel, people just went about their business, rarely did anyone ever come to the office, but this day was different. There was no way me and my sister being as young as we were could have known that Doug was using the motel as a front for selling drugs, but he was. On this one day that he left me and my sister alone at the motel a visitor came to see Doug. He asked questions about Doug and I did not understand why he was asking them. Holly had let him come into the office; after all he showed us his badge so we felt we could trust him. Once he was in the office he asked if it would be okay for him to look around, and again we told him it was okay. He had found a book and asked if he could take it, again we felt since he had a badge it would be okay. Doug and my mom should have given us clearer instructions about visitors with badges. After he found the book he left. It was several hours later before Doug and my mom got home and he had some people with him. He took them to his desk, and when he could not find his book he got up to find me and Holly. Holly and I were sitting on my bed, most likely playing a board game, when Doug walked in, his voice was raised and he was mad.

  He asked about the book and Holly told him about the man coming over with a badge and he asked if he could take the book. At hearing that Doug lost his temper, and control. Doug was in the process of building a wall in my room to make two bedrooms so there was a stack of lumber lying against the wall, and he reached down to pick up a piece. I can't say for certain how big it was or what size, but it would work for the job he needed it to do. He started swinging it at me and Holly, and we scattered. I managed to squeeze between the studs in the unfinished wall and got behind a dresser, but Holly; she got caught in the corner of the bed and wall. I watched as Doug brought that piece of lumber down on her, she curled into a ball and put her hands over her head, but he kept on hitting. I started pleading and screaming at Doug to stop, and after a while he did, but not before a few of the blows made contact with the prefrontal area of Holly's head. When he stopped he noticed where I had hidden and he knew I would not come out for hours so he picked up a table top record player and threw it at the wall above my head. It shattered and rained down on me, the larger pieces did inflect some pain and cuts but nothing serious. He then left the room out of breath and exhausted, the next morning we were on the road again, moving back to Santa Fe Oklahoma.

Chapter 6
The Farm

When we returned to Santa Fe Oklahoma Doug moved us into a house about five miles outside of town, it was in fact a farm. A small creek cut through the back side of the pasture that we kept cows in and the creek was also the place where I would go swimming on the last hot days of summer. All around the yard of the farm were small out buildings some of which housed chickens coops and in others we used to store equipment, but even here Doug ran some unlawful business on the side.

It was now late August of nineteen seventy five and my mom had enrolled me and Holly back into school. This was in fact the same school that I had seen my friend get hit by the car and killed just a few months before. Doug's abuse continued. He had in fact perfected an old form of punishment; he was drawing close to breaking me. At night after it got dark and if I did something that he thought was stupid he would send me to my room. I was not allowed to turn the light on, so my bedroom would remain pitch dark. He would tell me that he would be in there later to deal with me, which could only mean a beating. So I would go to my room, leave the light off and sit on my bed in the darkness waiting.

The waiting was unnerving, I never knew when he would enter or how long I would have to wait for him; so all I could do was wait in the darkness. I would strain my hearing, tilting my head in the direction of any squeak or the slightest noise. When he finely entered all I could hear was the jingling of his belt buckle, and the smell he gave off. The smell of beer and cigarettes would linger thick in the dark air, it would choke me and many times I would gag, trying not to throw up. He would never turn on the light; he preferred to hunt me in the darkness, his goal was to instill fear in me, a goal he achieved.

Once I knew he was in the room and moving in my direction I would scamper and hide under the bed trying to squeeze myself as far as I could against the wall in the corner. Sometimes I would hide in the closet, covering myself with clothes as if he would not think to look under them, but in the end he always found me. When I was sitting in the dark room waiting knowing I was being hunted, fear would grip me by the throat and choke me; I had to gasp for every breath of air. I would attempt to steady and quiet my breathing, but in fact every breath I drew in was a gasp for life and he heard every one of those gasps. That is how he always knew where I was and he would always find me. When he found me, or knew about where I was, he would swing the belt in my direction, and somehow the belt would always make contact with me. If he could not reach me with the belt he would reach for me with his hands. When he found me he would drag me from my hiding place, either by my arm, leg and sometimes even my hair. I could never tell from what direction the blow would come so when contact was made the entire ordeal was a surprise, even though I knew it was coming.

From these darkness beatings I learned to sharpen my sense of hearing and smell and it proved useful, and its usefulness would be put to the full test in just over a year. By sharpening these senses I was able to avoid contact with the belt many times. I learned to feel even the slightest movement of air against my bare skin and also hear the swish sound that the air made as an object moved through it. It is without a doubt that he had started this many years earlier, but it was on that farm that the memories of the darkened attacks are the strongest.

My mom had filled the backyard with chickens and every Sunday afternoon we knew we were having a fried chicken dinner; problem is the closest male child had to kill the chicken. So I tended to be gone around one o'clock in the afternoon. Nevertheless it was me and my cousin Todd that seemed to always be the chicken killers.

Todd spent a lot of time with us on the farm, I could never fully understand why he spent so much time with us, I suppose he just enjoyed being in the country out on the farm. But whatever the reason Todd and I had become friends and we had many good adventures on the farm. One thing that I remember very clearly, we had built a huge tree house in a field behind the house, and one day after climbing up we were met with a large surprise. A very large Western Diamond Back rattle snake had made its way into the tree house and there Todd and I were standing on a small, tight platform about ten feet above the ground. Todd did the only thing that he could have done. In lighting speed he reached down, picked up the snake and tossed it over the side. To this day I'm amazed that Todd never got bit, perhaps that snake was more surprised and caught off guard then we were.

Behind the farm house was the small creek that I mentioned earlier, too small to be a river, but it made a great swimming hole for me, Todd and other boys from nearby farms and homes. Nearly every day you could find me, Holly, Todd, Jason and some of our friends swimming. Some days while we were cooling off in the water we would see a truck back up to the creek downstream and unload some cargo. As I mentioned Doug was still engaged in some unlawful business and he was letting septic waste trucks unload their cargo in our swimming hole for a fee, to be paid to him. As long as they stayed downstream all was good as far as I was concerned.

My bed in my bedroom sat against the wall that had a window for a short time, it was moved to an inside wall after the window got broken. One night Todd and I were goofing off on the bed, just wrestling, when my bare foot went through the window. Blood was instantly everywhere. Doug refused to let my mom bandaged it. He felt that I deserved it for goofing off and breaking the window, so I lay there bleeding all over the bed. I tried to hold it to stop it from bleeding but it was no use, the cut was too deep. Finally, at risk to herself, my mom got up and bandaged it. I should have been taken to hospital and given stitches, but it made Doug mad that I broke a window and got blood on the sheets, so I had to learn my lesson.

Todd and I did have many great adventures together. While living in Santa Fe we would get inside a large tractor tire and roll down hills, I got very dizzy from doing this. We would build some of the craziest looking bikes, and they did work, although it took great effort, and we even built a mini-cycle. I have only fond memories during my youth with Todd on the farm, and I still miss those days.

One day Todd, Jason, me and another boy decided to go camping. We packed our gear and only one tent; we thought we were ready for anything. The month had changed from August to September, and in Oklahoma the September weather can turn from nice and sunny to cold and rainy in a matter of hours. We walked down the road, crossed a fence and set up camp in a cow pasture. That night a cold front moved through and the rain poured down, all of our firewood had gotten rain soaked. The next morning we needed to start a fire as the cold front had dropped the temperature and all four of us were very cold. There was not a stick of dry wood anywhere to start the fire with so we did the only thing we could think of. We all took off our underwear; our thinking was that we could start the fire with our hopefully dry underwear. It did not work, the underwear burned up too quickly and the wood was too drenched. We ended up packing up our camping gear and walked home in the cold rain, soaked and without a clean pair of underwear between the four of us.

I don't remember if we were asked or if it was just something that Todd and I set out doing on our own. There was a day that Todd and I were out in a field behind one of the out buildings and it was overgrown with tall weeds. We found some one-by-two's and we used them as weed cutters and started cutting down the weeds, Todd did not notice where I was standing when he swung back his stick and brought it forward. His stick came down and caught me at the base of my skull. I went down and for a few seconds I could not see, although I had my eyes open, everything was black, however I never passed out. That very same day Todd fell off the roof of the barn. It's a good thing that Todd and I were made nearly unbreakable back then.

It was while living on the farm that I had discovered mercury. In today's world if someone spills mercury they call out the hazmat crews. I remember I use to break open several thermometers for the mercury inside and once I had a big ball of it I would play with it for hours. I would carry it around in my front shirt pocket, where I felt it was safe. That farm house must have had a lot of mercury embedded in the carpet because I dropped it all the time.

There were so many events that happened on the farm it would take another one hundred pages to tell it all. Most of it was good; I did have some really good times on the farm with Todd. Times that I really look back on and miss.

I had quit wetting the bed by nineteen seventy five so now my beatings from Doug were less frequent. I had now decided to protect myself above and beyond all others around me, even my sister. I was tired of being beaten and taken advantage of; I had to look out for myself if I was to survive. However one day in the middle of September, not long after my mishap of a camping trip, things turned in my favor, or so I thought.

It was a hot day for September, more like early August, and hours had passed before my mom realized that Holly and Jason were gone. If two children that young went missing today a force of thousands would be out looking for them, but not then and not Holly and Jason. My mom figured out that they had run away and I decided to use this to my favor. I presented myself as having knowledge of their plans, but I was too afraid to tell. It worked; my mom gave me a Coke-a-Cola, sat me on the couch and asked me to tell her everything. I was never allowed to touch her Coke, so to get a whole Coke to myself was to be the top kid on the farm, the most favored kid, at least for the moment, she thought she had bribed me. I sipped small sips and spoke in broken bits and pieces, watching her for clues as to what information seemed justified. I didn't know anything about Holly and Jason and what they had done, they had told me nothing and I was just as surprised by their disappearance as mom was, but I had to play this out. I was guessing at every detail. I did know that Doug's German Sheppard was missing as well, so I just drew the logical conclusion and explained that Jason took the dog with him when they ran away. But up to this point no one knew if they had indeed run away. Finally I had played out my Coke and my mom sent me out to the yard to pull crab grass, which was to keep me out of her way. When Doug got home that evening my mom filled him in and then he questioned me, again I gave them nothing but made up assumptions, I just happened to have guessed everything correctly.

They had indeed run away, they followed the train tracks from the farm, on the north side of Santa Fe, all the way to Oaktown, where dad was at the time. Doug's German Sheppard did follow them and on a train overpass, about twenty feet above the rocky ground Jason tossed it over the side, killing it on the rocks below. When they arrived at dad's they explained why they ran away and early that evening dad pulled up with Holly and Jason in his car.

Doug ordered them both in the house and to the back room, he intended to beat them, but dad refused to let him touch Holly, so Doug took Jason in alone. I stood there, outside and listened to the beating and the screams of Jason, I suppose Jason took Holly's beating as well. I can still see my mom, dad, and Holly all standing around dad's car parked near the shade tree, no one saying anything or looking at each other while we stood by and let Doug beat Jason. After Doug came out I went in to see Jason, and Jason was in bad shape. For Jason to cower away from me could only mean that Doug had hurt him bad. It was only a few months earlier that Doug was paying Jason a weekly allowance to beat me up, and Jason was now cowering away from me. Holly went inside after Doug came out and started to pack her clothes and personal things, she was returning to live with dad. This would leave just me and I knew I would become the only and primary target of Doug, I asked to return to live with dad as well and was told no, by my dad.

Not long after Holly returned with dad, he took her back to Texas. He had come to Oklahoma for only a few weeks, he had left Donna and Kris behind in Texas. He had some unfinished business that Clifford and John asked him to take care of. He had written a letter to Holly to let her know he would be in Oaktown, but he never told me and told Holly not to tell me. Holly took advantage of his return to Oaktown and took her chance to escape from life with Doug. She had even used Jason to help her in her escape, knowing full well that he would have to return to Doug and Jason would have no escape. Holly knew that Jason would have to endure his beating as well as take one for her. She had learned to manipulate people and use them to her own advantage.

Chapter 7
"I Held My Breathing Steady"

In many ways, although it may seem odd, my mother was my protector during these first eight years, although not from Doug, she did protect me from a greater threat, my dad. As you may recall from my account dad beat my mom and left the family when I was six, I saw very little of him after that, and for good reason. So as I now take you through a transition in the telling of this story, pieces I have already told you may come to mind and start falling together, forming a picture of where I'm taking you. However I caution you, I don't believe it's possible for anyone hearing this story to know where it's going until I have told the entire story. From nineteen seventy three to this point in my story I have excluded telling you too much about my dad. Not only because I knew little of his life up to this point, but also because what he was and why he rejected his only son, me. From this point forward loose ends will start to tie themselves into nice little knots, and my story will start to make sense, at least that is my hope.

After Holly left in the middle of September and until December it was mostly just me at home on the farm. Although Jason and Todd spent many weekends there, they were away more often than they were there. I found myself alone with my mom and Doug and I was also the benefactor of all his anger and abuse. I had found myself in what many would call a prison camp, and I had no way of escape.

December twenty fifth nineteen seventy five, Christmas at Grandma Smith' house, this was a grand Christmas, perfect gifts, a meal fit for a family and my dad was back. He had brought Donna, Kris and Holly, it felt like a real family Christmas. While dad and Donna were visiting I told them both all the tales of Doug's beatings and what I was going through. Donna pushed my dad into a court hearing, she felt my dad should get custody of me; otherwise dad would have done nothing. Dad and Donna had contacted a lawyer the first week of January nineteen seventy six and for the first time I felt a ray of hope. I had allowed myself to believe in a better life and that I was going to get to tell my story for the first time and someone would listen, truly listen; and I would hopefully find some reprieve from the abuse. However a week before the hearing everything stopped and the meeting with the judge was canceled because my parents had reached a settlement; my mom was going to let dad keep Holly and I was to stay with my mom and Doug. Nothing changed, I gave up the last bit of hope a boy of eight could hold on to, my life was now completely hopeless.

    The settlement may seem odd; that my mom and dad would leave things the way they were, without asking me and Holly what we wanted, but there was a reason. Dad had not paid child support to my mom while she had me and Holly and in Oklahoma they had issued a warrant for his arrest, but dad knew Doug also had warrants out on him, but in several states. So it was a M-A-D situation. They both faced Mutually Assured Destruction if either of them did anything the other one disagreed with. What did surprise me was that dad did not want me, he choose my sister over me, in fact he made it known to me that he would never take me under any circumstances and then he wished me a good life with Doug, knowing full well what Doug was doing to me. So when Donna had wanted a hearing before a judge both my mom and dad wanted to do anything and everything to avoid being exposed and giving up the life they had, if you could call what they had a life. Each of them having one of us kids also meant money from state agencies. Whoever had a kid got food stamps and a welfare check every month, so the settlement meant simply keeping things the way they were. Donna was against it, but in the end she had no voice in the manner and when my dad had Donna in private he put her in her place, she never spoke of going to court again.

After dad, Donna, Kris and Holly returned to Texas, I returned to my life with my mom and Doug in Santa Fe Oklahoma and then – lost. The rest of January and the first part of February of nineteen seventy six my memory is filled with huge gaps; gaps that I can't seem to fill with anything, only white noise exists. I set out to learn what was missing from my memory.

Before my mom died I had a conversation with her about this time period.

"Mom what happened in January and February of nineteen seventy six?" I asked my mom, she was now sitting up in her hospice bed.

"Son, some things God does not intend for you to remember." Her reply was broken as breathing was difficult, and the hiss from the oxygen hose came with every word.

"But I can remember as much as I do about other times, why not this time?" I was pressing for details, I had to know.

"I will tell you this, this is one of the darkest time periods in your entire life, and it is best forgotten and not dug up." She said in between gasps of breath.

"How can this be the darkest, when what I remember about other times is as bad as it is? In fact the December of nineteen seventy six is the darkest time of my life that I can remember, nothing can be worse than that." I shot back.

I did have a love for my mother, but before she died I had to know the truth about January and February nineteen seventy six.

"You need to trust me on this one Brian, God is not letting you remember, don't try to."

She fell back on the bed, exhausted, unable to continue. My mother was not a religious woman, but her references to God were an inducement for me to stop with the questions, as if she was attempting to blame someone else for what happened in January and February.

So I gave up attempting to gain more information from my mom and left her in her misery. Much to my disbelief that was the last time I was to ever see her alive. In fact I was not even able to attend her funeral, and without me present she had no one to claim her body. She remains in a grave in a cemetery at the borders of Oaktown and Smith Counties in Oklahoma. Some of the local people and the police department in the community paid for a pine box and a metal plaque with her name and date of death, no birth date as she never gave one to the hospice.

I've not even been able to find the time to visit her grave, which I suppose I should find the time to do.

So left with no other choice for information, I asked my sister Holly, and her information was not going to prove too trustworthy, she was at the time I spoke to her addicted to prescription pain medications. What she was able to tell me helped shed some light on the matter and it also brought to my mind that there had to be police records, which there were. So from her account and obtaining and reading the police record of the account my memories were unlocked and I was able to clearly recall the events of the last week of January and the first week of February nineteen seventy six.

Holly told me that sometime in late January of nineteen seventy six Doug and my mom had gotten into a fight. They were at the Little Dixie Bar when the fight started. I personally don't know what it feels like to have a knife penetrate deep within my body, but I do know what it looks like. Doug and my mom had gone to the Little Dixie Bar for a night out, and as is true of most bars a fight broke out, but this one was between my mom and Doug. After I spoke to Holly I started digging deeper for more information and I have read so many variants of the story in newspapers that it's senseless to attempt to accept one version as the complete truth. But to get to the stabbing, during the fight either Doug or my mom, I don't know which one, pulled out a knife, most likely Doug. At first my mom pulled back, but since she was drunk and mad she changed direction and instead lunged at Doug, attempting to grab the knife from him; she intended to use it on him. As my mom moved toward Doug, Doug brought the knife up to his waist and the knife dug deep into my mom's right hip. She was taken to hospital and the wound was tended to. Since she had no insurance the emergency room stitched her up to close the wound and she was then sent home. However Doug was now on the run, fearing arrest and prison, so my mom had no one to tend to her at home. I was only eight years old and too young to give her the care she needed. My mom ended up calling the only person she knew that would come to her side, Steve.

  Steve picked me and my mom up at hospital and then drove us both home, to Kern Street. My mom could not stay in Santa Fe, she now had a real fear of Doug, the same fear that I had. Although the house on Kern Street was locked up and had no power or water, it was the only place my mom and me had left that we could go. In all her relationships, and the whole time she spent with Doug she never sold the Kern Street house or put another man's name on the deed, it was the last remaining thing that she had that was hers, and she held on to the house in case she needed a place to go to.

  The sun had just started to make its rise over the eastern horizon and streaks of light were starting to lighten the late January sky. Inside the house it was cold, very cold, when I would exhale my breath became frost, but like I mentioned this was all we had. Steve carried my mom into the master bedroom; it was the same room that Charles had built and shared with my mom. Steve put her into bed covering her with as many blankets as he could find. I then climbed in bed and lay next to my mother, placing my head on her chest. Steve was kind to my mom but it was also shameful that the only person she felt she could trust to call in a life or death situation was an old affair that she once had. Steve was holding on to his marriage, my mom was holding onto a fantasy.

When I woke up late the next day, the house was warm, meaning the gas had been turned on as well as the power and water; Steve had all the utilities turned on. After emptying my bladder I made my way to the kitchen and found it stocked with food, real food, not like the stuff Doug had been feeding me. I fixed my mom a bowl of Apple Jacks and a glass of orange juice and took them to her on a cookie sheet I found under the counter. I realized that from this day forward it was to be just my mom and me. I don't believe she would ever trust another man around her, after dad then Charles and now Doug, she was through with men.

Steve continued to come over while my mom recovered to ensure that she would be able to manage on her own. He took many photos of the stab wound; my mom wanted them in the event that the police ever found Doug, they would be needed as evidence. As January turned into February my mom continued to get stronger and as she did Steve was there less and less until one day he never returned, ever, he was out of my life and to never return.

There are a number of things about my mother's relationship with Doug that I've never been able to understand. The first was their sham marriage, how did they manage to legally pull that off? The second, why did no one in the bar attempt to help my mom when she was stabbed. So there is a lot about Doug and my mom's relationship that will now never be known. But as I said when I started telling you this part, there are many variations to the story and none of them make any sense. I also said that this turned out to be a dark time in my life, and it did indeed lend itself to that.

After Holly got my memory recall going, I was able to fill in the missing information, information that Holly would have no way to have known about. It also helped me to read through the police reports; there were two officers that made excellent notes in the reports. I believe what they wrote went beyond what was expected of them, but they both felt what they wrote was necessary.

After the stabbing and my mom and me returning to the Kern Street house our lives had settled down for a short time. It took some adjusting for me to get used to the concept that I would no longer be hit or beat for any perceived infraction on the part of Doug. The torture punishments also ended, as did me living in abject fear every second of every day.

By the second week in February my mother and I had found our routine, and she was starting to pick up her guitar again, but she just played, no singing. Maybe it took happiness for my mom to sing, and I knew she was not happy anymore. Before Steve left for the last time he had made a trip to our old house in Santa Fe and packed up all our clothes and some personal items, leaving everything else behind for looters and the landlord. It gave the landlord something to collect on for three months missed rent.

In four short weeks I had almost forgotten what my daily routine was like with Doug and was starting to find some sort of happiness for myself again. However the house on Kern Street also carried the worst memories of my life up to this point. It was here that I had to stop my dad from killing my mom. It was also here that I first met Jane, Josh and Charles. It was also in the Kern Street house that I had killed my little sister Beth. The house on Kern Street was a house full of the horrors that kept revisiting me, and the greatest horror to visit me in this house was only a week away, and my mom and I never saw it coming.

    February twelfth nineteen seventy six started out like any other day. My mom had recovered enough that she was now getting up and making me breakfast before I left for school, and this day was no different. The morning was warmer than it should have been and the sky was clear except for the rising of the sun, no clouds to cover the beautiful blue day that was taking form. My mom had made me gravy and biscuits with bacon on the side and she joined me at the breakfast table. Although I knew deep inside her she still saw me with repulsion, she was going to do the best she could to finish raising me. I was after all still only eight years old and very dependent on someone to take care of me, but I had also matured a great deal in two years.

    It was odd to be in the same house again that just over two years ago I had my sixth birthday and the following week watched as my life and family was torn apart. In the time since my sixth birthday I had traveled much of the central states and half way across the country and had experienced life at the hands of many peers and adults. What I had endured in the past two and a half years many would never see in a lifetime, but I was not proud of what I had been through, I was lonely and afraid. Sitting at the table eating breakfast that morning with just my mother in the house that once held my whole family was a reminder of that loneliness. I was now, as far as I knew the last thread of the tapestry of the family that once existed, the loose thread of which was pulled when I turned six. Looking back as an adult I now know that it was not my birthday or anything that I did that caused the tapestry to come undone, it was my dad, and that will become clear as I continue telling this story.

However for the time being I was sitting at the breakfast table with my mother eating breakfast prepared out of, if nothing else the duties of a mother. It was not out of love for me that my mom did what she did, raising me had now became her duty, like the job a trash man had to do. Sometimes we do a job and even a job we hate simply because we have to in order to survive. My mom continuing to raise me was that kind of job for her. Even though I was the last man standing, she no longer danced with me as she did in Walnut to Credence Clearwater Revival, she no longer held me when I had a nightmare, or hugged me when I fell and got hurt. She no longer played her guitar and sang folk songs with me, because now when she saw me, she saw the boy that was with Charles or the son that killed her baby daughter, she saw in me what she felt for my dad.

When I left for school that morning there was no goodbye kiss or 'be careful today', my mom did not even watch me as I got on the bus; I was just out the door and gone. My day at school was like any other day, learning the basics of reading, math and English, some art time and recess time then done, and I made my way back home. I kept to myself at school. The friends I had made two years ago I choose to no longer be friends with. After watching my friend get hit by the car in Santa Fe I no longer wanted any friends, I seemed to attract death and evil. It somehow seemed to me at that time in my life everything I did and everyone I came into contact with either died or turned out to hurt me or others in some way. So I felt it best to withdraw into myself and avoid people in general. At school I had learned to keep my head down, eyes to the floor and avoid saying a word to anyone, the more contact I avoided with others the greater the chance they had to live through the day they were in.

By the end of the day the temperature had dropped and a frost was in the air, it was after all the second week in February. When the bus let me off in front of my house I ran from the street to the door, the cold was cutting through the light jacket I had chosen, not expecting the day to turn cold. Inside the house it was warm and my mom was still in the process of turning the Kern Street house back into a home, even if just for the two of us. The stab wound was causing her to move slower than she was use to and unpacking the boxes that Steve had brought over was proving to be a time consuming task for her, but it gave my mom something to do during the day. When Steve brought some of our stuff back from Santa Fe he had also filled the kitchen with food, food that was now starting to diminish in quantity, we were running out of stuff to eat. And the money Steve left was also almost out, by the middle of March my mom would no longer be able to pay the utilities. My life was starting to take on a more desperate meaning for survival.

As the sun began to fade in the west my mom started to make supper, asking me to help her in the kitchen. Helping her in the kitchen brought back to my mind when me and my sisters help her with that last meal the family never ate on June fourth nineteen seventy three, in my heart I was crying for the death of my family, but on the outside I was letting my mom see the best face I could put on, but not for her sake, for mine. We both sat the table and then took our seats, she on one end and I set on the long side, but close to my mother.

"Brian?"

"Ya?"

My mom hardly ever started a conversation at the table, so I figured what she had to say must be important.

"We're bout out of food and money, soon we'll have notin' and I'm not able to go back to work yet."

I looked at her with a blank face. She got the point that I was attempting to get across with my expression, that she was not telling me anything I didn't already know.

"So what? We can't do anything 'bout it."

"Well in the morning after you leave for school I was going to use some of the money left and get a cab to take me down to the welfare office." My mother explained her intentions.

"So, we could've done that sooner, couldn't we?" I asked in return.

"No, not with my wound, I wouldn't have been able to move around very good and they might'of asked questions that I had no intention of answering."

She had a point, and I didn't want to end up in some boys home or worse foster care, well I'm not so sure which one would've been worse.

"So you think you can deal with'it 'morrow?" I asked her.

"Better than I could'of last week."

"Think we'll get anything from it?" I asked.

"Dun'no, but can't hurt to try, I can't see why we can't, we ain't got anything else, and I can't work with you being at home alone at eight."

My mom had made some good points and I knew she was right; we were likely to get approved under the circumstances that we were now living in.

After we had cleared the supper dishes and cleaned the kitchen we went into the living room and watch the evening news and some other shows that she enjoyed. Thinking back, as I tell you this story, I had not watched an episode of Star Trek since moving back in the Kern Street house with my mom after she was stabbed; somehow Star Trek had slipped my memory. We both sat on the couch, but apart, when I did attempt to sit close to her, she was cold and distant. Sometimes after Charles and Beth my mom was still my mom and yet at other times she made me feel hated and dirty. I look back today and wonder if my mother's mental state had not been adversely affected but all that our family had been through.

As the evening drew to a close and the hour reached ten at night my mom told me to go to bed, after all I had school in the morning and she was going to the welfare office, to get the help we were now desperate for.

At this point in the story I believe I should relate the events in as detailed a fashion as I can recall, as I want to ensure that I tell the account as correctly as I can.

"Brian, you need to get to bed, you have school in the morning and I'll have to be up early to get cleaned up for the welfare office."

"Sure, so you get the bathroom first in the morning?" I already knew the answer.

"And just what do you think?"

"Good night, mom."

"Night Brian."

I went to the bathroom, brushed my teeth, peed and then went to my bedroom. My curtains were open allowing the light of the full moon to fill my room with splinters of silver light in all directions. I removed my shirt and laid it on my dresser, then took off my blue jeans and placed them on my shirt; I would have to wear them for two more days before wash day. I left my socks on to keep my feet warm under the covers and walked over to the window in my underwear to peer out at the moon as it hung in the blackness of space. I stood looking up at the beautiful white diamond of a moon, light bouncing off of it giving us light to see, by night. I wondered if the men from NASA really did go there, dad had told me they faked the whole thing in New Mexico or somewhere out west, I could not remember. I wondered about other planets, and other children on those other planets, were their parents mean and was their life like mine. In an episode of Star Trek I had watched it was about a parallel universe, so I wondered if there was another Brian out, or over there, that was good and had never been treated like me and that never killed his little sister. As I continued to watch the moon, lost in thought, I could have sworn it blinked at me, but there was no one living at or in the moon, but there it was again, so maybe there was life out there after all. At least it did not hurt for a boy of eight years of age to have a small silver sliver glimmer of hope for a better life.

My room had no heat vent of its own, the gas furnace only had one outlet and that was in the living room, and with my bedroom door closed it was getting cold in my room fast. I ran and jumped on my bed and pulled the covers over me in one quick tug. I kicked my legs around under the blankets trying to warm up the cold sheets and then pulled the covers tight against my neck. I looked at the wall at the foot of my bed and at the moonlight as it made its nighttime dance with the imperfections in the plaster of my wall. The moon light also shimmered across the posters of Jim Kirk, Spock and the U.S.S. Enterprise. I let myself leave this time and this world and found myself on the bridge of the U.S.S. Enterprise, under the command of Captain James T. Kirk.

"Phasers locked and ready to fire Captain." I looked over my shoulder at Captain Kirk as I informed him that I was ready to fire at his command.

"Good, good Ensign, just hold it there until I give the order…"

Captain Kirk looked straight at me with his chin resting on his fist, as he slowly and methodically gave the instruction.

"We want no misunderstanding with these people; they have the power to destroy us in one salvo of their weapons." Captain Kirk Instructed.

"Ey sir." I reported to the Captain as I turned back to face my station.

"Any indication as to their intent Mr. Spock?" Captain Kirk swiveled his chair around to face the first officer's station as he asked the question.

"None that I can detect Captain, which is illogical, considering that they do have a great deal more firepower then four of our starships of this class and design." Spock reported in a matter of fact tone.

"No need to remind me of that fact Spock." Captain Kirk swiveled back around to face the main view screen.

"Ensign Brian, let's see if we can…"

From somewhere unknown to me I heard a scream fill the entire ship, and again I heard it, it sounded as if I could remember it from some another mission, but it was not a mission.

The second scream brought me from my dream and I bolted to a sitting position in my bed, blinking my eyes rapidly to adjust to the bright moonlight that still flooded my room. My ears perked at attention, trying to grab every sound wave that they could. It was all quiet, nothing; I was starting to think it was part of my dream. A dream, I didn't remember my dream anymore but I must have been dreaming because I did not hear anything while sitting up in bed. As I started to lay back down I heard it again, the scream, like the scream my mother had let out years earlier when my dad was trying to kill her in the room right next to mine, but this time it was muffled and more distant. I kicked and scrambled out from under the covers and ran to my bedroom door still in my socks and underwear. When I opened the door the screams were louder and no longer muffled. For a moment I stood paralyzed, unable to move forward or return to the safety of my bed, my knuckles turning white under the tight grip on the doorknob. The next scream sent me into motion once again. I bolted past my door and out into the living room trying to discern the direction of the screams and realized they were coming from my mom's bedroom. I slowed my pace and made my way quickly and quietly to her bedroom door. It would do no good to her or me if it was discovered that I was up. I knew that whatever was happening to my mom was not by her design.

    I had made my way to my mother's bedroom door, and again I stood unable to move, looking at my mother, Doug was beating her. The moonlight filled her room as it did mine and the blood that was being splattered and sent across her white sheets was not bright read as it should have been the scene between Doug and my mom was being played out in black and white. I had no idea what to do, when I encounter my dad trying to kill my mom I cried out, but I had no fear of my dad at that time. Doug I feared, in fact I feared him more than anything in the world at that time and that fear strangled me, forbidding me from calling out or moving. I slowly backed away until I was clear of the bedroom door and Doug's line of sight; I then turned and made my way back into the living room, all the time hearing the screams of death coming from my mom. I realized that if I did not act Doug would come after me next, after he was finished killing my mom he'd kill me. So no matter what, I had to act. If I did nothing he would kill me and if I did something he would kill me, at least if I did something I'd go out trying to do one last act of goodness for my mom.

    With the moonlight filling the living room and kitchen I looked around trying to find something that I could use against Doug, but nothing caught my eye, until the moonlight caught it. The light of the silver moon danced off the sharp blade of the carving knife sitting in the dish drain on the sink counter. I took the first step toward the drain and felt a tightness and resistance in my mid-section, then warmth running down my legs. At some point of seeing Doug beating my mom I had peed in my underwear, creating resistance in them as I tried to walk. I added a little more effort and ignored the inconvenience and made my way to the kitchen sink. I picked up the large carving knife and turned around to go back to my mother's bedroom; when nothing, no more screaming. Somehow I managed to pee my underwear a second time, realizing that Doug had just killed my mother and now he was going to turn his attention toward me. I did have one advantage however; he did not know I was up, unless he stepped in a puddle of my urine.

    I made my way to the area beside the stove and the half wall between the living room and kitchen and forced myself in the crack between. I could see out, but the shadows would hide me from Doug. I made myself as small as I could, and this time I controlled my breathing, something I had learned from Spock. I watched as Doug passed silhouetted in front of the big picture window, backed by the glow of the moon, he was walking to my room. I scampered from my hiding place and moved quickly to my mom's bedroom, I had to know for sure; I had to be sure before I ran from the house, that she was dead.

    When I entered her bedroom she was laying limp across the corner of her bed, a dark splattering covered her body and ran down along her arm and dripped from her hand that hung over the edge. I was sure now, Doug had killed my mom and if he found me in the house he would kill me too.

    "Brian."

    Doug had found my room empty and was now hunting for me; I could only hope he would not return to mom's room, he had other rooms to search first.

"Brian." Doug was dragging out my name, in a dark playful manner.

"Brian get out here NOW! I want to kill you and I'm too tired to go around hunting for you, so let's just get this over with and just let me kill you. I ain't got all night."

I went to the far side of my mom's bed and squeezed myself under it, still clinching the carving knife. My mom's bed sat low with her dead body on top, so I had to exhale and squeeze myself in tight. I pushed myself over to the same side my mom was hanging off of, so I could see when Doug entered through the door, then steadied my breathing and waited. As I waited my mom's blood was dripping in a pool right in front of my face and each drop splattered and splashed on my face, and with each splash I could hear Doug's taunt for me to come out of hiding.

"I'll tell you what Brian, if you come out now, I will kill you fast, go easy on you, make it quick, it'll be good for me to do it quick, I have to be at work in a few hours."

I held my breathing steady.

"Brian? Did you come into your mama's room to see if I killed her? Well I did, now where are you?"

Doug stood in the doorway to my mother's bedroom, holding his own knife, which was dripping black drops in my black and white nightmare.

I held my breathing steady.

I watched as he made his way across the room and toward the edge of the bed.

I held my breathing steady.

He stopped, his foot just short of the pool of blood next to my face.

I held my breathing steady.

I could tell he twisted his body in the direction of the closet.

I inched forward, just enough to put my left shoulder and left arm out from under the bed, and I held my breathing steady.

When his twisting motion was completed he called out again.

"Brian you hiding in the closet like you used too when I found your bed covered in piss? Come out..."

As I thrust the knife into his foot and through his shoe I had to make sure it pinned him to the floor. Doug let out a scream that sounded like no man that I had ever heard scream, and still I pushed down on the knife harder. In quick fashion I managed to pull myself out from under the bed, dragging my body through my mom's pool of blood, covering my chest, wet underwear and legs. As I pushed down on the handle of the knife with my full body weight Doug let out another scream, dropping his knife, but on the other side of his body and out of my reach.

"You little pansy. Well I take my generous offer to kill you quickly back; it will be slow, and painful."

His own words were stuttered as he hopped to keep his balance while reaching for the knife that he had dropped and trying to reach for the carving knife in his foot. He appeared to be indecisive as to which one to grab first. I raised myself on my hands and feet and as fast as I could I crawled on all fours to the far corner of the room. When I had found the safety of the corner I turned and pulled my legs into my chest and allowed my eyes enough room above my knees to watch as Doug made up his mind and pulled the knife from his foot, giving out another scream in the process. As he was pulling out the knife, I noticed that two new beams of moonlight were reflecting off of something on the bed that I had not noticed before, but I could not take my eyes from Doug long enough to see what it was.

Keeping the knife he had pulled from his foot in hand he limped his way over to me. My attention was locked on Doug and lost to everything else that was moving in the room around me. Doug did not bring the knife up and over head to drop down on me in a quick kill, instead he knelt down next to me, dragging the knife across my left cheek cutting deeply, I could feel the warm blood exit from the cut he had just made.

"Ya see Brian; I was going to do it quick and…"

Doug stopped talking, his voice became garbled and incoherent, his eyes closed and when they reopened all I could see was white, he fell forward and toward me. I brought my hands up in defense and at the same time pushing his body to the side, he landed at my right side, his back to me and I could see the knife he had used on my mom and intended to use on me sticking out of his back. I looked at his lifeless body in disbelief and wonder, and then I turned and fixed my gaze to where my mom was, and now was not. She was now lying in a tangled heap a few feet in front of me. Doug had not succeeded in killing her, somehow she had managed to survive and choose to save me from Doug. For that brief moment in time I allowed myself to believe that my mom loved me.

"Mama?"

I crawled over to her and placed my hand on her bare chest.

"Mama?"

"Call the police."

I bolted upright, check to make sure Doug was truly dead before leaving the room and went into the living room. I picked up the receiver to the telephone and I got no dial tone, the phone was dead. I ran out the front door and across the street to the front door of the house that the McCall's used to live in. I pounded and pounded on the glass window breaking it and shouting for who ever lived there now to call the police. When at last I saw a man approach the door with a ball bat, I yelled at him to call the police to come to the house across the street and took off before he could capture me. All he saw was a bloody eight year old boy in his wet underwear run back across the street and into a house.

    I made my way back to my mother and Doug, checking Doug again to ensure that he had somehow not managed to return to life. When I was reassured again that he was still dead I went back to my mom, her body was still warm, whereas Doug's was cold to the touch. I lay down on the floor next to my mom and rested my head on my mom's bare chest and at last allowed myself to cry. My tears flowed down my cheeks, the salt in my tears stinging the open cut along my left cheek. Soon my black and white nightmare was filled with blue and red lights dancing off the walls and ceiling of my mother's bedroom, the police had once again been called to the house on Kern Street after I stopped my mother from being killed.

    Once the police had secured the house the medical personal were allowed to enter and attend to my mother; by now every light in the house was on and what was black and white was now in full color. In the moonlight that filled the house all the blood was black and had little impact, but when the lights were turned on, the red color of the blood took on its full brilliance and it surprised me just how much blood had been spilled. My mother was covered and the wood floor of her room was streaked and smeared with it, mostly from when I had crawled out from under the bed and though the pool of my mother's blood. Doug had tracked it throughout the entire house as he looked for me, and me, I was drenched in my mother's blood. It was dried in my hair and my face, arms, chest, underwear and legs were stained red. The smell of iron filled the entire house. Iron from the blood and ammonia from the two times I had wet myself in fear.

    "Hey kid what's ya name?" A police officer asked me.

I said nothing, I was now feeling numb and cold looking at what I had just survived, and wondering if my mother would live. I heard the question the officer asked, but it sounded distant and out of reach. I felt his hand on my shoulder.

"Kid, what's ya name?" He asked again, giving me a gentle shake.

"Brian, will my mama live?"

"Don't know Brian, they're still checking her out. You need to get cleaned up before I take you."

The phrase 'take you' grabbed my attention and I cut off the officers next words.

"Take me, take me where?"

"We need to find a place for you to go. You got a daddy or some aunts and uncles we can take you to?" The officer asked me.

"Excuse me officer, the boy's mother is trying to say something." One of the medical attendants interrupted the officer.

I stood frozen as the officer left me and walked to the gurney that now held my mother. He leaned over and placed his ear just above my mother's lips so he could capture her whispered voice. I watched as her lips quivered, the officer giving me a glance as he continued to listen. When my mother was finished telling the officer what she felt she needed to they wheeled her out of the front door and loaded her up in the ambulance and then took her off to the Oaktown Hospital.

The officer turned his body to face me fully, he walked back over to me, and this time he knelt in front of me, so he could be eye level with me.

"Son, - Brian." The officer started off, attempting to make his gruff voice tender. He placed his arm around my back and rested his hand in the small of my back, again trying to be tender with his approach and words.

"Is there any reason that your mother would not what you to go to your dad's?"

The question took me by surprise, I couldn't think of anything, there was no reason that I could think of to tell the officer. I shook my head back in forth telling him no.

"Well listen." He tried to soften his voice a little more.

"You mother just told me that no matter what not to contact your dad and let him know about this, and that no matter what happens to her I had to make sure that your daddy never got you. You don't know anything about that?"

Again I just shook my head no.

"Hum, I...well your mother mentioned that you have a grandma here in town?"

"Ya, my Grandma Smith, she lives with my Uncle Mike, just down the street, I can walk over there." I replied.

"No need for that, go take a shower and put on some clean clothes. I'll have an officer stand outside the bathroom and as soon as you take off those bloody underwear you hand them out to him, okay?"

I'm unsure of the look I gave the police officer when he gave me those instructions, but I must have gotten the point across to him that what he just said sounded strange.

"We need to bag the underwear as evidence, even though Doug is dead we still have to collect all the evidence here and your bloody, and um well, pee stained underwear has to go into evidence as well. Got it?" He tried to explain.

I didn't get it, but I shook my head up and down, telling him yes. I walked to my bedroom, leaving bloody footprints behind me as I made my way through the house, to get some clean underwear and the pants and shirt I had taken off earlier. In my tow was a young police officer that the older officer had asked to go with me. The lights in my bedroom had also been turned on and lying on the floor, torn to shreds were my Star Trek posters, with bloody handprints in torn bits across the paper. Doug had ripped them off the wall while looking for me.

"You like Star Trek?" The young officer asked me.

"Ya, but this was all I had left of my Star Trek stuff, and he ever ripped that up."

"Sorry kid, some people in this world are just mean. You can get some more."

"Where?" I turned to face him when I asked the question and the young officer saw the tears flowing down my face and the look of abandonment that overtook me. The young officer could no longer hold back his own tears.

"I have nothing and no one, no one wants me or cares for me, so where do I get more Star Trek posters, and when do I get my Ken doll?" I asked, knowing that he did not have the answers or even understand the questions.

"Come'mere." The officer said reaching out for me and pulling me to him. He took me into his arms, and gave me a hug, blood still covered me. He let me cry out my feelings in the arms of someone I felt I could trust and that I knew would not hurt me.

I let all the hurt, anger and horror of that night out as the police officer held me, I had so much inside of me I didn't think I would ever stop crying, and his uniform was being covered with tears, blood, snot and spit. I pulled back a little from his shoulder and tried to wipe it off with my hand.

"Don't worry 'bout it Brian, it will wash. Get your clothes and I'll walk you to the bathroom."

I gathered my clothes and left my room to go to the bathroom to take a shower, again with the young officer in tow. I entered the bathroom and paused before I closed the door, I wanted to make sure he was going to stay by the door, just in case Doug was not really dead. I shut the door and walked to the mirror to look at myself, I was covered in smeared blood, my mother's blood. I reached up to feel my hair and I tried to run my fingers through the thickness of the blood but it was both dried and sticky. I started to cry again, now I was scared for my mom and about what would happen to me. I reached my fingers under the elastic of the underwear band and pulled them down, then stepped out of them, leaving them on the floor. When I rose back up I took another look at the strange boy in the reflection of the mirror before me. Covered with blood except for my mid-section where my underwear had been, there I was clean of blood and still had the flesh color of my skin. It looked odd to me, somehow out of place. I bent down and picked up my bloody and pee-wet underwear. I turned and walked to the bathroom door holding my underwear by the elastic waist and out in front of me, as if they were somehow diseased. I opened the door and while standing behind it I reach around and handed the underwear to the waiting young police officer, he held open a small brown paper bag and I dropped the evidence inside.

"Thanks Brian. Take your time getting cleaned up, I'll stay right outside this door, okay?"

I shook my head yes. I then walked back to the shower and turned on the hot water, I took a hot shower to wash what was dirty off of me. When I was done I got out, dried, got dressed and when I opened the bathroom door, there as promised was the young police officer.

"You know what?" I said to the officer as I exited the bathroom.

"What's that?"

"Can I come live with you?" I asked.

He forced a smile, pulling the corners of his mouth tight.

"It just wouldn't work and it doesn't happen like that. We had another officer go to your Grandma's and she is here with your Uncle Mike, they are taking you for now. Want to go get some your clothes and maybe some things out of your room?"

"These are the only clothes I have, and Doug tore up my Star Trek posters, so I 'spose I'm ready to go."

The young officer placed his arm around my shoulder and escorted me into the living room. When I entered I saw my Grandma sitting on the couch and I could hear my Uncle Mike talking to the older police officer in my mother's room.

"Brian; come over here."

My Grandma Smith held her arms open wide to take me in an embrace that only she could give. In all my travels in life, my Grandma Smith was the only force that made me feel safe and loved. I walked across the living room and fell into her arms, and again I started to cry. She started to stroke my blond hair, hair that a few minutes earlier was red with blood and sticky. Her hand felt good and relaxing as she gently scratched my head, and holding me tight with her other arm. In her warm loving embrace I was soon asleep.

When I awoke it was late in the evening and I was in a bed at my Grandma's. I was in the bed that she let me sleep in whenever I would visit, sheets that always smelled like a fresh spring day, and soft on the skin. She had taken off my shirt and pants and I did not see them lying anywhere in the room, but I did see a brand new shirt and pair of pants lying on the chair next to the bed. Since they were my size and I was the only boy present that wore that size I put them on and got dressed. This was the same house that when I was two I would pull my squeaky dog toy around, getting on my Grandma's 'last nerve'. This house, my Grandma's house was always a place that I felt safe. I walked into the living room, and found my Grandma and Uncle Mike, and sitting on the couch was the young police officer that helped me at the Kern Street House.

"Hi Brian, did you sleep okay." My Uncle Mike asked.

"I 'spose. What's going on? Why you here?" I directed my question to the young police officer.

"Well me and some of the guys on the force got you a few things. To start with, you found the clothes we got you, but we got you some more."

He started digging through some bags and pulled out two packs of underwear my size, two more pairs of pants, and four more shirts, all my size. He then pulled out two packages of socks and a pair of tennis shoes. I sat in the floor and put on the shoes without any socks and walked around, this was my first pair of new shoes, and they were my shoes. I remember for the Christmas of nineteen seventy three I hated getting clothes and all I wanted to find was my Ken doll, but now I was grateful to have clothes, but still there was no Ken doll.

"Got another bag here for you." The young officer reached around behind him and handed me a large paper bag.

I opened the top and looked inside, then sat down on my Grandma's green carpet and started to cry. I dare not touch what was inside.

"Hey Brian you okay, it alright, it's yours no one else's." It was my Grandma who spoke.

"Everyone at the police department and hospital chipped in and got it for you. It's okay to take it." The young officer explained.

I sat up on my knees and reached inside the brown paper bag, and pulled out a toy model of the U.S.S. Enterprise, along with a phaser, communicator and wall posters. I gently laid out the contents around me, and started to cry, in the last two years no one had even been this nice to me and I was unsure what to do or how to react.

"Thanks." It was hard to form the words through the tears.

The police officer got up and sat next to me on the floor, for a moment we just sat next to each other, more like a father would sit next to his son. He then reached over and picked up the box that held the toy model of the Enterprise and handed it to me.

"Go'head, open it up." The young office said.

I looked for the tab at the end of the box and carefully pulled it free and just as carefully opened up the box and slid out the U.S.S. Enterprise from its moorings. I held it in my hands as if it were the rarest material in the world, fearing any movement would destroy it forever.

"I can't stay Brian and my shift starts in a bit, but I wanted to give this to you myself."

I said nothing in reply, just reached up and gave the young officer a hug, and then he was gone.

It was about two weeks later before Uncle Mike took me to hospital to visit my mother, when I saw her I knew I would never be going home with her again. She was connected to several machines, some going into her arms and one going in her mouth, her eyes was taped closed. Uncle Mike told me she could hear me if I talked to her, but she would not be able to talk back. I said nothing, just stood by her bedside. Doug had stabbed her twenty five times, and all over, he had even cut her face up, like he had done to mine but worse. As I looked at the bandages on her face I reached up and touched mine, Doug intended to do the same to me.

Uncle Mike told me that one of the stab wounds had hit her spine and shattered some of the bones in it. Had she remained on the bed and never moved, they could have most likely saved her ability to walk, but when she choose to pick up the knife and stab Doug to save me, a chipped bone finished cutting some nerves in her spine, she was paralyzed from the waist down, Uncle Mike had to explain what paralyzed was to me. That was the last time I was to ever see my mother until I interviewed her for this story. After the visit I returned to Grandmas and Uncle Mike's house, that night after watching Star Trek I asked my Uncle Mike about me.

"Uncle Mike?"

"Brian?"

"Will I live with you and Grandma from now on?" I asked them both.

Grandma was sitting in her rocker, spittoon on the floor next to her and a wad of chewing tobacco in her mouth.

"We talked about that Brian." Was my grandma's reply, but she cut herself short.

"And?" I pressed.

""Your Grandma and me live off my war pension; it's all we have every month." Uncle Mike explained.

"What's a war pension?" I asked wanting to know more, my fate was at stake.

"I get a monthly check for fighting in World War Two, over in Germany." Uncle Mike explained.

"Well if I stay here, won't you still get it?"

"Yes, but it won't be enough to support you as well as me and your Grandma."

"Can't you ask for more each month?" I asked, knowing where the conversation was going.

"No, what I get is what I get."

"So where is mama going?"

"She is to be placed in the nursing home to be looked after; I'll be going in everyday to check on her as well." My Grandma told me.

"Can I stay with her?" I was crying now, the plea could be heard in my voice.

"No son you can't."

"So what is to be done with me?" I asked already knowing what my Uncle Mike was going to say.

"I know your mother gave instructions to the police and to me not to send you to your dad's, but she never said why, so I don't see a reason that you can't go to live with your dad. Can you?" Uncle Mike asked.

"No but mama told me not to go to Texas to live with him."

"I understand that Brian, but it's the only place for you to go. I gave him a call last night and arrangements have been made for you to go to Texas." Uncle Mike told me.

"Is he coming up here to get me?" I asked.

"No, he's sending the money for a bus ticket. When the money gets here I'll take you to the bus station, buy a ticket and send you to Texas. It's a straight shot, only one bus."

"Can I take my clothes and Star Trek toys the police officer got me?"

"Yep, I'll pack all that up for you." It was my Grandma that spoke up.

"That's your stuff, and no one can take it from you." She continued.

That was the end of the conversation, I was sent to the bathroom to take a bath and then to bed. When I was in bed I stayed awake for hours, scared of what lay ahead of me. It was only two years earlier that I was part of a family of five, that went to two and was now I thought going back to five, but two of which

I did not know anymore. I was afraid of what life was going to be like in Texas. But no fear, not even the fear that I felt when I ran for my life from Doug would match the fear that I was to face in Texas. Everything in my life up to this point had been training for the horror I was soon to face, but no amount of training could prepare me from what I had to face. My life in Texas would take me down a path darker than any path I had yet walked down. Although I would have some good times in Texas and meet new friends, it was my dad that altered events in my life to such a point that I don't think I have ever recovered.

My fate was now sealed, I was about to learn a truth about my dad that my mom fought hard to keep me from learning, and in December nineteen seventy six that truth would be fully exposed.

Chapter 8
Texas

Although much of the story that I've just told you may seem detailed, it's necessary to tell you all that I have told you, as you will soon understand. Without me telling you what I just told you it would be very difficult if not impossible to understand what I will now tell you. Without knowing what you now know you would not be able to understand the choices I had to make over the next year, and what my dad did to me and what he made me do. In the remainder of my story I will delve into the darkness of my dad, and what I tell you will without a doubt be hard to believe, but I have made it easier for you to accept by telling you all the things that I have just told you. Also what my mom did for me would be impossible to understand without this background information. In fact as I go deeper into the story you will even start to understand why my mother told the police and my dad the lie she did about me killing my sister, and why she lied again in my behalf.

***

The money for my bus fare to Texas did not arrive until March third nineteen seventy six. As soon as my Uncle Mike got the letter and money he drove to the bus terminal to purchase my bus ticket. I would be boarding the bus and leaving for Texas on March fifth. When the day for me to leave arrived my Grandma packed up my few belongings and loaded them in Uncle Mike's car; she then gave me a hug and kiss goodbye and I climbed in the front seat. When my Uncle Mike drove off, I propped myself up on my knees to watch my Grandma as she waved goodbye to me, not knowing it would be the last time I would ever see her.

Just after my ninth birthday in nineteen seventy six she slipped and fell, breaking her hip. They placed her in the same nursing home as my mother, where she died a few months later. My Grandma Smith was the only constant in my childhood and now she was gone.

The bus ride to Texas was scary for a boy of eight. I closely watched everyone around me, I was sure someone was going to kill or snatch me, but that was not the case. I arrived safely at the bus station in Alta Loma Texas, where waiting for me was my dad. He helped load my single suitcase into his car and then opened the back door for me to get in. I climbed in the back seat and we drove off. The trip to his house on Avenue J was driven in complete silence.

He brought the car to a stop in front of a small yellow house that sat atop stilts about two feet off the ground. There was no under pinning, the crawl space below the house remained open. I later learned that it was to allow water to flow freely under and around the house during tropical storms or hurricanes. The front yard was empty and bare, not even a single shrub, the driveway was loose gravel with grass growing through it. Behind the house was a single small out building that held tools and yard supplies. To the left of the building my dad had built a dog pen and inside was three hunting dogs. Dad loved dogs but he hated to name them, so for the three he had in Texas he named them, Dog, Gone, and It. And you guessed it; if you say all three names together real fast you got 'Dog Gone It'. But he usually just named his dogs, 'Dog'.

The back yard had trees and lots of them, small ones and big ones, excellent for climbing in and building tree houses. Around the back yard was a fence that enclosed a pasture further back and to the right of the house, pastures that once held horses but were now vacant.

Inside the house it was plain and bare of furniture. Entering the house from the front was the living room. Directly ahead was a door to the front bedroom. The bedroom was large for its outside appearance; it had four large windows across the back wall and two on the far wall. From the living room and turning left was a small hallway. The first door on the left was the bathroom, and across from the bathroom was the kitchen. Going straight to the end of the hall was the second bedroom which was dads.

Dad carried my suitcase inside and dropped it on the floor in the front bedroom, which became my room. It was empty except for a double sized bed that sat directly on the floor pushed up in the corner where the windows met, and a small chest of drawers.

"This is your room." My dad told me in a gruff voice.

When he dropped my suitcase I wanted to tell him to be careful because my Star Trek toys were inside, but living with Doug taught me to never reveal things of value to anyone, they will use it against me. I walked to where my suit case lay and picked it up and laid it on the unmade bed. I sat down on the bare mattress and looked at my dad.

"Where's Donna, Holly and Kris?" I asked my dad. There was no trace of them living in the house.

"Moved out." He replied.

"Are we moving to where they are?"

"No. Now quit asking questions. Put your stuff in that dresser. Tomorrow I'll take you over to the school and get you enrolled." He walked out of my bedroom.

I walked over to the dresser and opened each drawer one at a time, as if I expected to find something someone had left behind. When I had completed my inspection I started to unpack my suitcase, putting my underwear and socks in the top drawer, shirts in the second, shorts in the third and blue jeans in the bottom. With extreme tenderness I placed my U.S.S. Enterprise on the top of my dresser and carefully set my other toys around it. I left my posters on my bed; I needed to ask my dad for tape to put them on the wall.

"Here."

The 'here' was unexpected and when I turned I was hit in the face with a set of bed sheets. My dad had tossed them in my direction and they were followed by a blanket and a single feather pillow.

"Dad?"

"What."

"Do you have some tape so I can hang up my Star Trek posters?"

It was then that he paused in the doorway to take note of the U.S.S. Enterprise and other toys sitting on my dresser. He locked his gaze on the starship; he became fixated for a brief moment in time.

"Dad?"

"So you like that show?"

"Yes sir. Will I be allowed to watch it?"

"I don't care what you watch. I doubt I'll be here. Best be careful so that toy ship of yours doesn't get broke."

My dad said it while pointing at the starship; it was more of a warning.

"I will."

Again he left me alone in my room, never answering me about the tape. Since I was used to being ignored I turned around and set about making my bed. I carried my empty suitcase to the closet and laid my Star trek posters on the closet floor. Once I had made my bed I again sat down on the edge of my bed, not knowing what to do.

"Here."

My dad had remerged in my doorway and had tossed some clear tape on the bed next to me.

"Don't mess up the walls, I rent this place, it ain't mine."

"Yes sir."

"I ain't no sir; so don't call me that, just say yes."

"Yes si...yes."

Doug had insisted that I use sir when addressing him; it would take me some time to change this pattern.

With tape in hand I collected my Star Trek posters and hung them at the foot of my bed, I wanted them to be the last thing I saw at night and the first thing I saw in the morning. After I had completed making the room mine I set out to explore my new world. In the kitchen I found my dad opening some cans of dog food.

"Want me feed the dogs?" I asked my dad.

"No, I don't want you near my dogs, ever. Got it?"

"Yes. Can I go outside to explore?"

"I don't care what you do. But stay away from my dogs."

"Okay."

I left the house through the back door and started to explore my new world. I had never lived in Texas and every sight and sound was going to be a new adventure. Next to my dad's house on the left was another house, it too was yellow in color but a darker yellow. Behind that house was a long building with a door at each end. I wondered if the people that lived there had any kids and I hoped that if they did they had a boy my age. On the opposite side of my dad's house was a fence that went around a large pasture that was now empty. There were no other houses in sight. Other than that there was nothing as far as I could see down both directions on the road. The pastures and fields would be interesting to explore, but for now I stayed within the confines of my dad's yard.

The rest of the day I spent climbing trees to see which one would be best for building a tree house in. I wanted to build another tree house but I needed to find the material to do so first. While in the house, I had turned through the television channels to see how many reached my dad's house from Houston, in all he got four channels.

Around two thirty I started to watch the house next door to see if any kids would show up, school should be getting out about two thirty and it would be around four if they rode the bus before they got home. But I never saw anyone go in the house or come out of it. When five o'clock approached my dad called me in the kitchen for supper. On the table sat two boxed dinners.

"You sit on that end of the table. Can you read?" My dad asked.

"Yes."

"Good. I won't be here most nights, so you need to make these yourself. The freezer is full of them, they're supposed to be different kinds but it all tastes the same. Just follow the directions on the back. Do you know how to use the stove and oven?"

"Yes, mom showed me ours on Kern Street."

The reference to the Kern Street house caused my dad to look up at me and he locked his eyes with mine in a cold dead stare.

"You're to never mention that house or that woman again. Do you understand me Brian? Never!"

I swallowed hard; I started to feel fear again.

"Yes."

"So do you think you can make these dinners on your own?"

"Yes."

"There'll be a box of corn flakes in the cabinet for your breakfast."

"Can you buy Apple Jacks?"

"Corn flakes are good enough. I don't have the extra money for you to put sugar on them, so eat them with just milk."

"Okay."

I had resigned myself not to ask for more from my dad, I quickly learned my place. If this was as bad as he got, I could take it, it was better than being beat, as I was with Doug.

"I'll be leaving around six o'clock every night; I won't be back before you go to bed, so you'll have to take care of yourself. Make sure the dishes are done up every night before you go to bed. I'll be here when you get up, but except for tomorrow morning I'll be in bed, so keep things in this house quiet."

"Yes, I will. May I ask? Where do you go at night?"

"I tend a bar at night called Dee Jays."

"Do I get a key to the house?"

He reached back and stuck his hand in his front pocket and slid a key across the table toward me.

"Good you asked, I nearly forgot."

"Brian? I mean what I say about the kitchen; have it cleaned up every night, not a single dish left. Got it?"

"Yes." I said with slight frustration.

After we had finished eating he got up and left me alone while he went to Dee Jays to tend bar. After my dad was gone I turned my attention to the dishes and cleaning the kitchen. Living with Doug I learned to clean a kitchen well and I continued that practice when I started to clean the kitchen for my dad. After I was done I went into the living room and started to flip through the channels on the television, trying to find something to watch. I watched television until I was too sleepy to understand the dialog. When I was too tired to stay up anymore I went to the bathroom, brushed my teeth, emptied my bladder and then made my way to my bedroom.

I removed my shirt and pants, tossing them in the corner, a place that I choose at random for my dirty clothes and walked over to the window in my underwear. It was only about a month ago that I had stood and looked out of my window on Kern Street, up at the silver light of the moon, on the night that altered my life course that sent me here. Now here I was again standing in my underwear and looking out of another window that was now my bedroom wondering what this turn in life would bring upon me. I turned off the light, and walked to my bed with the glow of my nightlight filling the room and climbed under the covers. I looked around at my room, my eyes landing on my new Star Trek posters one of the U.S.S. Enterprise and the other of the entire crew standing around Captain Kirk's command chair. I was alone in the house and the sound of silence was deafening. I had never been alone in a house, all by myself that is.

As my dad had said he was up when I got up, and a box of corn flakes was sitting on the table. I poured me a bowl and covered them with milk and then ate them without any sugar. I would in time get used to the taste, but for the first few weeks it was going to be an adjustment.

"Once I get you enrolled I'll leave. I'll make sure what bus you're supposed to ride before I leave, make sure you're on the right bus after school."

"I will."

"I don't want to have to come down there because you got on the wrong bus, savvy?"

"What?"

"When I say savvy, you reply savvy. It means you understand. Savvy?"

"Savvy."

"I mean it Brian; I don't want to have to come down there to get you. I'm not like your mom or that Doug; I won't hit you or beat on you. But I don't want to have to track you down because you're too stupid to understand either."

"I understand. I'll get on the right bus."

After we had finished eating breakfast he drove me to the school and he enrolled me. I was now enrolled in another school and had to make all new friends. I decided to adopt my no interference with other people policy. My first day at school went as expected and I avoided everyone and every question that I could and I survived the first day. I did manage to get on the right bus, and when it dropped me off at my house, dad was not at home. I let myself inside and changed clothes into some shorts, to keep my school clothes clean and to make sure they lasted longer. I then went out the back door to see what adventures awaited me.

In the far back corner of the backyard stood a tall huge tree that I felt was the best tree to build a tree house in. I started to look through piles of wood that my dad had to see which ones would be best for use as a tree ladder. I took my perfect finds and made a stack of them at the base of the tree and all the while I had the feeling that someone was watching me. I ignored my feelings and continued to hunt and gather the needed supplies.

"What'ya goin' to build?"

The voice and question caught me off guard and scared me.

"Who are you and where are you?" I asked.

"Names, Scott, and I'm right here."

Through the bushes that grew between my house and the house next door stepped a boy about my size. His hair was as blond as mine was, but his eyes were blue to my hazel.

"Hi, names Scott, like Scotty on Star Trek."

He flung his hand in the air and gave a lazy wave as he introduced himself.

"Hi, yourself. Names Brian. You like Star Trek?"

"Who doesn't? What'ya makin'?"

"Trying to see if I can find enough stuff and wood lying around to build a tree house."

"I don't see that'ya goin' to be able to do it with what'ya got there. I got lots of wood at my house. We can use some of that."

I followed Scott through the bushes and into his backyard and then out to the edge of the long building that I had noticed the day before. Stacked up against the building was a huge pile of wood, and sheets of wood were stacked up under a lean-to.

"That's a lot of wood." I exclaimed.

"Ya, we have to keep it around in case we need it for the rabbits, in there." Scott nodded his head toward the long building.

"That's what you have in that building, rabbits?"

"Yep, we show them, gots 'bout two hundred and fifty 'supose."

"For real? Two hundred and fifty. Can I see them?"

"Don't see why not. Come'on."

Scott led me to the far end of the long building and through a door that entered into the feed storage area for the rabbits. In the small room were floor to ceiling shelves that held rabbit food and supplies to treat the rabbits. The far was wall covered with blue ribbons and trophies.

"You won all those for the rabbits?" I asked pointing to the wall of ribbons and trophies.

"Yep, well me, my mom and step-dad. Follow me."

Scott exited the small dirt floor room through a curtain to the right of where we entered the room. Once I passed through the curtain I had stepped into a large room that housed hundreds of rabbits. Scott walked me up and down row after row, all the while explaining what each type of rabbit was, and what had to be done to each one to get them ready to show. I hung on his every word, and found the rabbits fascinating to watch. After he had showed me each and every rabbit we exited the long building out the back door that was close to the stack of wood we had been working on.

"That's a lot of rabbits." I said.

"Yep, should be here to feed them and scoop up their poop."

"I'll help, I don't care, I ain't got anything else to do. You're the first friend I've made since I moved here."

"When did ya move here?" Scott asked.

"I moved down here yesterday. My dad lives alone in that yellow house next door."

"THAT'S YOUR DAD!"

"Ya? Why you say it like that?"

"You don't know? You really don't know?"

"Know what?"

"That man next door, your dad, nearly killed the woman that lived there with him. An ambulance had to come take her away, and the two little girls have never been back."

I was quickly taken back to when I was six years old and had to stop dad from killing my mom.

"So what happened? What happened to the two little girls?"

"After the woman, I think her name was Donna?"

I shook my head up and down to tell Scott he was correct.

"Well after she got out of the hospital she returned with some cops and they loaded up her stuff and the stuff that belonged to the two little girls. She moved out with the two girls. I've never heard another word about that house or the man that lived there until just now."

"Ya, I kinda know what my dad is like. But I've nowhere else to go and no one else wants me." I explained to Scott.

"What 'bout your mama?"

"She's in a place like a hospital for the rest of her life. And my Grandma could not keep me, so I had no choice but to come live here with my dad."

"Man, I feel for ya. Keep one eye open at night, I hear stories 'bout that guy, your dad."

"Probably all true."

"You say I'm the first kid you met since you moved here? Well I hang out mostly with two other boys that live down the street named David and Chris. If you got'a bike we can ride down there." Scott told me.

"Na, I ain't got no bike. Can we walk?" I asked.

"'Bout a mile down, too far to walk. I have two bikes myself, my one from last year and the one I got this past Christmas; you can have my old one. I'll check with my mom to make sure, but I think she will let me give it to you."

"I just met you like a few minutes ago and you're givin' me a bike?"

"I got to live next door to you right, might as well be friends. Com'on let's get going, you'll like them two."

Scott kept both of his bikes in the garage and they were both in excellent condition. I didn't want to make the first move, as it was hard to tell which one was the old one and which one was the new one.

"That green one there is my old one."

It was a lot like my old bike that I had to leave behind in Santa Fe, but this one was better. It had a full laid back banana seat, with a high arch back bar. The handle bars were fully extended and had nice arched curves as well, and Scott had left a card in the spokes.

"Let's ride." Scott said as he peddled out of the garage.

I followed close behind, glad to have made a new friend, and to have the freedom that a bike offered. We rode down the street and past my house and the pasture that had a fence around it; the pasture was now overgrown from not being used. We continued to ride, following train tracks that had curved just past my house and now ran parallel with the road. Once we passed the pasture the terrain opened up to expose a newly built sub-division. We turned down the first road to the left and then in the driveway of the second house on the left. We both coasted our bikes under the carport and stood on our peddles to break.

"Hey Chris; what's going down?"

"Notin' just my raccoon won't eat; think he might be sick or sometin'. Who's that with ya?" Chris replied.

"This is Brian; his dad is that freaky man that lives in the yellow house next to me." Scott replied.

The statement caused Chris to direct all his attention to me and for the moment he forgot about the raccoon he was holding.

"I feel for ya man. With your dad, life has to be rough." Chris said.

I just gave him a forced smile.

"David home?" Scott walked to the edge of the carport as he asked the question while looking across the street toward the ranch style house that sat on the corner lot.

"Na. He's inside turdin' up my bathroom. Drive's my mom nuts with the smell he leaves behind. Something dead lives up his butt." Chris answered.

"No doubt man, no doubt. Brian here is tryin' to build a tree house in a tree behind his house. Wanna help?"

"And go in that freaks yard. No; you, you're not a freak, but your dad is." He directed his comment toward me.

Chris was a typical boy, had a small muscular build and sandy brown hair with brown eyes. He had all the features that in the future would draw most girls to him, but he also had no leadership qualities. Chris was a follower, and a cautious one at that. If he felt threatened he would back off to save his own neck.

Chris' mom had put a real stove in the carport so his sister along with David's could make Shrinky Dinks. These were small plastic toys which had many different popular cartoon figures and you painted them and then baked them causing them to shrink. Somehow David's sister always talked me into making them with her. However for the ones I made she had to tell me what color to put in each section, so in reality I made mine for her.

"Well I'll get David's opinion and then we'll see if we help Brian." Scott replied.

"It's not a big deal; we don't have to build it." I said.

"It's not you, it's Chris. Chris is a wimp'o. Unless we all vote first to do something, he chickens out."

The comment took me by surprise, these boys were supposed to be friends and here Scott was cutting down Chris in front of a stranger.

"Don't think nothin' of it Brian. Scott's right I'm a wimp'o, I hate to decide anything, and if something might get me in trouble, I prefer to run. I live by the thought, 'better to run away and live then to stand your ground and get beat for it.'"

Scott said the phrase at the same time that Chris had said it.

"That's right stuff."

A new voice entered the conversation. David had finished his business in the bathroom and was now coming down the two steps that exited the side door.

"Did you stink up my house again?" Chris asked.

"What else; smells better in there after me anyway, better than your stink." David replied.

David turned his gaze toward me.

"David."

He stuck out his hand in a gesture for me to shake it. I looked down at his hand and wondered if he had washed after wiping.

"Take it. I washed my hands."

Regardless if he did or not I needed friends so I reached out and shook his hand.

"Brian." I said as I shook his hand.

"Now we're friends Brian. You, me, Scott there; and even Chris. We needed a forth anyway. And as far as that tree house I heard mentioned, we'll all help build it, won't we Chris?" David said,

Chris shot a sideways glance at David, and then just nodded his head in agreement.

In one day I had gone from no friends to three, and I could tell that there was something about David that appealed to me, a brother that I needed and I knew I had found. Of the four of us David was the plainest; he was the type of boy who could easily get lost in a field of kids. But he had an awesome personality, he was a leader, and a dare devil. He seemed to always come up with brilliant ideas for fun things to do. I really enjoyed David as a friend. He had a little sister who I always got upset with because she was what I called a tag-a-long. And for some reason she formed an attachment to me. She had to always be where I was and that got on my nerves.

David's hair was black and his eyes were green, but he did not have the cute boy looks that one would imagine to go with that combination. He was about my build and skinny like me and his facial features were simple, nothing outstanding caught your eye. If he were in a crowd he would go unnoticed, in fact if he were alone he would go unnoticed.

"So how old are you Brian?" David asked. I picked up right away that he was the leader of the group, but not in a bullish way.

"I turn nine in May." I answered.

"Well you and Scott, you're 'bout the same, he turns nine in April. Chris is nine in August, and me, I'm ten in June. So we're all 'bout in the same age area. But really Brian; before we can let you into our group; there are two requirements that you have to meet."

David was about to outline requirements for being friends with him, Scott and Chris, I felt I was about to lose the three friends I had just made.

"He already likes Star Trek." Scott interrupted.

"Well then one more requirement. What do'ya think of The Beatles?" David asked.

Right or wrong I felt I had to stand my ground on this issue.

"I think they're the grooviest group around." I answered.

"And the Rolling Stones?" David continued.

I just shook my head no.

"Well that confirms it boys, he's one of us. You're in Brian." David affirmed.

With having David, Scott and Chris as friends I was hardly ever home and therefore I did not have the chance to get in my dad's way. Dad allowed me to spend weekend nights with any of the three new friends I had made; he said it got me out of the way when he brought his lady friends over. I was just glad to be away from him. Although he never hit me, being ignored and neglected by my dad made me feel as bad inside as being abused by Charles. So any time away from the yellow house on Avenue J was time I took advantage of.

Of the four of us, Scott, David, Chris, and me, Chris was the odd one, I've been told I'm odd, but Chris had a personality that I had as yet to encounter up to that point in my life. He was quiet and preferred to sit back and watch what was going on and then if he had a comment he would, but mostly he kept his thoughts to himself. But more important I was never comfortable around him. His quietness made me uneasy.

The four of us boys did go ahead and build a tree house in my back yard over the span of two weeks, and with my dad's permission. Again it got me out of the house, and the tree house proved to be a place he would ground me to when he got tired of looking at me. In April me, David and Chris went to Scott's birthday party at his house and then in May David's mother gave me a ninth birthday party at David's house. David's mom and dad were the perfect parents. They showered both David and his little sister with love and attention when I was there. Even when I was not at his house I could tell by the way David spoke about his parent and little sister that he loved them. I envied David, but in a good way, for the family he had and sometimes at night before I drifted off to sleep I would dream that David and I were brothers and that his family was my family.

Chapter 9
These, Those, and Butter Knives

David and I quickly became best friends, I needed an older brother, someone with a take charge personality, and he stepped up to fill that role. It took no time for me to form an attachment to David, as if he had always been my older brother, and David returned that feeling. But I had a lot to learn about life in Texas and one lesson that I will never forget was learned in the hills.

I was at David's one day in early June and we were playing in the back yard when I first noticed the hills, I had noticed large mounds of dirt all over the back yard. Now if you recall; I told you earlier that I hated anything on my feet so if I did not have to, I did not wear shoes. I had no idea what these mounds of dirt were so I took to kicking them down, and within seconds I learned what those mounds of dirt were. David's mother heard me screaming as the big red ants covered my feet biting as they made their way up my legs. She bolted out the back door, picked me up and dropped me in a kiddy pool and doused me with the water hose. I had welts all over my feet and lower legs; I never kicked over an ant hill again. From that day forward I paid more attention to David's lead and started asking him more questions about things in Texas that I did not know about.

In late June David's mom gave him a birthday party, he had turned ten, he was now a year older then I was. David started to teach me about life in Texas and he and I started to ride our bikes everywhere. Although there were many stories about boys being mistreated in Houston Texas throughout the entire nineteen seventies, his parents never worried and they allowed him to ride his bike anywhere. My dad could care less, even if I did go missing.

Avenue J, the street my house sat on, as well as Scott's and the street that David and Chris's connected to was also notorious, as I will bring out later. At the time that I lived there in nineteen seventy six however, neither I nor any of the other three boys knew what was happening along Avenue J. Avenue J had the unique distinction of looping off of Interstate forty five. From Interstate forty five a person could exit and take Avenue J, which was mostly marsh on either side and within a few miles be back on Interstate forty five. Someone could dump something in the marshes and never have to back track and be miles down the Interstate and gone. Avenue J was the go-to loop off of Interstate forty five if you needed to get rid of something or dump something in the marshes. Nevertheless this was the road that all four of us boys lived on and we never knew the secrets that lie in the marshes as we rode by.

So not knowing about the under life around us, David, me, Scott and Chris had many adventures in and around Alta Loma, sometimes we even rode as far as Galveston Island. But David and I would sneak off many times on our own adventures. Our personalities were very much the same and we both had very vivid imaginations that allowed us to escape the confines of reality easily. David also taught me many other tricks about life in Texas.

David showed me how to go crabbing by just using a string. It was simple enough; I would lower a string off the side of a bridge and dangle it in front of a crab, once the crab latched onto it with its claw you gently pulled up the string while lifting up the crab. Once the crab was off the ground it would not let go of the string. That was crabbing. He also taught me how to go shrimping. For that we had to go down to the shipyards and the docks. We would climb over the edge of the concrete outcroppings and lean over the edge, holding onto a mooring or another object and reach just under the edge of the water and pick shrimp off the concrete dock below the water level. David did it first to ensure that I watched him to learn how to do it properly. If I fell off and in the water I could easily drown or worse be caught in the wake of a passing ship; and that would have been bad. While one of us was hanging off the dock the other one would be sitting on the dock, within grabbing distance, holding a bucket to drop the shrimp in. I ate a lot of shrimp and crabs while living in Texas.

    David also taught me that if I picked up a shell to make sure that the crab was not still inside, they tend to stink after a few days sitting around the house. David's mom took me and him to an old Pirate Castle, and even under the ocean. The Pirate Castle sat on Galveston Island, so we had to cross from the mainland to the island. There were several ways to get to Galveston Island; David's mom usually took the bridge. But this time she took the tunnel under the ocean, so I could be under the ocean. While going through the tunnel I noticed water leaking in along the walls and asked if the tunnel was going to flood. She told me no. David's mom explained that water seeped in all the time and it was allowed to drain out through the bottom of the tunnel. It was impressive to see all that water seeping in, and scary. She took me and David to the naval shipyards where I saw some of the biggest ships that I would ever see in real life.

    These, those, and butter knives. Sounds like the title to a funny movie. I had been having trouble in school with writing, but not reading, it would be a few more years before it was discovered I had a mild learning disability. The disability centered around the mechanical translation of converting words in the mind to written words on paper. Most people are aware of dyslexia, or other learning disabilities, it would be a teacher in another school; in another state that would pick up on mine.

When we write, not type, things on paper it involves a complex series of events between the brain and mechanical abilities of the hand, it's far more complicated than one would think. Our thoughts and words have to be translated into electrical impulses that act on muscle cells to then be converted into a form of writing. At the same time all this is going on, the ability to make all of what we think of as words has to appear on paper. This proved to be a monumental task for me. I could read anything put before me, but writing was a near impossibility. Certain words or phrases caused a greater degree of trouble as well, and two words that I could not tell apart were these and those.

    I could read words and understand them and their place as I read them, but I could not translate them into a written word or understand how to tell them apart. My dad concluded that I was doing it on purpose to make him look foolish. So the kitchen butter knife became a favorite tool of my dad's to teach me the difference between these and those. Dad would have me sit at the kitchen table and write on a piece of paper the words these and those hundreds and hundreds of times; all the while he was standing behind me with a butter knife. If I made a mistake he took the butter knife and smacked me on the back of my head. He held the butter knife by the blade and hit me with the butt end, whack, crack, over and over each writing session. Soon the butter knife became his favorite way of punishment it did not leave any apparent marks. He would come up from behind me when I was unaware of it and whack, smack, right on the back of the head.

    Because my dad would sneak up from behind me I never knew when a blow to the back of my head was coming. Therefore I started to sit in chairs that had their back to the wall. I'm still easily startled when approached from behind, and sometimes I've been told my reaction seems a bit dramatic, but my reaction is always very real.

Even with all of my dad's efforts to teach me how to tell these and those apart I still have trouble, so I suffered at his hand for nothing.

***

Through June and the first part of July; David, me, Scott and Chris had a blast. Once while riding my bike down Avenue J at full speed toward David's house I had a most terrible crash. David had a St. Bernard and when you're nine years old your body mass is far less than that of a St. Bernard. I only had on a pair of red shorts and shoes that summer day, so nothing was on my legs to protect them in the event of a crash. As I approached the street corner David's dog ran right out in front of me. I hit hard. I don't remember how high in the air I went or how I landed, but I do remember the bike coming to a sudden stop. I flew over the handle bars and landed with my left leg folded under me. My left leg landed first and a large stone cut a hunk of tissue out of my leg, blood was everywhere. David's little sister had already run to get her mom, who then took me inside and cleaned up the wound and bandaged it. I asked her not to tell my dad, I didn't think he would care, but for the fact that it left a physical mark. My dad was odd that way; he did not mind me getting hurt, as long as no physical proof existed. David's mom agreed. To this day there is a crater scar on my leg where I landed on that rock.

We had finished building the tree house and with the extra lumber we built a small club house at the base of the tree. Both the tree house and club house were in my backyard and David, me, Scott and Chris conducted our boyhood secret meetings and planned the activities of summer things. I had at last settled into a normal boyhood life.

As the days dug deeper into the month of July, my friendship with David grew stronger. I had found in David the brother that I so desperately needed, and he returned that friendship. The darkness of living in Oklahoma was now far behind me and I felt free to be a normal boy. And as long as I stayed clear of my dad, I did not have to deal with his verbal abuse or the belittlement that he meted out to me. I had, at last, found freedom in Texas.

David was a well-adjusted boy, a quality that he obtained from his parents; parents that loved him and treated him with kindness. He returned that quality to me and I started to see in David the boy and person I wanted to be. David taught me real boy things, nothing like Josh and Charles had taught me.

David took me to a skating rink and he did his best to teach me to skate, but for some reason I could not get the hang of skating. I tended to walk with the skates. I had tried to learn to skate many times before but just did not have the legs for it. I even tried to learn with a pair of metal skates that attached to your shoes, but it proved useless. I ended up taking off the wheels and nailing them to a board. Now skateboarding, that was my thing. David did not know how to ride a skateboard so this was my chance to teach him something. He was able to grasp it quickly. David also tried to teach me how to shoot a bow and arrow, although I never got the hang of that either. But the greatest adventure of my entire childhood was when David took me flying.

David knew of an old World War Two airbase island near Galveston Island. It was long decommissioned and shut down, but he knew of a way to get on the island. One day toward the end of July David told me he had a surprise, but it would require a long bike ride. I trusted David completely and if he said it was a surprise worthy of a long bike ride, I was ready to ride. I had stayed the night with him so we could leave as early as possible.

We packed some sandwiches and water and headed out. I had no idea where he was taking me but it took over two hours to reach the edge of a canal that I knew we could not ride our bikes across. He stopped short of the canal and dropped his bike in the tall grass, I did likewise.

"It's over there, across the pipe." David was pointing across a large pipe that connected the mainland to a small island.

"I don't see anything on the other side." I said.

"Trust me on this one Brian, it's there and it's far out. But let's rest a bit before we cross the pipe." David said.

We both sat down in the grass and took small sips of water from our canteens.

"How are we going to cross the pipe?" I was concerned, the pipe crossed over an ocean inlet canal.

"Walk, or if you're too chicken, sit and slide you butt across." David instructed while giving me a smile.

"I think I'll sit and scoot my butt across." I answered.

"Good thinkin'. If you fall in the sharks will eat you."

"Really?"

"Yep. They did a story on one boy who fell into a canal; a shark jumped up before he hit the water below and ate him in one gulp." David reported.

"You liar." I replied while kicking him with my foot.

David could not contain his laughter after that; he started rolling around in the tall grass holding both of his sides while laughing.

"Finished yet?" I asked.

"Just 'bout." David replied still laughing.

From the mainland to the airbase was an old oil pipe, it crossed over an ocean inlet. After we got done resting David went across the pipe first, and he walked it foot over foot. When it was my turn I slid my butt across inch by inch, all the while David yelling at me from the other side and telling me that if I fell in the sharks would eat me, and still laughing. After I had made it across the pipe we ran across an open field and up to a chain linked fence. David had already made a hole in the fence from a previous visit and it was still open. Once we both made it through the hole in the fence we were standing at the edge of an old airbase.

At first I just stood in absolute amazement, everywhere, on the runway and in rows were old fighter planes; they were prop planes. David took off running in the direction of the closest one, and I fell in behind him. He had boosted himself up through the missing side door and then turned to help me climb up. At ten years of age he was already starting to grow and was bigger than I was. As he helped me to climb in he gave me one word of caution.

"Watch for snakes, rattlers are bad to get in the planes and hide out." David said.

My eyes widened at the statement, and I started to move through the plane with deliberate caution, keeping my ears tuned; in case I heard a rattle. We climbed in and out of different planes for hours, running all over the air base and in and out of old buildings. He then found his fighter plane, and not too far away I found mine, it was facing his.

***

I climbed into my plane; all geared up with cap and goggles I had found and eased in behind the wheel, and then I started my engine. Looking out across the tarmac I noticed David had done likewise.

I had received reports of enemy fighters in the area and my orders were to take out as many of the enemy planes in the air as I possibly could. I had just been given charge of Eagle Squadron, and this was my chance to prove that I had the right stuff. I intended to bring all my boys back safely to the base. I gave the order and we took off in formation, within seconds of gaining altitude I eyed my enemy; at my one o'clock.

David peered at me through the broken glass of his fighter; he knew as I did that we were about to have a dog fight. When I could see the whites of his eyes I opened the protective flap of my trigger and unleash my guns on him, and let him have it. I had to have fired off hundreds of rounds, but somehow he was able to avoid my barrage, I could not bring this one fighter down. I attempted to come up from behind him for another run…..

***

David and I played for hours before the sun started to steal the day. Reluctantly we had to leave. This time I was invincible so I walked, at least part way, across the ocean pipe. David was one of those few people you come across in life that gives you more than they take. David gave me some really awesome childhood memories and for that I will cherish his memory forever.

That summer with David, Scott and Chris had been great, and I had made some great new friends. I was able to reenter boyhood without any fears of being beaten or abused, but I had really let my guard down, I should have heeded the warning that my mom gave me about dad. Sometime in August dad suffered a near fatal fall.

Dad worked in the shipyards and also on smoke stacks, he was a welder through the week and tended bar on the weekends. While he worked he was never without a bottle of cheap whiskey in his pocket, and he stayed drunk as long as he was awake. One day while working on a smoke stack, without a harness, he lost his grip. He was drunk, and he fell. He was heading toward the ground about a hundred feet below. It's odd but it seems that the drunks always get the breaks and he got a break. He had the presence of mind on the way down to lodge his leg in some runes of the ladder on the smoke stack, and snap, he broke his leg and stopped his fall. After he was rescued and his leg set, he was fired. The money he earned tending bar at Dee Jay's on the weekends could not cover all his bills. With no way to pay any of his bills; he was in a desperate position. Dad did, however, have several options, and he used all of them.

His first option was to turn to his lifelong friend Clifford. As I had mentioned earlier, once Clifford arrived in Houston he quickly started a powerful business. Clifford ran a legitimate business and that business served as a cover for all his other activities. Clifford also had his hands in real-estate, trafficking guns into Mexico, and selling boys. Dad approached Clifford for help, and Clifford was all too ready to help my dad. Dad was able to still drive with his broken leg; he had broken his left one. So Clifford asked dad how he felt about making regular trips into Mexico. My dad agreed; knowing that he was running guns across the border for Clifford. This was dad's first step into Clifford's world and it would lead to the worst encounter of my life.

***

While all this was going on with my dad, David's mom had formed the four of us boys into a Cub Scout troop. David, Scott and Chris were able to get uniforms, but dad wanted nothing to do with the Cub Scouts; so at first I was attending den meetings in my summer clothes. One day during a den meeting at David's house I noticed a box was sitting on the kitchen table; it had my name on it.

"Go'head and open it, it's got your name on." David said as he pushed the box toward me.

I reluctantly lifted the lid of the box and peered inside. The first thing that caught my eye was a brand new yellow Cub Scout hat laying on top of a yellow scarf and under that the full blue Cub Scout uniform. I was excited.

"Well; take it in David's room and put it on. I want to get some pictures of all you boys together in uniform." David's mom told me.

The four of us boys ran upstairs to David's room and once inside I sat the box on his bed. Scott and Chris quickly emptied the contents, laying them out on the bed for me. After I had removed my shoes, shirt and shorts Scott and Chris started to hand me my uniform. Chris handed me my new pants, which I put on, then Scott handed me my blue shirt, already with my name and den number on it. I quickly buttoned it up. David was ready with the scarf and tied it around my neck. I then picked up my hat and proudly placed it on my head.

"How'd I look?" I asked my three best friends.

"Like a real Scout." Was the answer; multiplied by three.

David put his hands on my shoulders and pushed me toward the mirror above his dresser.

"How do you think you look?" David's reflection asked my reflection.

"Like a real Scout."

"Let's go show my mom." David turned and bolted out of his bedroom door.

Scott, Chris and I followed David downstairs and back in the kitchen.

"Well what'd you know, now all four of you boys match. Line up there across the far wall. I want a good picture of all four of you boys." David's mother instructed.

We all walked to the wall, lined up nice and straight, then broke file and tossed our arms around each other's necks and just hung in the air. SNAP, the last picture of our happiness ever to be taken. Chris was to the far left, then Scott, David and lastly me. That picture was the last picture all four us took together willingly, and with smiles. It was also the last picture that all four of us would ever take together. In just a few months the four of us boys would make a decision that would cost us our friendship and one of us would have to pay with his life.

But that was still a few months away, right now we were the four Cub Scouts of den number twenty four.

When dad went to work for Clifford his life and temper changed quickly. He appeared to be living on the edge of fear. He gave off the attitude that he was always being watched, and that sense of paranoia filled the entire house. Dad was new to Clifford's way of doing business and Clifford was concerned with dad's loyalty, so an arrangement was agreed upon. John was still working for Clifford, as a handler of ones who did not agree with Clifford; and it was John that Clifford used to test my dad's loyalty.

I had come home one evening and in the kitchen was my dad with two other men. They were Clifford and John; two more men were waiting outside in a white car. This was the first time I had ever seen Clifford or John and I had no idea who they were. Thinking they were friends of my dad I went to my room and grabbed my camera. I took one single picture. As quickly as I snapped the shutter button Clifford was all over me. He shoved me down on the couch hitting me with his open hand across my face and all the while telling me to never take another picture of him. He then stood up and smashed my camera, destroying the film inside as well. I fell back on the couch with my hands covering my face, and tears of a familiar fear running down my cheeks. Dad walked up to me and told me that I shouldn't have taken the photo without asking permission. I gave my dad a look of total hate and went to my room to cry and worry about tomorrow. My old fears had returned.

Clifford did not give my dad an option, it was more of a command, John was moving in with us. Clifford did not trust my dad, what had happened back in the late sixties was still a scar on their relationship. Although the three were friends, Clifford would not sacrifice his business or money for their friendship. He wanted my dad's loyalty. The next day John moved in.

The first few days after John moved in I slept on the couch. I kept a separate area for my things in my old bedroom which John had taken over. But I made my resentment known to both my dad and John. John made an offer to set up a cot on one side of my room, and use two dressers as a partition and let me have the other side. It seemed like a good idea at the time, but it was just the beginning of what my dad, Clifford and John had discussed a few nights before.

It did not take long before John made his move. John was hateful and aggressive and he was only interested in himself. Since I knew the rules of the game, Charles had taught me, I did what I had to, in order to survive. When I was away from home, I did my best to keep from my friends what lingered in my bedroom. I had stopped inviting David, Scott and Chris over, and I even refused to let them come to the tree house or club house behind my house. I took every measure that I could to protect the three of them from the nightmare I was facing every night. But I could not keep the change in my personality secret from David, he saw right through my façade.

"Brian; what's up? Something 'bout you has changed." David asked one day while I was staying all night at his house, something that had now become rare because of John.

"It's nothin' David, and I don't want to talk about it."

"I ain't gonna leave you alone until you tell me." David replied.

"I can't tell ya." I answered back.

"Why? We're supposed to be best friends; best friends can tell each other anything."

"If I do, you have to swear as my best friend that you won't tell." I said.

"Okay, I swear."

I told David everything; about my dad and John. I also told him everything back to when I was six years old, at least what I was able to remember. All the time I was telling him I was crying, and soon he was crying as well.

"Brian you have to tell. We can tell my mom." David said.

"Can't David, you promised. If you do they will put my dad in jail and I'll have nowhere to go."

"You can move in with me. My mom and dad will let you." David offered.

"Don't work like that David. Besides when my mom caught Charles with me, she hated me and if your parents find out; they'll look at me the same way my mom did. David you promised; keep your promise. Please."

David shook his head yes. After more talking we both finally drifted off to a restless sleep. I wish we had told his parents that night.

Chapter 10
Cub Scouts; Den 24

Although forming a den troop was the idea of David's mother, it was my dad that somehow managed to take it over. Scott, Chris and David never told their parents just how bad my dad was, so their parents agreed to my dad being in charge of the troop, just as long as John was present at every meeting. The wolves were now in charge of the four little sheep, and they intended to eat us alive.

United States history shows that throughout the decade of the nineteen seventies thousands of boys in the Houston area were used in the sex trade. Ages ranged from five to twenty years of age. In truth there is no accurate record of just how many boys were used in the trade and the exact ages. Many of them were killed in the process and dumped in the marshes south of Houston, some off of Avenue J. The "Houston Boy's for Sale Trade" as it later became known was not run by a single person or by organized crime. Individual business men managed their own outlets; mostly they catered to the rich, powerful and political. Clifford ran such an outlet, and that was what I was used for. I spent the rest of nineteen seventy six in such an outlet, being taken to many of the finest homes in and around the Houston area. I even had the chance to meet some of the most famous people of the seventies, people every boy wanted to be when they looked up at the moon and wondered about who went there. I will not name names or go into detail, after all that account has been told; I'm telling you the story of David's mark.

Some of these homes I was taken to were opulent, old money and powerful people. I cannot remember how many houses or places I was taken to; but after the first house I could care less how grand the house was when I realized what I had to do there.

I remember one place that I was taken to in vivid detail. My dad had gone into another room to make arrangements and there was another boy already there and he was playing a piano. I walked over to him and sat next to him on the bench, I had by now learned not to ask names. I watched him play for a little while and then he taught me some basic notes. It was my introduction to learning how to play the piano. I remember having learned to play the piano; but I don't remember ever taking a formal lesson. I wonder in reflection if those boys that taught me, played out of their own misery?

The trips to other houses continued, nearly daily, and I could not take it anymore. I had to find an escape; my old escape was no longer working. I found that escape one day at a house I was dropped off at. Inside the house were two other kids and they were a lot older than me and both of them were already drinking to cope with their lives. The oldest boy asked me if I had ever had a screwdriver. I had to ask him to explain what it was and after he explained I asked him to make me one. At nine years of age I took my first drink, and throughout my childhood I choose to drink to cope with what my dad was doing to me.

As August turned into September it became clear why dad took over my Cub Scout troop. He was told to by Clifford and during one of our den meetings my three best friends were brought into my world. My dad used the cover of the troop to market me, David, Scott and Chris. My dad was the front man and John our handler. I really can't explain what a handler does, he more or less presents the product to the potential customer. Sometimes we had to work together, but more money was made when we were worked alone. This was the life my dad made for me and my friends.

Dad was also involved with gambling at local horse tracks, all under the control of Clifford and sometimes I would go and spend all day wandering around the track while dad tended to business. I only went on days when I had to be dropped off somewhere else later in the day.

I'm not going to speak anymore of the abuses that David, Scott, Chris and me suffered, it serves no purpose. But I will visit one more account with John later that changed the direction for all four of us boys. But before my dad got control of our Cub Pack, there were two camping trips that I got to go on that really stand out in my memory.

The first one was a huge Jamboree Camp. Hundreds of boys from Cub Scouts, Boy Scouts, and even Eagle Scouts all converged on one location. I don't remember the exact location; I just remember it was on a huge hill overlooking a valley.

It was the largest Jamboree I had ever been too; hundreds if not thousands of boys. We had built a massive bonfire on the first day at the edge of the hill and we built our own benches. That night we sang songs until the stars filled the sky, and filled our bellies with Smores and hot dogs. We had pitched our tents when we first arrived so when bedtime was called everyone headed for their tents. David and I tented together and Scott and Chris pitched their tent right next to me and David. Before going to sleep that night we all stripped to our underwear and got in our own sleeping bags for a first night's sleep and then talked of the activities that would fill the next day.

Without any warning in the darkness of the middle of the night the earth blew apart. The camp had suffered a direct hit from an overhead tornado. The tornado never touched the ground where we were camping but skipped over the tree tops by only a few feet. Nevertheless the destruction was incredible. The tent David and I were sleeping in was torn away from us and we both managed to find our flashlights and started running; but we had no idea where to run. Once out of our tent the confusion was rapid. Everywhere there were beams of light going in every direction bouncing off the densely pack forest of trees, and screams, screams from all directions, even up. Boys crying out for help because they were hurt, and some were hanging from branches in trees. Within the swirls of confused light beams; ran boys in all states of dress and undress, most were in their underwear. Panic and fear ruled the darkness of the night. As the beams of light fell upon twisted trees the pouring rain warped the lights' direction. Fear gripped all of us younger boys as our minds filled the dark forest with monsters, in my mind I was back at the house on Kern Street.

      Through the driving and pounding rain someone yelled out that everyone should head for the busses; David, me, Scott and Chris turned our direction and flashlights toward where the parked busses should be. As we ran we were dodging undefined items dropped in the path in front of us, it was a gauntlet of items from the lives of thousands of boys. When I came into view of the busses a new terror struck. What was left of the busses would not provide much in the way of shelter. I ran among the busses trying to discern which was the safest to get on. Some of them looked like a giant fist had punched them several times, not a single bus was left with a full pane of glass. I found what appeared to be a safe bus and called out to David, Scott and Chris, we all then climbed aboard. Everywhere we walked we were leaving foot prints of blood as we had all cut up our feet in the debris field. I had cut my own feet up pretty badly as did my friends. I found an empty seat and sat down, holding the spot next to me for David. Scott and Chris took the seat behind us. Along with all the other boys on the bus we sat shivering form the cold rain beating down on us through the shattered windows.

I don't remember how much time passed before the red and blue swirls of lights were added to the confusion, but I was glad when they appeared. After the blackness of the night was filled with the blue and red lights, new voices and shouts filled the air. A uniformed medical person walked up the steps of the bus, peered over the polished chrome railing and then disappeared. Seconds later several uniformed medical personal made their way down the isle of the bus. One of them draped a blanket around me and David. With the blanket now keeping our warmth in, we cuddled together to try and stop shivering. A young woman in a black uniform with a red cross on the sleeve asked if I was alright. I told her about my feet being cut and bleeding and spoke for David, Scott and Chris. She then asked all of us if we were brothers, after an exchange of a quick smile with the other three I told her no, but David told her that he and I were. She then started to treat our cut feet.

Not long after the rescue personal arrived the rain started to taper off and then it quit. By the time the rain had stopped the young nurse had finished with our feet and moved on to others. David got up and motioned for me and Scott and Chris to follow him. David led the three of us outside and once we stepped off the bus we all three stopped and looked up into the night sky. The sky was now completely clear of clouds, rain and any threatening weather. When I looked up I looked into a black sky full of beautiful stars, whatever happened was now over.

With the morning sun it looked as if a bomb had hit our camp. Almost all the trees were broken and what was not broken was pulled up and laying everywhere. Tents and clothes filled the broken trees that were left standing all the way to the highest branches. And everywhere you looked was debris; there was no safe place to take a step. The four of us had been given some oversized medical clothes, although much too big they provided some covering. The devastation to the camp was so bad there was no way to tell one person's items from another's, so we were forced to abandon all of our camping gear. I was also forced to leave behind my Cub Scout uniform, something I would never be able to replace.

We were escorted to an area that had several newly erected tents, all of them white with red crosses on them, and we were taken into the largest one. Once inside we were taken to a long table and told to stand in line. When we reached the front of the line we had to give our names and phone numbers so our parents could be reached. The tent was packed with boys, many wearing the same oversized clothes we had on, some had managed to find enough to wear lying on the ground. Yet some other boys were standing around in their underwear, shivering from the cold. There were not enough clothes to go around. It was then that I realized just how well off I was with my oversized medical clothes.

When we reached the front of the line Scott and Chris gave the names of their parents and phone numbers and then David and I stepped up to the table.

"Names please?" The attendant asked.

"David and Brian Foster." David spoke for both of us.

"So you're brothers then? Home phone number?" The first question was rhetorical.

David gave the attendant his phone number and she wrote our name and number on a tag, as she had done for Scott and Chris. She then handed us the tags with the instructions that we were to hang them around our neck. We then exited out of the back of the tent to find Scott and Chris waiting.

"Why did you tell her we were brothers?" I asked David when we were clear of the tent.

"Do you really think your dad will take the time to come get you? And what do you think he will do if he does and gets you home? Beside my mom will know who my brother is and keep it cool. She just understands." David explained.

"Did you tell her David?" I asked

"No Brian I gave you my word, our word now. Me and these two are in this crap with your dad just as deep as you are. None of us can ever tell. She just worries about you." David replied.

David put his arm around my shoulders and the four of us walked off in the direction that just the night before we sat around a large bonfire. There we waited until our parents arrived to claim us.

There is only one other Scout camp trip I remember going on with David, Scott and Chris. Several small troops converged on a Scout Camp location. David's mom was still our Den mother so David's dad and Chris' dad took us to the camp site. It was nothing like the Jamboree. There were perhaps only about twenty boys at the camp site, including the four of us. As was the case with each camping trip we were paired off, so there were two of us in each tent. Again I paired off with David and Scott and Chris teamed up together. David and I scouted around until we found a nice spot to pitch our tent. We wanted to avoid any wind from blowing against the tent like at the Jamboree. We found a nice low spot that had ridges on each side. When David's dad saw our choice spot he asked if we were sure we wanted to pitch a tent in a ravine. We were sure we had found just the right spot. We were out of the wind, and any apparent direct danger.

That night the rain poured and poured, and by the time David and I exited our tent there was several inches of mud where we had been sleeping. We made our way to a wooden picnic table and there the two of us sat in our mud covered underwear. We had mud caked on our arms, legs, backsides, and hair. When David's dad saw us he stood and laughed for the longest time; I now saw where David got his ability to laugh in times that I found stressful. There were showers on location so we took a shower and room was made for us to sleep with Scott and Chris. In the morning all the boys at the camp location went back to our tent and we became the "mud patch boys". Our tent was firmly stuck in place by a thick layer of mud. David's dad forwarded the account to the headquarters of the Boy Scouts. It was not long after that David and I received a patch to add to our collection. It was called the 'Mud Patch'. I sometimes wonder if the patch is still in the Boy Scout list of patches to this day. And if it is has someone else ever earned it.

    By the last week in September and toward the first week of October life was getting hard for the four of us boys. In many ways I had it worst, I had John to contend with in my house. I'm going to censor the next bit of this story the best I can, but it has to be told to understand the events that led up to David's mark and that dark December nineteen seventy six.

    John escalated his abuse of me and what he was doing was more painful. Because of that I started to put up resistance to his abuse. Then one night it all came out. John tried to unleash all of his anger on me. I was asleep in a fetal position in my bed with my back to the wall, and John was sleeping against the wall. He had long since taken the cot down and was sleeping in the same bed as me; I figured he might as well. I was nearly asleep when he tried to hurt me. The shock of what he tried to do caused me to scream out. I was never allowed to scream out. My scream woke up my dad and he came to my doorway and there he stood in his underwear looking right at me; and John in bed with me. I was whimpering and fighting back tears when John whispered in my ear that if I told my dad what he tried, I would regret it.

"What's wrong with you?" My dad asked with full impatience.

I lay there, trying to think of something, but my mind was blank, but then in an instant the monster appeared that would be with me long into my married life.

"There's a monster in bed with me; it's green with brown spots."

When I turned to look at John I did indeed see a monster. He was green and his form resembled a blob of a man. All over his green body were brown spots, like huge scabby sores that were seeping with puss.

"There's nothing there but John. Now go back to sleep." My dad demanded.

Dad left the doorway, I was now alone with the monster, and the monster went to sleep.

I don't believe I slept that entire night; my fear was far too great. If my eyes grew heavy I would pop them back open. I also played games in my mind to keep myself awake. I was terrified to fall asleep and all night long I could feel the pounding of my heart. I kept this up until the sunlight of the morning started to fill my room. When I got up that morning, I quickly got dressed and headed outside. I did not want to be in the house with John at all. For the entire day I did my best to avoid him. I spent most of my time with David, Scott and Chris. I had told them the entire account and they too helped me to avoid going into the house. It was late afternoon when we watched John as he left the house and for some reason I went back in. I simply don't remember why. While I was busy doing whatever I was doing, John pulled up and I was trapped inside.

I was in my bedroom when John entered, with no way to escape. I watched as he walked over to my dresser and picked up my toy Enterprise and started breaking it into small pieces. I could tell that John was mad and I was going to pay a heavy price for his anger. John took his rage out on me at that very moment. He ripped my clothes off then pushed me backward on the edge of the bed. I had no time to mentally prepare for the shock, and I had no time to run to Tasana I was there and there for the entire event.

    When it was over John left the house. When I heard his car pull out of the driveway I rolled over onto my side, pulled my legs up to my chest, and cried. I don't know how long I stayed there, but it could not have been too long. I had to take a bath. I made my way to the bathroom, plugged the tub and turned on only the hot water. As it was filling I got in, and within seconds I noticed the color of the water had changed to a brownish red. I pulled my legs to my chest, put my head on my knees and started to sob. When the tub was full I turned off the water, resumed my position and continued to sob. I asked over and over what I did to be here in this life. I rocked myself at times, then I would stop and try to quit crying, but I would start again. God was not someone to me; He had forgotten me when I was six years old. My mind wondered about my existence, why I was born to such hateful parents and why did they do this to me. I wanted my life to end that day, I wanted to never have been.

    I sat in that same position until the water had turned cold and then I heard a car pull in the driveway. My first thought was that John had returned to finish me off but it turned out to be my dad. From the conversation to follow my dad and John must have met somewhere and talked. Dad went first into my room looking for me, because when he came into the bathroom he had an alarmed look on his face no doubt he saw the mess my room was in. When he entered the bathroom, he took a seat on the toilet. There was a long silence; then he looked at the water, then at me.

"What happened?" He of course already knew, but he wanted to hear my version of the story.

I told him everything; holding noting back, hoping it would move him to help me. He then went into his "what happens in this house stays in this house" speech. He explained what would happen to him if I ever told and what he would do to me. He sat there and talked and talked and talked, while I sat in a tub with brown and red water mixing into one color. The water was getting colder and colder. When he finished talking he asked for my agreement, he was going to wait until I complied.

"Savvy?" My dad asked.

"Savvy." I replied, resigned.

He stood up, ran his fingers through my hair, and left me alone. I don't remember getting out of the tub or drying off, but I know I did and I did it alone. When I entered my bedroom I found that my bed was made with fresh clean sheets and any mess on the floor was now cleaned up. I walked over to my dresser and took out a clean pair of underwear and tried to put them on. The first few attempts failed, the pain was too great. I carried them back to the bed and in a slow gently motion I sat down on the edge and started to cry all over. I lay back and covered myself up, letting the underwear fall to the floor.

When I woke up the next day it was already late in the afternoon, and in my bedroom floor sat David.

"Hey." I said looking at David.

"Hey yourself. Got you a shiner in the deal I see."

He twisted his face in a crooked smile. He was trying to find a sliver of brightness to this horror.

"David? Don't make me laugh, it hurts."

"Don't you think I know that? Listen Doc asked John to move out, it will still be business as usual; but Clifford was ticked."

"I can see why, the merchandise was damaged." I replied to David's comment.

"Well; to hear Doc tell it, John went for a ride in the marshes. Clifford told that stupid jerk to never damage us. He has it coming as far as I'm concerned."

"Is my dad here?" I asked David.

"Na. Clifford called him back over. I think they are going to make him point man since John is now feeding the fish in the marsh. Clifford also said that we, all four of us were to get a week off. He knows we're friends. Clifford figures that way it will help you recover faster."

"It's all money to Clifford. Me and Scott are his biggest earners, no offense." I said.

"Believe me, none taken. Here, I brought you a sandwich and a Dr. Pepper."

David handed me a small plate and a bottle of Dr. Pepper. I attempted to sit up but was having trouble. I had already bruised all over my body.

"Let me help." David offered.

"Can you help me on with my undies?"

"As long as you don't mind me seeing you in the buff?"

"Get for real." I replied with sarcasm.

David helped me on with my underwear and then with a shirt. He then went into the living room and took the pillows off the couch to prop me up in bed. Once I was sitting up I started to eat.

"Hurts to eat." I told David.

"No doubt. Brian, we have to tell. They'll kill us. Do you know how many boys are found every day in Houston, dead?"

I shook my head yes, and I really did know.

"The four of us can't go on like this, we have to tell."

"David I can't, not after yesterday, I'm too scared. Clifford will kill us even if we do tell. Think about John, he's somewhere out there along the loop under water. I don't want to join him." I answered David.

"Wanna keep living like this?" David asked.

"It has to end sometime."

"Who's gonna make it end? We are. Please Brian, I can't stand to see this happen to you. Me, Scott and Chris, got it bad, but you, you don't have a prayer." David said.

"I'll live David. But what happens if we tell and one or all of us are killed?"

"Would being dead be worse then what you are feeling right now, or what you felt yesterday?" David answered.

I had no answer, because the truth was, we were all better off dead.

"We'll have to talk it over with Scott and Chris." I replied.

"We will. We just need to wait for the right time to talk."

"And place." I added.

"Definitely 'and place'" David agreed.

By the end of October I had recovered enough to return to work for my dad and Clifford. I did feel better that John was lying in the marsh; at least now at home I would no longer be abused, except by my dad's words.

As the days of October passed the four of us had not found the time or the place to talk. But every day both me and David looked and waited for the perfect chance to make our break from the life we were in.

Somehow we managed to keep our friendship separate from what my dad and Clifford had us doing with each other. I can't explain how David, Scott and Chris managed it internally, but I just viewed what I was forced to do as something I was forced to do. But when the four of us were away from work, we were the best of friends.

With John gone and out of my house David managed to build the courage to start staying the night with me. Scott and Chris were always worried about my dad, and I can't blame them. But dad never got that involved; he was mostly interested in the money side of what I had to offer. With David staying the night and spending more time with me our friendship grew stronger; somehow we had managed to become closer than brothers. I was thankful for the short time our lives crossed. We had still not told Scott and Chris of our plan to tell someone, and one of the reasons that we had not told them yet was that we had to figure out who to tell. Some of the people that Clifford did business with were the very ones that we should have felt safe to tell. So we both felt like we had no one to turn to.

The four of us stayed in the Cub Scouts, we really had no choice it was the means that Clifford was using to gather boys for his business. But we also never recruited anyone or introduced any of our friends at school to our Den Master.

Regardless of the life David and I were forced to live in the darkness, we remained the closest of friends and continued our bike riding adventures. As much as he had ridden his bike in the surrounding area, we still managed to find new and unexplored areas to venture into. Some of those areas proved to be extremely dangerous.

Throughout the entire marshlands were canals, some were of concrete but most were rock or dirt bottom. In the dry hot days of summer many were dry and hardly a flow of water ever ran through them, but they were also very unpredictable. It could rain miles away from where we lived, and in our location we may not see a cloud in the sky. But the canals could fill suddenly and without warning. Although signs lined the canals warning people of that fact, few heeded the warning, including David and me.

It was toward the last days of October that we both learned the importance of those warnings, and the danger of ignoring them. October is normally a dry month around Avenue J, but it proved to be wetter further inland. We had rode our bikes to a rock and dirt bottom canal and decided to see if we could catch any crabs or shrimp along the rocks. Small shrimp and crabs would hide in the shallow waters left in pools as the water drained from the canals and it made catching them easy. We dropped our bikes in the now dead grass and climbed down the steep embankment. We were filling our pouches that hung off of our belts and had been hunting for hours, not even paying attention to how far we had walked, when we heard the sound of thunder. The sound of water rushing through a tight and confined area over rocks sounds very much like distant thunder. The sound was unknown to me, but David knew it well.

"BRIAN! RUN"

David shouted as he started running back in the direction of our bikes and away from the sound of thunder.

"Why." I asked as I too started to run, falling in behind David.

"Water, the canal is filling upstream, soon it will catch us and the water will wash us out into the ocean." David explained as we both were running.

I started to look at both sides of the canal and could tell the banks were too steep to climb up, we were no better off than the mouse I had found in a trap years earlier, the spring had sprung.

I was starting to see that we had come too far from the slope that allowed us to climb down easily and we were running out of time. I did not see how either of us would make it out of the canal. I started thinking that I hope we both drowned quickly. As we ran through the canal bottom we both had to be careful of large rocks and pools. Pools of water were everywhere along the canal bottom and they appeared shallow, but some of them were deceiving. When the canal was running at full capacity the water would twist, flip and turn over the larger rocks and debris that was washed out to sea. In that process softer dirt on the bottom was dredged out and deep pools of water were left behind. If the dredging went deep enough it could meet up with an underground water pool and a strong downward current ran constantly. With this in the back of our minds David and I ran carefully through the bottom, but it was costing us time.

The sound of the rushing water was getting closer and closer with every step we took and I could see nowhere along the bank to climb up. Fear was winning control of my judgment. I had caught up to and was running beside David when the fear won out.

"David we have to ignore the pools, the water behind us is worse than the pools." I was straining for each breath.

"No there not. If you step into an underground pool you're just as gone. Stay with me Brian."

We continued to run, and then David vanished from my sight.

When I opened my eyes my vision was blurry and it stung. I had fallen into a pool, and was being pulled under. I tried but could not touch bottom and the current was pulling me down. I had fallen into an underground pool. I was terrified. I kept looking up through the murky water and I could see the edge of the pool above me but just barely out of my reach. At that moment I knew I was going to die in this small pool and be washed out into the ocean. David of course had seen the whole thing and he quickly stopped running and dropped down on the canal bottom near the edge of the pool. He thrust his arm in as deep as he could and when I saw it I grabbed hold of it. He pulled me up to the edge and I grabbed the edge with my free hand as he then reached back behind me and grabbed my belt and hauled me onto the canal bottom bed. I lay there for a few seconds trembling from the cold, but only for a few seconds.

"GET UP!"

David screamed at me.

"RUN!"

Again we started running, the October wind cutting through my wet clothes, causing me to shiver. David and I were both franticly looking at each side of the embankment for a place to climb up, but nothing appeared hopeful. The sound of thunder continued to beat down on us, getting louder and louder. I had to force myself not to turn around, it was better not to see my own death approaching. Both of us were exhausted and about ready to just stand still and get it over with when David pointed toward the embankment.

"Look, there!"

David was pointing to a shallow washout a few feet ahead of us and to our left; we veered in the direction of the washout and picked up our running pace.

"You go first Brian; you're more tired and wet." David told me.

With every bit of strength I had left, I started climbing up the steep embankment, all the while kicking the dirt and rocks loose. When I had reached the top, I turned and looked down at David as he was trying to climb up, but I had loosened too much of the embankment. David could not get a firm hold of the embankment anywhere and the water was now within sight. I took off my shirt and dug my heels into the edge of the embankment. I kept hold of one end of my shirt and dropped the other end to David.

"Can you reach my shirt?" I hollered to David.

David looked up and just above his head lay my shirt on the embankment, he reached for it. On the first try he came up short, I leaned forward and fluttered the shirt further down the embankment. Again David reached for it, this time he got it and as he climbed up, holding onto my shirt, I dug my heels in deeper and held on tight. When he reached the top he collapsed forward and onto me. We both turned to look at the canal and the water as it rushed by. We had somehow managed to cheat death by drowning.

My pants were still soaked from falling into the pool, as was my hair and body. David took off his shirt and held me close to his chest for a few minutes. We had learned in the scouts that bare chest to bare chest was the quickest way to warm someone up. He then gave me his shirt and I put it on. I was starting to warm up somewhat. We then lay back on the grass so I could dry off and listened to the rushing water as it passed us on its way out to sea.

When my jeans were dry enough we got up and started walking in the direction of our bikes; the ride home would finish drying my jeans and my dad never had to be told of my close encounter with death.

My dad was not home when we got to my house, so we had some time to clean up and see if I was hurt anywhere. We went to my room and I undressed and David looked me over for any damage. Each scratch would have to be explained, but he found none. I took a shower, dressed and went back to my room where David was waiting; he had made us some sandwiches.

"I'm staying the night. In case you wake up screaming." David told me.

"Sure. Dad will be drunk when he gets home."

"I'm use to that."

We finished eating our sandwiches and after we were done gathered some of my Star Trek toys and went into my backyard to play.

It was around nine at night when my dad got home from Clifford's. He reeked of whiskey and cigarettes and was in a hateful mood. And I was the target of his hate.

"Brian!"

Both David and I heard the slurred yell from the kitchen.

"Stay here." I told David as I got up.

"He does anything and I'm in there." David said.

"What can we do, we're too little to hurt him?" I reasoned.

"Don't care, friends stick up for friends." David replied.

I left the room and walked to the kitchen.

"Why ain't these dishes done?"

I looked at the spotless kitchen and didn't see anything that I had missed hours earlier. But when I glanced at the counter again I saw a glass that I had used for Dr. Pepper sitting next to the sink.

"You mean that one glass?" I asked pointing at the glass.

"You mean that one glass?" My dad mimicked back in a slurred drunken voice.

"Yes I mean that glass you idiot. Why did you leave this kitchen a mess when you know it's to be cleaned when I walk through that door?" My dad used the same voice he had on my mom when I was six years old. I started to worry.

"Dad its one glass, I'll reuse it before I go to bed and then wash it. I promise."

"You calling me a liar?" My dad replied.

"No; I was just telling…"

My dad's fist was unexpected and I didn't even have time follow it through. He had caught me on the left side of my jaw and the force of the impact knocked me hard against the wall. When I hit the wall the sheetrock gave way and cracked under the impact of my body. I fell to the floor and immediately started crying and reached up with my hand to cradle my jaw.

"You stupid, stupid boy, you busted the wall." My dad said with the voice of the monster.

The kick knocked the wind out of me, but the pain was what sent me into blackness. It was David's face and voice that I heard, checking to see if I was still alive.

"What happened?" I asked David.

As I drew in each breath my ribs felt like they were on fire.

"After he hit you, he kicked you in the ribs. I guess at least two times. Can you sit up?" David asked.

I was unable to without David's help. Once I was in a sitting position David lifted my shirt to look at the damage that my dad had done.

"Man Brian; if Clifford sees this, your dad may end up in the marsh." David said.

"Where is he? My dad." I asked.

"Passed out on his bed. Your side is really bad. It's turning black and red. You have to have some ribs broken. So how's your jaw?" David asked.

"Hurts, want me to punch you so you know? Sorry. Hurts, it also hurts to breathe in." I said.

"He beat you bad Brian. Clifford is gonna be mad. Brian if Clifford drops your dad in the marsh, you're gonna have to move in with me and we have no choice but to tell."

"We'll have to tell Clifford that I got beat up at school." I offered.

"And have Clifford pick up some other kid for this? Get for real, we have to think of something else to say." David reasoned.

"Bike wreck?"

"He'll take our bikes away."

"We'll think of something. Help me up." I reached my hand out to David.

Standing up was harder than sitting up, but I managed with David's help.

"I'll get you some water. Stay there." David said.

David walked to the sink and picked up the glass that started my dad's rant. He rinsed it out and filled it with water. When he turned around he dropped the glass which shattered on the hardwood floor. My dad had awaked from his slumber and was now standing before me, the barrel of a twelve gauge shotgun resting against my chest.

"Dad, please don't." I pleaded.

"Shut up you stupid freak. You took my life so I'm taking yours." My dad said.

"What do you mean I took your life, it was just a glass?"

"Not the glass you stupid dummy. My life. And now yours is mine."

"I don't know what you mean dad."

The pleading was evident in my voice. David watched, waiting for his chance to make a move against my dad.

"What do I mean? What do I mean?" My dad repeated sarcastically.

"Yes. What do you mean that I took your life?" I repeated the question.

"Let me tell you, you stupid little screw up. Before you were born I had my chance at my dream. I got picked to play baseball, I was gonna' be somebody. Your mom and me had it all worked out and I was going to be a great baseball player, I was gonna get my dream. Then you came along. Your mom, that stupid woman, made me give up my life, MY LIFE of playing baseball to be a dad to YOU and help raise YOU. Well guess what you stupid little screw up? I did give up my life of baseball but I was not going to be a dad to you. YOU took my life away from me so I intend to take yours from you. You wanted me to be a dad, to toss you the football, to let you play with my dogs. Well NO, not for you, you stupid screw up. So for six years I left you alone. I went to work, I paid the bills, but that stupid mom of yours wanted me to be a daddy to you. I was not goin' to be. I did not want to look at you every day and be reminded of what you took from me. I wanted to take everything away from you like you took everything from me. And now with your mom like she is, here you are, here for me to screw up. Boy have I messed you up, and your little screw up friends as well. Ain't that right David?"

Dad paused in his rant to look at David. With each YOU he jabbed his finger in my chest. His words were laced with hate and sarcasm.

The shock of his words hurt me and the hurt ran deep. I had wondered why my mom did not want me to live with my dad and now I knew. Apparently, what my dad just spewed out was something he and my mom had discussed in their marriage, and my mom realized the danger it posed to me. With the barrel of the gun still resting against my chest I knew I was standing in front of nine years of built up anger and hate.

I also realized that no one on this Earth wanted me.

"You're such a stupid little screw up of a boy, I bet you thought that you were gonna have a good life here. Why do you think your mama told everyone not to send you here? Well B-r-i-a-n, I'm gonna take your life, I'm gonna kill you and drop you in the marsh right next to ole' Johnny."

"DOC!"

David approached and put himself between me and the barrel of the shotgun. After my dad's rant, David realized that my dad's anger was toward me and me only.

"Move you little screw up." My dad shouted at David.

David did not move.

"Doc, listen. You can kill Brian, but if you do what do you think Clifford will do to you? Clifford will drop you in the marsh right along with John and Brian. Don't throw the rest of your life away over Brian. If he already took your dream, why give him your life?" David was attempting to reason with my drunk dad.

David's words stung me, but I knew he was fighting for my life. His words also impacted my dad. My dad's eyes took on a distant stair as he thought through David's words. After what seemed like minutes but were just seconds my dad turned the butt of the shotgun toward me and brought it down hard against my forehead. The impact from the gun knocked me to the ground again. David dropped to cover my body with his body to protect me from another hit.

"Stop it Doc; you damage him too much more and Clifford will drop you." David turned his head and looked up at my dad. David was now holding back his own anger and hate toward my dad.

Dad stormed out of the kitchen and left the house. He would not return until early the next morning. He went to Dee Jays to drink some more.

"Come'on, I'm taking you to bed." David said.

David reached down and helped me up. He put his arm around my upper back and under my arms and escorted me to my bedroom. He helped me into my bed, leaving me dressed, and pulled the covers tight to my neck.

"I'm gonna' go clean up that broken glass and then bring you back some water." David told me.

I nodded my head yes.

Every time David and I faced such a life and death ordeal our bond grew closer, we were somehow more than brothers, I just can't explain how. And we had proven we would die for each other.

"Here."

David handed me a glass of water.

"Brian, we talk to Scott and Chris tomorrow. Maybe between the four of us we can find a way to tell someone." David said.

"Agreed. You still staying the night?" I asked.

"Yep."

David climbed into bed next to me and we both laid there and talked of Star Trek and a better life on some distant planet. We were soon both asleep, hoping that by telling Scott and Chris of our plan, our nightmare would soon be over.

We should never have planned to tell.

Chapter 11
"Rocky" The Last Round

The truths my dad revealed to me about why he was doing the things he was doing was difficult for me to comprehend. Regardless of what happened when I was born a father should still love his son. But in truth my dad never felt any love for me; his words before my sixth birthday were mechanical, and a lie. Nevertheless he must have felt something, not for me but for himself. In the presence of others he needed to maintain the guise of a father and son relationship. It was in that light that he attempted to make amends with me three days after he beat me and held the shotgun to my chest.

David and I had been out on an adventure when we stopped by my house to eat lunch. Dad was usually out doing jobs for Clifford but when David and I walked in the house dad was there. He was sitting at the kitchen table, sober but working on getting drunk, and in a wire cage on the floor next to him was a small puppy.

"Whose puppy?" I asked my dad.

"Yours. I'm sorry for the other day." Was my dad's mechanical reply.

David and I both bent down and started petting the puppy though the wire cage.

"Go ahead, take him out, he's yours after all."

I opened the cage door and the puppy jumped into my arms, knocking me back from my sitting position.

"Easy there boy. Don't get too excited." I told the puppy.

"What'ya gonna' name him?" David asked.

"Don't know, but you're gonna' help me pick out a name. He's our dog." I told David.

"Can I take him to my room?" I asked my dad.

"Ya, but Brian you're gonna' be cleaning up his crap. I better never step in any." My dad said.

"K. Let's go." I said to David as I picked up the puppy and we went to my room.

"Shut the door." I told David.

After the door was closed I set the puppy on the floor. It was shades of brown all over and its fur was full and thick. Its face was round and its nose and snout were black.

"What do we call you boy?" I asked the puppy while holding him up in the air.

"We named our Saint Barnard Samson." David offered.

"Ya and he's as strong as Samson. But we got to think of a good name for this guy." I countered.

"Put him on the floor again and let him run around." David told me.

I put the puppy back on the floor and we both watched him as he ran all over my bedroom, getting the layout.

"Snoopy?" David suggested.

"Na, don't look nothin' like him. Bandit?" I offered

"From Little House, that's a stupid show." David said.

"You're right."

"SPOCK!" We both said at the same time.

"Then Spock it is." I said to the puppy as I picked it up.

David stayed the night that night and the puppy slept in the bed with us. I learned quickly that house breaking a dog was going to take time and patience. But unlike Doug I was not going to beat Spock if he had an accident in the floor.

The next morning after David and I ate breakfast we went to Scott's house and then rode our bikes to Chris'. November of nineteen seventy six started off warm. The four of us were dressed in summer clothes and enjoying a Saturday with no appointments with either Clifford or my dad. The entire day was ours to play. It was the day that David and I had chosen to tell Scott and Chris of our plan. We rode to an open field that was bordered on one side by a marsh and the other side by Avenue J; we could see in all directions. In the middle of the field we dropped our bikes in the dead grass and then sat down in a circle.

"What's up with all this not telling me and Chris what's going on stuff?" Scott asked.

In order to help Scott and Chris understand why it was now urgent that we get help, David told them about what John had done to me and the beating my dad gave me. David left out no detail, even expounding deeper in the story than I have told you. Both Scott and Chris started to cry, knowing full well and having complete understanding of the pain I had endured. Although David, Scott and Chris had never been handled the way John handled me, it was a fear they all had and understood.

"Who do we tell? Our parents?" Scott asked.

"Can't." David replied.

"Why, they'll be the first to help us." Scott continued.

"You tell him Brian." David said to me.

"Your step-dad; was over at the house the other day. He had a meeting with my dad and Clifford." I explained to Scott.

"Oh crap. They got him to replace John. He told mom he got a new job. He was fired two weeks ago. Crap Brian; that means it's in my house now." Tears started to form in the corner of Scott's eyes.

"Hey I know man, see the problem we have, we can't trust your parents anymore. And if we tell mine or Chris', well you know, they don't know who to tell or trust and they may end up in the marshes." David explained while pointing in the direction of the marshland behind us.

"We have no one then. I mean there are cops, businessmen, those politicians, all kinds of powerful people in

Clifford's book, we're screwed. I'm scared. I mean, if we tell, we're dead." Chris said.

"Not if we stick together, and find the right people and tell many people." David explained further.

"You two are nuts; we can't take the chance." Chris was on the edge of panic.

"What choice do we have Chris? Keep letting these people do this garbage to us or take a chance to get out?" David said with a raised voice.

"Hey guys; we can't turn on each other over this; let's keep it cool." I said to all three of them.

"I'm in. With them getting my step-dad to work for them I'm no better off than Brian. No offense Brian." Scott said.

"None taken, 'cause I know what you mean. What about you Chris? You in?" I asked Chris.

"Crap guys, you're all nuts; they'll kill us, you know they will." Chris said.

Chris had lost it and was starting to break down. His voice was squeaking and cracking when he spoke and tears filled his eyes. All of us understood his fear and all of us knew that fear, but we had to end this nightmare we were in.

"They'll kill us; they will make us suffer, drag it out." Chris repeated.

Chris was crying nearly uncontrollably. I pulled him to me, giving him a hug, David and Scott joined in.

"One for all and all for one." Chris whimpered out between sobs.

"It'll work out. Somehow it'll work out." I tried to sound upbeat.

"Brian?"

"Ya David?"

"What do you think about God?" David asked.

"I told you about what Charles did. Well on the night of December twenty fifth nineteen seventy three when I did not get my Ken doll like my mom promised, and after Charles left my room. I sat and watched the lights on the Christmas tree until I fell asleep. But before I fell asleep I told myself that there's no Santa Clause and God does not care for little boys. Look where I am today." I explained.

David understood my point and he never brought up God again. But to be clear; I did not give up on the topic of God and after I got in this wheelchair I had time to learn about him. But this story is about David's mark.

"All right; we have to figure out who to tell. Let's try to meet again about this subject in two weeks; here in this field. No matter what we never mention it at any other time or around anyone else. Agreed?" David instructed.

We all agreed and then rode our bikes home. But David, me and Scott was worried about Chris; he looked sick from the decision.

The following Saturday David's parents were taking his little sister to Dallas for a Girl Scout meeting so David was staying at my house from Friday to Sunday. We had the entire weekend to ourselves. Business was slow for Clifford through November and December; most men were home with their families for the holidays or on vacations. So once more we had an entire weekend off. I was starting to heal after my dad's beating but I had some differences in my body. My rib cage was shifted and off center. David figured my dad had kicked me hard enough that it somehow twisted everything. And my jaw seemed to always hurt. David figured that he broke that as well. David did turn out to be correct on both accounts. When I turned twenty two I had to get a physical for a job and during the physical the damaged from that beating showed up. I had three ribs that had been broken, and my jaw was also broken and had never set correctly. I told the doctor that did the physical that I was in an accident as a child; he took it to mean a car wreck.

It had been only a week since the four of us boys had the meeting and planned to tell someone, but none of us had been able to find someone we could trust. Nevertheless David and I still were looking; we wanted this life to end.

Saturday morning David and I were watching cartoons on television when we were both called outside by my dad.

Little boys and dogs just naturally go together. Puppies and boys are what convey ideas of purity and innocence. But that Saturday my dad had other ideas. Once David and I were outside we noticed that dad had Spock back in the cage. The puppy was wagging its tale and was barking its high pitched bark as it saw David and me approach. Both of us sat in the dirt next to the cage and I asked my dad why the puppy was back in the cage. Dad told us that the puppy was sick and I needed to tend to it. I believed my dad since he got the puppy in the first place.

I was eager to do what was needed to help my puppy. Dad told us the puppy had worms and that they had to be drawn out and to do this I had to do a series of steps. Without going into to detail, my dad had me kill my own puppy. When I had finished what my dad made me do to the puppy; it ran to the ditch along the road, and flopped over from exhaustion. David and I ran to the ditch and we both dropped to our knees and sat next to our puppy, watching it. Slowly Spock died at our feet. Dad was standing behind me and he put his hand on my shoulder, I looked up at him as did David, both of us crying without restraint.

"Did you see that boys?" My dad's question was stupid.

We nodded our heads yes.

"Remember it well; because if you tell anyone, and I mean anyone what business me and Clifford are in and what we do with you boys you will be just like that little puppy. Savvy?" My dad explained.

"Savvy." We both replied at the same time. David had already learned what savvy was.

Dad walked away leaving me and David to watch our puppy as it finished dying. When the puppy took its last breath I carried it to the back yard and buried Spock beneath our tree house.

"Get your bike; I'm getting Scott." David instructed.

I ran and got my bike as well as David's and walked them both over to Scott's. When I got there Scott was already outside on his bike with David waiting on me for his. David got on his bike without saying a word and the three of us rode to the field we had met in a week earlier.

"This is crap; Chris is a wimp." David was walking around swinging his fist at the air.

"What's up guys?" Scott asked,

I explained what my dad had just done and it was then that the light went off for Scott; Chris had wimped out and told.

"You know what this means? They won't stop; we have no choice but to go ahead and tell. That little pansy of turd Chris. He screwed us over; we either tell or don't; we're dead either way." Scott said now walking in circles as David was.

"So what do we do David?" Scott asked.

"We keep the plan; but without Chris. No matter what we keep the plan. Agreed?"

"Agreed?" Scott and I answered at the same time.

The rest of November went by slow; we were determined to tell, but could find no one to trust. I spent Thanksgiving with David and his family, and after the meal we watched football with his dad. During a commercial break an advertisement for the upcoming release of the movie "Rocky" was shown, and as soon as it ended David and I were at his mother's skirt. She understood that telling us we could not see the movie was useless, so with David's dad's permission we started making plans to see the movie "Rocky" in December. The next day we told Scott about the movie and he had also seen the commercial and he wanted to go as well. The three of us made plans to go see "Rocky" but without Chris.

     December third nineteen seventy six, "Rocky" was released. The following Sunday December fifth David's mom took me, David and Scott to see it. She loaded the three of us up in her green station wagon and off we went. After the movie we could not stay still in our seats, we had all decided to be famous boxers. When David's mom pulled into their driveway the three of us tumbled out of the car and quickly sprang to our feet. We then started throwing punches at the empty air. We would pair off and fake box each other. The movie had infused within us hope and power, and that turned out to be a very bad thing.

Chapter 12
David's mark

The movie had inspired David, me and Scott; it gave us courage and the first day of Christmas break the three of us had another meeting in the field.

"The first day back to school after Christmas break we tell." David started off.

"Who?" I asked.

"All three of us have different teachers at school. All three of those teachers are girls."

Scott and I nodded our heads following David's reasoning.

"We all tell our teacher's at the same time, say one o'clock. Since our teachers are girls, I don't remember being taken to any girl customers. You guys?"

"Na." We both said.

"One o'clock then it is. We need to plan a…" My voice trailed off with the approaching of a car.

A white Lincoln drove slowly past and nearly stopped when in a direct line of sight with us. The three of us watched with keen interest, knowing full well that Chris had betrayed us; again. The car belonged to Clifford, all three of us knew it well, and there was only one reason for Clifford to be out here in the marshes. Clifford never dumped anyone off, he always had my dad or someone else do it, and so the only other reason for Clifford to be here was that he was led here.

Chris' had not simply betrayed us, but fully exposed us to the most feared man in our lives. Nothing was said between the three of us as we watch the car disappear in the distance. When the car was gone, David spoke first.

"I'll take the fall." David said.

"Like crap you will." I said while standing up.

"Ya like Crap." Scott added.

"We're in this together and till the end." I said.

"Even if it means being dumped in that marsh behind us?" David asked.

"We'll be together and that's what friends do, stick together. Remember David, those are your words." I explained further.

"Brian you're nuts, you're stupid crazy nuts. It's better for one of us to take the fall then all of us." David explained.

"David, look at us, stop and look at us. We have value to Clifford; we bring money in for him. He would be stupid to kill us. The three of us combined are a gold mine for Clifford." I explained.

"That's true of you and Scott, Brian. But not me; and you both know it." David replied.

"Crap David; do you always have to be right about everything." I shot back.

By now all three of us were standing. David was correct, Clifford would spare Scott and me, but David was always the last boy standing, or used as a fill in. He just did not have the looks to make the cut.

"I agree with Brian, David. We make the stand together." Scott added.

"You both are nuts, and I'm glad to have you for my friends. Well we best get back before it gets too dark. Never know what someone will do to us if he kidnaps us." David said.

The ride back to Avenue J was quiet, none of us said much as no one had much to say. The early December sunset was creating beautiful colors across the sky; almost like Northern Lights, but I learned in science class that they could never reach this far south. That sunset of December was the most beautiful I had ever witnessed, and it is forever etched in my memory. It was the last bike ride that the three of us took.

Once we were in front of David's house on Avenue J we all stopped and dropped one leg to the ground to brace ourselves in a standing position while remaining on our bikes.

"Christmas break is two weeks." Scott said.

"Ya." My voice was somber.

"That's a long time." Scott said, his voice cracking under the strain of holding back fear.

"We'll be alright guys. I don't think Clifford will do anything this quick. He'll want to find out if we talked yet." David said.

I nodded my head in the direction of Chris' house. A moving van was parked in his driveway and his family's belongings were being loaded inside. Chris was watching us through his bedroom window.

"Little crap'o." David hollered while giving Chris a gesture.

"Where do you think they're moving?" Scott asked.

"Clifford prob'ly movin' them." I added.

"I would think that Clifford released Chris for his loyalty and if that be the case, I would go as far from this nightmare as I could." David reasoned.

"Lucky boy." I added.

"But at what cost Brian. Think about it; I mean really, one or all of us is going to pay for Chris betraying us. How and when we just don't know. So he might be lucky, but he has to live with the guilt." David explained.

"If the freak has a conscience." Scott added.

"You two better ride home; still have a bit to go." David said.

"David..." I started off.

"No one is saying goodbye this time. Got it? Just ride off Brian."

Scott and I stood up on our peddles and rode home, both of us with tears in our eyes. We had lost the final round and were down for the count. Over the next few days the three of us lived in fear, waking each morning hoping only to live to go to bed that night.

December thirty first nineteen seventy six I woke up early, eager to survive to the end of the day. I forsook a shower, quickly slipped on a pair of shorts and my shoes and then rode my bike to David's house. The day was unusually warm for the last day of December, but a thin layer of clouds hung high in the sky, casting an ominous feeling within me. Once at David's I jumped from my bike and allowed it to roll to a drop stop. I ran up the sidewalk and rang the doorbell. I pushed the doorbell button four times before I started knocking, and still I got no answer. I could hear the television, but heard no movement. I ran to the side yard, opened the gate to the backyard, where Samson greeted me.

"Hey boy, where's everyone at?"

I halfheartedly spoke to the dog. I made my way into the screened in porch and knocked on the back door, no answer. I tried turning the doorknob, locked, which I found strange, they never locked the backdoor. As I made my way back around the house fear started to grip me. I knew it had started. David was right, the price would have to be paid from what Chris had done, and one or all three of us would pay it. The collector had come for his due.

I picked up my bike and rode back to my house faster than I had ever ridden my bike before. Once in my yard I jumped from my bike, letting it crash on its own, somehow I knew that was the last time I would ride the bike that Scott had given me months earlier. I ran to Scott's house and pounded on his bedroom window. I was relieved to be greeted by a sleepy face peering back out at me.

"Get out here quick." I said to Scott.

Scott stepped out of his front door dressed only in a pair of pull on shorts; he didn't even take the time to comb his hair.

"What's goin' down?" Scott asked.

"David's not home." I said.

Scott just shrugged his shoulders.

"No, you don't get it. TV's on, doors locked, but no answer. I buzzed the bell over and over. Then I knocked. I went to the backdoor and knocked." I explained to Scott.

"Backdoor locked?" Scott asked.

I raised my eyebrows and nodded my head yes.

"David's was right; their gonna' make us pay." Scott said as he let his small body drop against the house.

As soon as his body had touched the house he jerked back up as if he had fallen backward on a bed of hot coals. Terror etched across his face and his eyes widened and the whites of his eyes turned red. I spun around to look in the direction that gripped his attention. Leaning against a tree on the property line was my dad. He had a cigarette hanging freely in the corner of his mouth, the smoke drifting in his eyes forcing him to squint while he watched us. Fear now griped me as it did Scott and I was paralyzed. I tried to tell my legs to run, but the transmission lines were down, I felt a familiar warm sensation run down both of my legs.

My dad pushed his body away from the tree and stood looking at us as he would a rabbit that he had in the sights of his gun. He removed the cigarette from his mouth and flicked it in our direction. He then started walking toward us.

"Looks like you pissed yourself Brian." My dad told me what he reached us.

I knew I had wet myself but I looked down anyway to confirm what my dad reported. When I looked back up he smiled at me and then at Scott.

"Looks like you have the same problem there Scotty." My dad said to Scott.

I turned to look at Scott, he too had wet himself. We were both now running on fear alone.

My dad took us both by the shoulders and escorted us in the direction of the feed storage shed behind Scott's house.

Once we were at the door of the shed my dad held it open for us. Scott went in first and then I followed. As soon as I entered the room I came to a complete stop, looked down, and then raised my head to look at those standing around. I noticed that Scott's step-dad and Clifford were already in the room. My dad walked over and took his place beside Clifford. Scott had been pulled to the far side of the room by his step-dad, and I was left standing where I had stopped with the door closed and locked behind me.

On the dirt floor, at my feet, was David. He had been stripped naked and his wrist and ankles were restrained to keep him from moving. From personal experience I already knew what each of these men was capable of; but with David now restrained before me I was about to learn just how far they would go to keep what they were doing a secret. I was so frightened that I broke down and lost my composure completely. I started to shake; as if in a cold shiver, and started crying is winded bouts. I was crying so hard that the mucus from my nose and my tears was streaming in a constant flow down my face and dropping from my chin to the dirt floor below. I didn't know what was about to happen but I knew there was no way this was going to turn out good for me and more so for David.

My dad handed me a large knife, when I looked down at it, it reminded me of the carving knife I had used on Doug about a year earlier. I brought my gaze up from the knife and I looked over to see my dad, I was pleading with my eyes. I was not able to form words, as fear griped my throat, so I slowly shook my head back and forth telling my dad no. My dad told to get on my knees beside David, but I refused. The tension in the room was thick, and it was filled with the smell of urine from Scott, me and David. As far as I was concerned my dad no longer carried the authority that a parent would to a child, so I did not feel obligated to obey him. I realized that if he would force me to hurt David, he would have no problem hurting me. Again I shook my head no. I had now reached a point that disobeying my dad was acceptable.

My dad then placed both of his hands on each of my shoulders and forced me to my knees. I struggled under his pressure, but I was too small to resist my dad. When I felt the cold dirt on my knees I turned from looking at my dad to David in front of me. I found myself looking at David in the face. I was now dripping snot and tears on David and begging for these men standing around me to show mercy, any kind of mercy. I started begging, pleading and bargaining with my dad. This was the greatest and hardest I had ever pleaded for anything in my life. At the same time I would turn to David and I kept telling him how sorry I was. I was doing anything and everything I could to buy time; I had to stop this from happening. My thinking and thoughts were fast and erratic. I was looking for an out, any out. I was willing to make these men any deal they wanted, but nothing was forthcoming.

David was also crying and begging just as hard as I was. All the leadership in him was now drained out. And to David's other side sat Scott; he too was doing the same as I was. I don't remember who explained it to the three of us boys, but we were told that because we planned to tell, an example had to be made of one of us and David was to be that example.

That information changed the direction of my pleading, as did for Scott and David. I can't put into words how hard I begged and pleaded, I can't find the right words that can capture the feelings I had, and I can't convey the absolute loss of control and helplessness that I felt. When I think back to this event I can feel all those things again, yet I can't explain them.

Dad instructed me to press the edge of the blade into his upper left shoulder and drag it crossways down to his right hip. Again I starting begging and pleading, all the while I was slowly shaking my head back and forth. I was crying harder than I had ever cried in my life, but nothing I did or was going to do would stop this from happening. With reluctance I leaned over David while bracing myself with my left hand in the dirt. I was hoping that simply scarring David was the intent, and if I did what I was told David would just end up with a huge scar across his chest.

I placed the edge of the knife against his skin. All the time I kept telling David how sorry I was, and kept asking David to forgive me. Over and over I asked for David's forgiveness. He said nothing but just cried. He knew as I knew nothing could be done. As I pulled the knife toward me I felt and saw David's body heave, and I slid my left hand over to his hand to hold it. It was all the comfort I could give my best friend. Turning my attention back to the knife I noticed my tears and snot was dripping on him and I moved my head so it would not drip in his face. I then gently finished pulling the knife across his chest and belly, the cut that was left behind allowed David's blood to seep out and flow down the sides of his body and onto the dirt floor. When I had finished my cut, David let out his last whimper of a cry, he appeared to be sleeping. When I had completed what I was forced to do I let the knife drop to the floor beside me. Then I sat back with my legs folded under me, exhausted. I slumped forward toward David and bowed my head in disgust. Dad bent down and picked up the knife and handed it to Scott's step-dad.

Scott was forced to do the same to David, but from the other side. And as I had done, Scott did all he could do to find a way to stop what was happening. When Scott had completed the task; he did as I did, and slumped forward exhausted. David was still breathing, but there were no more tears and he no longer had the ability to cry out from the pain that Scott and I had inflicted.

David lay motionless, except for the slight movement of his chest with each shallow breath, as if he were at rest. Looking back I could only speculate that he had passed out when I had started my cut. Blood was flowing down both of his sides and it had started to form red pools in the brown dirt. Me and Scott were then pulled to our feet and ushered out the back door that led to a pasture behind his house. Once we heard the door close and the latch lock we collapsed under a big tree.

Scott and I sat with our legs folded under us and cried, neither of us knowing what to do. David was the one we looked to, it was his advice and words that always led us in the right direction, and now he was gone, by our hand. I left that room fully believing that I had just been forced to take the life of my best friend, but now as an adult I know that a child of nine could not have inflected that much damage.

Scott realized that he still had the knife in his hand; they had forgotten to take it from him. I looked at my right hand, it was covered in David's blood, then I looked at Scott's right hand, it too was covered in David's blood. We both knew what we had to do. In turn we each made a cut in our own blood covered hand, and then pressed them together. We thought that David's blood would mix with our own blood and from that act we would carry David with us as long as we lived. I learned later that the blood of

David never mixed with our own, but it was the only act we could think of to keep David alive.

I then dug a hole with the blade of the knife and buried it beneath the tree in a forked root. We both stood and walked carelessly down the pasture and made our way to a dry creek that at one time flowed behind our houses. We found a dead tree on the ground and sat with our backs to the tree and our houses.

The death of David is the single, greatest reason I don't view myself as a victim of anything I endured. The three of us had planned to end our abuse by going for help. David gave his life because of that plan, and I never carried it out. David's death was therefore worthless, in vain. Had I chosen to continue with the plan and go for help David's death would have held some merit. As it was I chose to let his death become empty and meaningless. Therefore by allowing David to be murdered I forfeited my right as a victim forever.

"It's not over." Scott broke the silence.

"I know that's what I was thinking myself." I replied.

"They'll come for us, sooner or later they will."

"I know."

"We can't go back to the house."

"I know."

"Brian?" Scott turned his face to me.

"You have to figure out what to do." Scott said.

I had not noticed it before but drops of blood had splattered on Scott's face. I wondered about my own face, and then thought about telling him, but decided not to.

"We're not going back, but I don't know what to do. It's December and we have nothing on but shorts." I explained.

"Maybe David's parents are home now; let's walk over there though the fields and woods and see." Scott suggested.

"Let's go." I said standing up and putting out my hand to help Scott up.

The woods in this part of Texas consisted mostly of small trees and twisted vines and thorns. It was more like attempting to walk through a briar swamp. But we pushed through it. The trek to David's house had cost us dearly in cuts to our entire bodies and feet. It took us nearly two hours to make the short trip, a trip that on my bike took minutes. The woods exited from behind Chris' house and we both knew that if Chris saw us we would be as good as dead. We crouched down to scout out the area.

"Brian?"

"Ya Scott?"

"Whatda' we do?"

"Do you see anything around Chris' house?" I asked.

"Na notin'. No curtains on the windows either."

"Ya, I'm thinkin' there already gone, you?"

"Same." Scott answered.

"I think we should just walk out like nothin', try to be casual. Go right into David's back yard." I suggested.

"If the door is still locked?" Scott asked.

"Get the rock key."

"Brian, I'm scared and I got to pee."

"I'm scared too. How many times do you think you've peed in your shorts already?" I asked.

"A lot. You?"

"'Bout as much, just pee in your shorts. Let's go." I said.

We both stood up and walked out of the woods on the far side of Chris' house, to avoid being seen by any neighbors that might be home. As we made our way into the street I noticed that the clouds had thickened and it was starting to sprinkle. Once we were in David's back yard we relaxed our posture and I found that I needed to pee as well, and I did.

"I'll check the door. If it's still locked grab the key and bring it on the porch. I'll give a thumbs up or thumbs down, down means grab the key" I told Scott.

"K."

I made my way onto the porch and tried the back door again, it was still locked and the television was still on. I gave Scott the thumbs down. He walked over to a rock that only David, me and Scott knew about; we had moved the key after Chris betrayed us. Scott turned the rock over and dug through the dirt until he found the key. As he approached the door with it he was wiping it off on his wet shorts.

"Sorry." Scott said as he handed me the key.

I took the key from his hand and pushed it into the lock.

"No need to be sorry, all you could do."

I opened the door and the first thing that hit us was the smell. It was not all that bad, but it smelled of rotting fruit.

"David's mom would never leave food out to spoil. That smell is sick." Scott said.

"Let's go in." Was my only reply.

As we entered the kitchen I noticed that Scott reached to turn on the light and I was able to stop him before he did.

"Better not turn on any light or anything." I said.

"Why?"

"Don't know, just a feelin' I have."

We continued into the house. As we made our way through the living room I noticed that the daytime soaps were still on, I looked at the clock and it was fifteen minutes after two.

"Crap; the day's almost over. We got to move." I told Scott. "Upstairs, David's room."

We walked upstairs and straight into David's room, we were hunting for clothes.

"We should wash this blood off of us first. Don't you think Brian?" Scott suggested.

"Ya, sorry."

David shared a bathroom with his sister; they each had their own door. When we entered the bathroom I walked to the sink and started to wet a washcloth. Scott froze staring at the bathtub. I turned to see what he was looking at and quickly put my hand over Scott's mouth to muffle his scream.

"Shush. Don't scream, and be quiet." I whispered in Scott's ear.

In the bathtub was David's little sister, dead. She happened to be taking a bath when whoever entered their home found her and took advantage of the water, holding her under until she drowned.

"You think..." Scott left the question unfinished.

I nodded my head yes.

"Wet a few washcloths and take them back into David's room, be quick about it." I instructed.

We both wet several washcloths and carried them back into David's room, tossing them on his bed. We both then removed our wet, blood soaked shorts and underwear and started to wash ourselves with the washcloths. Once we were clean enough we found some of David's clean underwear and other clothes. We put on blue jeans and two shirts, in case we had to be outside all night.

"He only has one pair of tennis shoes; the other pair is a pair of dress loafers." Scott said.

"You take the tennis shoes, I'll wear the loafers." I suggested.

"No, I'll take the loafers."

When we had finished dressing we took a minute to sit on David's bed to catch our breath.

"I miss him." Scott said.

"Yep, me too. We had some great times here in this room. Playing games and just having fun, my Cub Scout uniform."

"Do you think we'll make it?" Scott asked, looking at the floor.

"I don't know Scott. I have no idea what to do or where to go." I said in reply.

"Do you think they killed his mom and dad?"

"Yep." I dropped my head when I answered. I wanted David's parents to be my parents and I felt the loss.

"Let's see if we can find them. But be quiet." I said as I stood up.

We walked through bathroom and into David's sister's room, but found it empty. We exited her room and turned left toward the master bedroom. We both stopped in the doorway. Bent backwards on the bed laid his mom, dead. She had been beaten and from the looks of the marks on her neck, choked to death. My thoughts returned to when I was six years old and I walked in on my dad trying to kill my mom.

"Brian who did this?" Scott asked.

"I know who did it, my dad. Let's go." I answered.

We exited the master bedroom and looked in the master bathroom, but found it empty. We then walked back downstairs. We already knew the living room and kitchen was empty, so we made our way to the den. In the den we found David's dad. He had been shot, but we did not approach his body to see where or how many times. We both turned our faces to the wall and threw up.

"We got to get out of here." I said, pulling on Scott's arm.

"I need some water Brian."

"Crap, I do too."

We went into the kitchen and I got both of us a glass of water, we continued to drink until we had three glasses each.

"They'll come back here looking for us?"

"My dad will, ya, he will. He's intent to kill me now." I answered.

"What do we do?"

"We have to stay alive, Scott. Somehow, I just don't know how."

"I'm hungry. Can we eat?"

"Ya, let's make a sandwich."

We found the bread and peanut butter and grape jelly and each made a sandwich. I also poured us a glass of milk; it would go to spoil anyway. Although I knew staying in David's house was dangerous, I also needed time to think. Scott was now looking to me for advice and help, and I had always turned to David. I was not the decision maker David was, and now I was forced to be the decision maker. By the time I looked at the clock again it was approaching four o'clock in the afternoon; the sun would be setting soon.

I stepped out onto the back porch and noticed that a chill was now in the air that was not present before, and the rain had picked up. It felt and looked like a rain storm was moving in. I walked back inside the house.

"I hate to say it, but I think we need to spend the night here, or somewhere." I said.

"Brian, it stinks and it's gonna get worse. And your dad?" Scott said.

"I know, but it's raining now and it's gonna get cold." I replied.

"Chris' old house?" Scott offered.

"We'll have to break out the back window." I answered.

"So, who'll care, what do we care?" Scott offered back.

"Fill up some bottles with water; I'll go grab two of David's coats." I instructed.

"Brian; hurry."

"I will."

We put on the coats and then put the water in the coat pockets. Under the cover of the twilight of the evening we made our way back across the street to Chris' old house. We walked behind the house and to the window that was in his sister's bedroom. I felt around on the ground in the darkness until I found a rock that I thought was big enough to break through the window. I tossed the rock at the window, causing the window to shatter, glass to fly and the sound of the shatter to travel. At the moment that I let the rock go I caught what I thought was a flicker of light out of the corner of my eye. I choose to dismiss it. I reached in through the broken hole in the glass and unlocked the window, then lifted it up. I boosted Scott inside, and he in turned pulled me up and through the window. I turned around. Lowered the window back down; locking it.

"Did you get any cuts coming through the window?" I asked Scott.

"Na, you?"

"No. Let's go to the living room so we can keep an eye on David's house." I said.

"What about Chris' room, it looks straight across?" Scott suggested.

"I'll never go in that coward's room again." I said through clinched teeth.

"Sorry."

We walked into the living room and made our way to the picture window that covered most of the outer front wall that faced David's house. We then sat below the window and watched.

"We need to take turns. One sleeps; the other watches." I said.

"Can I sleep first Brian? I'm really tired." Scott asked.

"Ya, use my leg as a pillow if you have too."

Scott stretched out on the floor and put his head on my thigh and in seconds he had drifted off to sleep. I propped my arm in the window sill and rested my head, while keeping my eyes fixated on David's house, I did not notice my dad's car parked at the end of the road.

Chapter 13
We Will Survive

As I drifted off to sleep I remembered the Christmas tree of nineteen seventy three. The red, green and blue lights winked at me until I lost touch with reality. I kept telling myself that that was three years ago, how could I be seeing the tree lights wink at me again, here in Chris' old house. This was nineteen seventy six and I was fighting to keep me and Scott alive, there was no Christmas tree around.

I jerked my head up off my arm. I looked out across the street at David's house. The winking lights were coming from David's windows. I watched as my awareness started to return from my sleeping. I soon realized that my dad and Scott's step-dad were searching David's house for us. Their flashlights were intermittently appearing in my line of sight through openings in the curtains. I shook Scott awake.

"We got to go. Our dads are searching David's house." I said as Scott regained his awareness.

"Crap; they'll see our dirty shorts and the mess we left behind. They'll know we were there." Scott said the fear evident in his voice.

"Ya, but they don't know where we are now." I assured Scott.

"How long they been there?"

"Don't know. But come to think of it. I think I saw some car lights or a flashlight when I broke Chris' window." I answered.

"They could have heard the break?"

"Crap. I didn't think of that."

Scott was correct. If they heard the breaking of the glass it would only be a matter of time before they come across the street to check the outside of Chris' house.

"Back to the room we came in." I said, helping Scott to his feet.

We walked back to Chris' sister's old room and stood looking out of the broken window. The rain storm had moved in, and it was now raining hard, with a strong north wind. Even with David's coats we were going to get soaked and be cold. We had no choice.

"I'll go first, then help you out. We go back into the woods until 'bout halfway down back to my house. We then turn to the street and make our way across. Once across we run like mad through the open field to the train tracks. Got it?" I instructed Scott.

"Then what? Once we make it to the tracks." Scott asked.

"The tracks go into Alta Loma; we follow them." I added.

"Crap Brian. That's miles. We can be walking all night, in this." Scott replied.

"Any other ideas?" I asked.

"Why not go to another house around here?"

"If we do and my dad sees us he will just tell them we ran away from home and drag us back." I explained.

"I'm scared Brian, really scared."

"Ya, me too. But if we follow the tracks, no matter how long, we will soon be in town."

"K."

I unlocked the window and raised it, being careful so no more glass fell out. Once I had it up all the way I helped Scott out and then I climbed out. We then reentered the thick woods. It was harder to make our way through the twisted thorns and vines. The rain quickly soaked our heavy coats, slowing us down. I noticed that Scott's coat was getting entangled by the thorns.

"Take the coat off and leave it." I said.

We both took off our coats, leaving them behind. Although it was colder, we were able to move a little quicker. The rain was turning the ground below us into thick mud. With each step our feet sank and stuck. When I lifted my foot out of the mud a sucking, sloshing sound was made. I realized that I may lose my shoes. I turned to face Scott.

"The loafers?"

"Already lost them. Figured no use in saying nothin', nothin' could be done." Scott replied.

The thickness of the woods, and the entangled thorns and vines were once again digging into our flesh. The pounding rain stung the freshly made cuts in my face and arms, each drop of rain renewing the pain. We continued to push through, making our way slowly to the road. The mud buried us about two to three inches with each step. I didn't realize that I had lost my shoes and socks until we had cleared the woods. The mud kept my feet encased. Once we had reached the edge of the woods that exited onto Avenue J, we squatted down to scout out the area.

"I lost the tennis shoes and my socks."

"Ya I lost my socks too. I got cuts all over my face and arms."

"Me too. See any cars?" I asked Scott.

"No. But don't mean they ain't out there watching from somewhere."

"Ya, and to think of it, we left a great trail for them to follow." I answered.

"What do'ya mean?"

"The broken window, the muddy footprints leading into the woods, we dropped the coats and somewhere we left behind our shoes and socks. Not to even consider all the broken branches." I explained.

"Crap Brian. So what do we do?"

"Keep to the plan." I said.

"Here's what we do. We get a good grip on each other's hands. If I fall you drag me, if you fall I'll drag you. We stand and bolt across the street and squeeze through the barbed wire fence. Then we bolt for the train tracks, keeping a grip on each other. Got it?" I explained.

I took a deep breath.

"Ready Scott?"

"Let's go."

I took Scott's hand in mine, reflecting back to my friend in Santa Fe and the price he paid for letting go; I tightened my grip on Scott's hand. We stood and bolted out of the edge of the woods and into the street. When we made it to the fence on the other side we pushed our way through the barbed wire. I ignored the barbs as they dug into my flesh. Once on the other side of the fence and in the open field, we reconnected our hands and bolted for the train tracks. The thickness of the clouds forbade any moonlight to help us see clearly, only a dimly pink ambient light reflected off of the clouds. Rocks and thorns cut our now bare feet.

We continued to run.

The wind had died down and the rain was coming straight down instead of sideways at us.

We continued to run.

I heard a car door slam in the distance.

We continued to run.

Suddenly Scott's hand was no longer in mine, at the same moment I heard Scott let out a piercing scream. I stopped and turned, but I could not see him in the darkness. In the corner of my eye I saw the flicker of a light. I carefully started backtracking, whispering his name.

"Here." Scott's voice was full of pain.

I got on my hands and knees and started to feel the ground until I reached Scott. He was curled in a fetal position holding his right leg to his chest.

"What happened?" I asked.

Scott was crying, and letting out whimpers of pain.

"I tripped and when I came down my knee hit a rock." Scott explained.

"Can you stand, or walk?"

"Help me try." Scott reached his hands up and toward me.

I stood up and then reached out and took Scott's hands, carefully pulling him up to a standing position. He shifted his weight to his good leg. As he stood he let out another cry of pain.

"Keep it quiet if you can." I said.

"It hurts Brian."

"Put your arm around my shoulder and keep your weight on your good leg. I'll drag you if I have to."

"I would tell you to leave me here, but I know you wouldn't and besides I'm too scared to stay." Scott said.

"Right. Listen. Go to your safe place. Like when you're on a job. It'll help control the pain. I'll worry about staying in the real world."

I waited a few seconds to allow Scott to go to his safe place and then resumed our trek to the train tracks. I now noticed the flicker of light again, it was brighter and closer. It was moving in our direction.

Supporting Scott had slowed us down to less than a walk, but I was not about to fail Scott as I did David. If worse came to worst I would lay Scott in the grass as bait, while I lay in wait with the largest rock I could find. But for the moment I pressed on, with Scott hanging from my shoulder. When we made it to the train tracks I helped Scott down to sit on the rail. I turned my attention back in the direction we had just crossed and noticed the flicker of light was still cutting through the rain. I was sure it was my dad but the rain was distorting the beam of light, making it difficult to determine exactly how close he was, but I knew he was closing in. I sat down next to Scott.

"Change of plan." I told Scott.

"What?" Scott asked.

"With my dad behind us he'll catch up to us if we stay on the tracks. Up ahead the tracks curve to the left and when they do we will be out of his sight for only a few minutes."

"He can see us?"

"He may not be able to make out anything, but with the flashlight he can see our outline. He will be able to see our outline until we take the curve. Once we take the curve we leave the tracks and go in the woods on the other side." I explained

"I've never been on that side. Where do they go?"

"David and I explored it once. The woods are like what we were in behind Chris' house, but after a while they come out to a highway that has a gas station and some other businesses." I explained.

"How long is a little while?" Chris asked.

"Chris; it's thicker, thornier and longer. It will be a hard push through the woods, but I figure it's our only chance, it'll be quicker in the end because of your knee."

"It's like the Battle of the Wilderness." Scott said.

"I had not thought about that, but it would be just like the Battle of the Wilderness and we are at war."

One of the hardest battles of the Civil War was called the Battle of the Wilderness. The Confederate and Union armies converged on a narrow road that was surrounded on both sides by a wilderness much like the one that Scott and I had just left behind and now faced again. In the Battle of the Wilderness, the wilderness itself claimed the lives of solders. Now Scott and me were about to fight our battle of the wilderness.

"Brian; if your dad gets close, bury me under some bushes, leaves and vines. He won't suspect it and I'll stay wherever you bury me until you come back." Scott said.

"We stay together, no matter what." I replied.

"So he can kill us both!"

"Let's go."

I lifted Scott up and he put his arm back around my shoulder. Before we started walking toward the curve I looked back at the approaching beam of light. It was closer and less scattered by the rain.

"Double time Scott. Just like in the Battle of the Wilderness."

We marched toward the curve in the track.

Sticking with the metaphor of the Civil War battle seemed to help Scott. Scott was the history buff of the four of us and I doubt there was anything about history that he didn't know. During our march toward the curve I kept the Battle of the Wilderness fresh in his mind. Scott knew that many of those fallen in that battle had to clear the wilderness or face being burned alive. Camp fires left burning from the night had set the entire wilderness ablaze and those fallen that were still alive burned to death if they were unable to crawl to safety. I started to realize that Scott was now fighting that battle in his mind. The pitch darkness of the night, pounding rain and the enemy behind us made it real for him. Regardless, it helped him deal with the pain he was in and allowed us to increase our pace.

When we made it to the curve I sat Scott back down on the rail and turned to look for the beam of light. It was not within sight. Although my dad had a flashlight, he did not know our plan and direction. I was also used to trekking through this area, my dad was not. Although our advantage was small, it was enough to give us a slight edge over my dad.

"Ready?" I asked Scott.

"No, but no choice."

I helped Scott to his feet and we then left the tracks, carefully making our way down the steep embankment. We walked across a small clearing and stood at the edge of the wilderness. I turned to look back down the tracks and in the far distance I thought I could make out a faint flicker of light. I shifted Scott's weight and we entered the wilderness. The final battle for our lives had begun.

Chapter 14
The Battle of the Wilderness

We inched our way into the wilderness. The deeper we dug into its thicket, the deeper the thorns dug into our flesh. I had to fight for each step we took, disentangling both myself and Scott every few feet. I was reassured by the fact that if it was hard for me and Scott it would be hard for my dad. I could only hope he was drunk, it would even the odds. Although it helped Scott to mentally be in a battle fought nearly one hundred and fifty years ago, the pain in his knee was winning. He was sweating profusely and a few times we had to stop so he could throw up. I looked for a chance to take a rest. That opportunity came sooner than I had expected, and Scott welcomed it. We found a large dead tree that had fallen near a ravine creating the perfect hiding place. The tree had fallen at the edge of the ravine creating an overhang; shelter from the rain. I helped Scott down the muddy slippery slope and then up and under the fallen tree. I climbed up after Scott was settled in and I sat as close to him as I was able to preserve our body heat.

"After you rest for a bit I want to see your knee." I told Scott.

"Okay. Brian? How much further to the highway and the stores?" Scott asked exhausted.

"It's still a ways. David and I had nothing to do for a whole day and we explored this area. I remember it was getting dark by the time we made our way back out onto Avenue J. We'll be alright. My dad is probably drunk, and if he is he's having a harder time then we are." I tried to sound upbeat.

"But if my step-dad is with your dad?" Scott replied.

"Every time I looked back I saw only one flashlight. I saw two in David's house. I bet they split up, and now your step-dad would not know which way my dad went." I answered.

"I hope so, and I hope your dad is drunk."

Scott struggled in an attempt to pull up his rain soaked pant leg, but it was no use and causing him a great deal of pain. The fall had ripped open the fabric of his jeans around his knee, but not enough for me to see anything in the darkness.

"I'm going to rip your pant leg open more so I can try to see. Okay?" I said.

Scott nodded his head yes.

I carefully reached into the torn opening and pulled the tear further apart. Once Scott's knee was exposed I realized just how bad the damage was and how much trouble he was in. Although it was dark, there was enough pink ambient light reflecting off of the clouds to allow me to get an idea of how bad the damage was. The flesh was cut and flayed from around the knee area. The area where no skin remained appeared to be too white. I was not sure but it looked as if the bone of his knee cap was exposed. It did not look broken however. The light provided by the reflection of the clouds was not enough to tell if it was still bleeding.

"How bad is it?" Scott asked.

"I think they are going to have to cut your leg off just below your sac." I said.

"REALLY?"

"Na, just trying to rib you. It's hard to tell in the darkness. But I don't think I see any fresh blood. But I'm going to tear off a piece of my shirt and pull that skin back up to cover what I think is the knee cap. I'll tie a strip of my shirt around your knee. Okay?"

"It's going to hurt really bad, that's why you're telling me so I won't scream out."

"Ya. Listen, find a stick and put it between your teeth, like in the movies." I suggested.

While Scott felt around in the mud for a stick I ripped off a strip from the bottom of my shirt. Once Scott had found a stick and wiped the mud off as best as he could he put it between his front teeth.

"It's gonna hurt." I said one last time.

Scott shook his head yes, he understood. I had noticed that he had started crying, tears of anticipation.

With as much care as I could I took hold of the flap of skin that had been flayed and laid it back over his knee cap. Mud had encased itself in some of the folds, so with extra care I wiped it away with another piece of my shirt. Once I had the flap of skin back over the knee cap I took the strip of shirt that I had torn off and wrapped it around the flap of skin and his leg to hold it in place. I then tied the strip of shirt, being careful not to over tighten it, but enough to hold the flap of skin in place. Although Scott's tears of pain had increased and he let out a few moans, he took the pain better than I had expected.

"Alright?" I asked.

"No. Can we wait here until the sun comes up? There's no way your dad would find us here." Scott pleaded.

"I was considering that as an option. It may not be a bad idea. We both could use some sleep anyway. At least the rain's not beating right down on us anymore." I said.

"How much longer can it rain? I wish it would stop." Scott said.

"You and me both."

I looked out over the area in front of us and noticed that the ground was now covered in water, like a shallow marsh. When we started moving again we would be treading through water, with inches of mud underneath. I was losing faith that we would survive with each passing hour.

We leaned against each other and attempted to sleep.

***

"Captain'? Life support is off line. We have at most one hour of oxygen left." The ensign next to me reported.

"Mr. Scott, if we shut down all unnecessary decks and move those personal to the other decks will that buy us some time?"

"Ey' Captin' but no enough." Scotty said from his station on the bridge.

"See to it." Kirk ordered.

"Ey sir." Scotty exited the bridge via the turbolift.

"Mr. Spock. Please tell me that you have found a way to penetrate their defenses?" Kirk said as he spun his command chair around.

"No sir, I have not. It appears Captain that we are all doomed to die." Spock reported as he got up from his chair and started to dance.

"I think I'll join you Mr. Spock." Uhura said as she made her way over to Spock's station.

"Captain; that noise, sounded like the ship cracking in half." I reported.

***

The crack was from a stick close by being broken. Since it cracked it had to be a dead limb still attached to a tree. Everything on the ground was too water soaked to crack. Scott had heard it also and I noticed that he opened his mouth, I reached over and placed my hand over his mouth to stop whatever was about to come out.

In the distance, or what the rain distorted as distance, I saw the flicker of a light as it bounced its bent waves off of the trees and underbrush. My dad had managed to venture this far, we must have left a trail. If he managed to turn the light in our direction, our white skin would reflect the light and he would find us. I reached down and scooped up some mud and speared it all over Scott's face. Since his hair was dark I left that alone. I then smeared his exposed arms. I did the same to my face and arms, but I had to smear the mud in my hair as well. My blond hair would reflect the light.

"Keep still and quiet." I whispered right in Scott's ear.

I watched as my dad inched his way in our direction.

We held our breathing steady.

His flashlight bouncing twisted beams off of the dead tree above us.

We held our breathing steady.

I watched as he brought the beam of light toward our hiding place.

We held our breathing steady.

The light came to a stop at our feet and then swung around and in the direction we intended to continue walking after our rest.

I held my breathing steady and emptied my bladder.

The beam of light moving off infused Scott with mild excitement. Again he was about to speak. I held my index finger across my lips, gesturing for him to remain silent. I watched as the beam of light disappeared in the distance. Dad had walked a few yards in the direction of the highway, and then turned to his right. I had never been in that direction before and I was hoping that he thought we had circled back and that was what he was doing.

"I think he's gone." I said to Scott relieved.

"So we can go now?" Scott asked. Fear surging through his blood and making him want to run.

"No. He may double back or turn back toward the highway. We're safe for a few hours. Can you sleep?" I asked.

"I don't think so. I'm too scared. Please Brian, he's going back toward the tracks, please can we move again?" Scott pleaded.

"Okay."

I helped Scott to his feet and then down the muddy slope and into what was now a shallow marsh. With each step our bare feet sunk several inches into the wet heavy mud, only to be rinsed partially clean when we extracted them from the mud. The short rest and the adrenalin running through Scott's blood gave him the strength he needed to press forward at a faster pace. We were making good time, and if Scott's fear could keep the adrenalin flowing, we might be able to reach safety.

The beam of light reappeared.

"Oh crap Brian. I thought he circled back." Scott exclaimed.

"Me too. Jerk, he turned his flashlight off when he was far enough away, waiting us out. He must have figured we were hiding. Can you run? The wilderness clears up a lot ahead. No more thickets, just trees." I asked Scott.

Scott could and did run. Although the thicket tripped us both many times, we made our way out of the thorns and vines and into the clearing of just trees. We still had to contend with a shallow marsh and thick mud, but at least we would suffer no more shreds of our flesh and being beat down by the vines. Behind us the beam of light was bouncing up and down in a frantic manner. My dad gave chase for us.

"How much further to the highway from here Brian?"

"I remember when we cleared the thickets it went easier, but still took some time. I don't see any lights or hear any cars yet. Stay with me. Remember this is the Battle of the Wilderness, the enemy is approaching, he might even set the wilderness on fire." I attempted to encourage Scott.

"Brian, I'm tired, too tired. Go without me."

"You know that that will never happen, so shut up sayin' it." My anger was not at Scott but the situation we were in.

"I'll drag you Scott if I have to. I'll make one of those Indian medicine beds out of sticks and pull you behind me. But you're not taking the easy way out and quitting. Now find some fear in you and let's move." I ordered.

I had turned to face Scott who was behind me and when I turned back around I noticed a flicker of light. I knew we were too far from the highway for it to be a car, so it had to be Scott's step-dad. I turned back to look in the opposite direction and saw my dad's flicker of light. Scott had also noticed the additional beam of light.

"They did split up. My step-dad drove around to the highway and entered the wilderness from the other side." Scott explained the obvious.

I placed my hand on Scott's chest, motioning for him to stop walking. I had to think this through.

"What do we do now Brian?"

"I don't know."

The clamp on the mouse trap had slammed down on both me and Scott.

"Scott listen. My dad is still coming from the far side; your step-dad is coming from in front of us. If we cut in the opposite direction, arch our turn, we can go around your step-dad and be running away from my dad. Once out of the direct path of your step-dad we can make a run for the highway." I explained.

"Go."

We both ran as fast as the mud, rain and marsh would allow. Scott's blood infused with another rush of adrenalin, deadening the pain from his busted knee. We ran in a line away from my dad and at and arch to Scott's approaching step-dad until we were clear enough to turn back toward the highway. We continued to run, splashing water and kicking up mud, and falling face first with every few steps in the marsh. The noise of our departure alerted Scott's step-dad and he too changed direction and bolted off after us.

"Brian I hear something."

Scott had heard something, the blare of a truck horn from the highway up ahead in the distance. The horn gave us both hope and somehow we were able to increase our pace. The thickness of the wilderness still blocked the light from the highway and surrounding buildings, but we both knew we were close. We continued to run.

Scott held out his hand, pointing ahead of us, lights in the distance. The wilderness was now thinning out enough so that the lights from the businesses were able to penetrate it. Exultation filled us both, and we quickened our pace. We were now close enough that we could hear the sound of cars as they sped down the highway, and make out the shapes of buildings.

We both were going to survive the Battle of the Wilderness, our battle.

At first I thought Scott had run into a low hanging tree limb, until I heard the voice of his step-dad. Scott's step-dad had managed to get ahead of us and waited until our path crossed his hiding place behind a tree. As we approached he stepped out and smacked Scott in the chest with a tree limb, Scott went down, the wind knocked out of him. I stopped, turned and then looked around my feet for anything that I could use as a weapon. Finding nothing I ran and jumped on Scott's step-dad's back. I wrapped my arms around his neck and started to squeeze with what little strength I had left. He flipped me over his head and I went flying through the air to crash against a tree and fall at its base face down in the water.

Scott had gotten his second wind and picked up the limb that his step-dad had used on him. When his step-dad smacked Scott across the chest the limb broke, leaving behind a jagged point.

Scott's step-dad approached me, removing a knife from its sheath. I lifted myself up on my hands and feet and attempted to crawl away, but the mud and beating rain caused me to slip back down into the marsh. I heard Scott holler at his step-dad. His step-dad stopped his advance on me and turned to face Scott.

I saw that Scott had braced the stick against the ground, with the jagged edge facing up. From behind I ran and pushed his step-dad toward Scott. His step-dad rushed forward from my shove and landed on the point of the stick.

His death was quick. He fell forward, landing on Scott. As he fell the limb broke again, the break piercing Scott through the leg and pinning him to the ground. I rushed to his side, glancing back to see how far back the other beam of light was. I did not have enough time. I remained with Scott.

"Run Brian."

"No."

I tried to pull the limb out of the ground, but it was deep. The rain and mud had softened the ground which allowed the limb to penetrate deep into it. But the same mud and rain had formed suction, forbidding me to pull Scott free.

"Brian; when your dad gets here he will kill us both; please run."

"No Scott. I failed David. I won't fail you."

"So you'll die instead and then no one will know the truth about us, or even know we existed? Brian if you run you can survive and someday tell this story to someone, anyone who will listen. If you stay here and die with me, then who we were will never be known. David will die again." Scott said.

I turned back in the direction of my dad and noticed that the beam of light was getting closer.

"I'll buy you as much time as I can Brian. Besides I'm too hurt and I'm tired of living. If I were to survive the battle of this wilderness I'll just kill myself later. Brian; I don't want to live anymore anyway. It's better to just die than to live with what happened to us always in my mind." Scott reasoned.

"So I have to live with it in my mind? I asked.

Beams of light were now bouncing off the trees around me and Scott.

"Scott. I'm sorry for what my dad is and all that happened to us."

"Brian, tell this story to someone."

"See ya later Scott; no goodbyes."

"No goodbyes. Now it's your turn to run, so run Brian."

I stood up, looked down at Scott one last time and then ran. I ran as fast as I could through the rain, water and mud. The closer I got to the edge of the wilderness the easier it got for me to run. I did not want to hear Scott scream when my dad found him, so I ran faster.

The rain stopped, the wilderness grew quiet. I stopped to listen and heard nothing. Through the thinning trees the clouds started to allow slivers of moonlight to pass through. I could see the highway, I could see freedom, and I turned around. I ran back in the direction to where I had left Scott laying in the mud. Since I never heard him scream out I thought maybe my dad figured he was dead already, and I did not see a beam of light follow me after I ran away from Scott.

When I reached the spot where I had left Scott, he was gone. His step-dad's body still lay where it fell, but Scott was gone. I saw a set of boot prints walking back toward the tracks so I followed them. The boot prints stopped. I saw noting, and I could not find Scott.

"Who you looking for stupid?"

I didn't turn around, I knew who it was, and I could smell the stench of his cigarettes and whiskey. From his slurred speech I knew my dad was drunk. I ran and then curved back toward the highway. I never saw the tree when I made my turn back to the highway and I ran into it, scraping the right side of my face. The impact spun me around and I fell face first in the water and mud. The mud worked its way into the deep cuts of my face. I screamed out from the pain.

I scampered to my hands and knees, moving slowly to ensure I had not damaged anything else. I brought my hand to my face to wipe away the mud, but the act itself brought on more pain. I stood up and then turned around to find my dad standing behind me. He brought his fist down hard against the right side of my face and the open flesh. I screamed out again as I fell once more into the muddy marsh.

"I'm gonna leave your ugly butt out here Brian, to rot."

My dad said as he brought his boot into contact with my rib cage. I screamed out again, wondering why I turned back. I should have realized that dad finished Scott off and he was now lying face down in the muddy marsh somewhere.

"Just get it over with, just do it." I said through my clinched teeth.

"Not that easy. You have no idea what my life has been like because of you, do you? Brian I had it all, I had everything. 'You took my life so now I'm gonna take yours', and I will enjoy it.
"

"I was a baby; I had no choice in being born."

"No but it's because of you that I lost my life. There's not a day that goes by that I don't think about what you did to me."

"Then let me walk out of the wilderness. I'll blame everything on Scott's step-dad. You walk back to Avenue J. I'll leave your life. When I find help I'll give a fake name and say that I'm a run away or something. You can have your life." I offered.

"Nope Brian. See I can't play baseball now, it's gone forever, and so you'll be gone forever. Come on."

My dad reached down and grabbed me by my hair and started dragging me through the muddy marsh. I figured that he was taking me to where he took Scott. My shirts had suffered several tears through the wilderness, and being dragged through the muddy marsh with sticks and limbs passing under me ripped the rest of my shirts off. Scott and I had put on two for extra protection, and it worked to a point. Now my flesh was being torn from my back as my dad dragged me. He let go and dropped me in the mud.

"Stay there." My dad said, pointing at me while walking off.

"Now where did he go? I left him right here. SCOTT!" My dad yelled out.

I now knew Scott was still alive.

"If you see Scott, tell him to stay right here. I want you to watch me kill your friend, like you did David. Remember?"

I realized that my dad had gone crazy. For nine years he had been thinking about the life he lost, or what he thought he had. And for nine years he allowed that hate to fill his heart, and now he was intent to extract that hate out on me. I watched as my dad walked around in the muddy marsh looking for Scott and I was glad that he got away. My dad's revenge would be incomplete without Scott around.

I wanted to get up and run, but my dad kicked me in the same area of the ribs that he did weeks earlier. When I moved, my head would spin and part of my vision would go black. I could not possibly walk out of the wilderness. I pulled my body up so I could rest against a tree and watched my dad as he walked around in the muddy marsh. Every few steps he kicked mud and water up in the air in frustration. He walked back over to me.

"Where is he Brian?"

"How would I know?" I answered with sarcasm.

It was the wrong answer; he gave me another kick to the same side of my ribs.

"Get up."

"I can't. You busted my ribs and every time I move I nearly pass out."

"Pansy."

"SCOTT! Where are you? He's your friend; tell him to get over here." My dad told me.

"Ya right, like I'm just gonna help you."

"Why not, you did with David, both of you did."

The sound of the crack was louder than I had expected. My dad swayed and then fell face down in the water and thick mud. I watched him as he fell and when I looked back up I saw Scott standing there with a huge stick in his hand.

"Think he's dead?" Scott asked.

I looked over at my dad he was face down in the water, blood flowing from a gash in his head.

"It looks like he hit his head on a rock. Even if he ain't dead yet he will be. He's face down in the water."

"We best get going." Scott said as he held out his hand to me.

"I can't walk, he busted me up bad."

"Well look at me. Get up. We help each other."

Scott pulled me forward as much as he was able. I also pushed my back against the tree and walked myself to an upright position. Scott reached down and picked up the stick that he used to knock my dad off balance. Scott now used it as a cane. My dad still lay face down in the muddy marsh. By now he was dead from drowning.

I held on to Scott and Scott held on to me as we walked out of that wilderness on that clear bright morning of January first nineteen seventy seven. Together we had fought our own Battle of the Wilderness and together we walked out. As we exited the wilderness we saw a Denny's restaurant just off the highway, we both walked toward it, free of being Houston Boys.

Resources

With a story such as this, and as unbelievable as it sounds I feel it only right to tell you my source material. True the foundation is my own memories, but as everyone is aware, memories can't be trusted, completely.

Interviews
Susan Smith (Mother)
Holly Smith (Sister)
Josh
Donna (?) [Smith]
St. Andrews Catholic Church (Staff Member)
A retired agent in Galveston County Texas
Police officers
Uncle Mike

Records:
Hospital; Alta Loma Texas
Alta Loma Elementary School Texas
Police reports (Oklahoma & Texas)
Period News Paper Articles: Oklahoma and Texas
Period Personal Letters: Susan to her sister Mary
Period Personal Cards: Birthday Cards, Christmas Cards and personal cards
Misc. School Records: Oaktown; Oklahoma and Texas
Misc. Hospital Records: Oklahoma, Texas and other medical records from private doctors
Photos: Taken by family, friends and others
Videos: Taken by family and others
Internet Web Sites: Social media; area local sites; forums; and other sites
My Baby Book: Kept by my mother until I reached age six
Smith Family Tree Published May 1975
School Yearbooks: Oklahoma and Texas
Total time in collecting and researching the information contained in this account is equal to over seven years.

The End

Authors Reflection

Although the events and places in this novel have been fictionalized, they are based on my childhood. My birth dad died of cancer in 2010 or 2011, and with his death I felt a measure of release, although limited. Some in my family will nevertheless dispute how I have portrayed my dad, suggesting that he was never guilty of such acts, or one should not speak ill of the dead. Those that make such notions did not know him as well as he let me know him. My dad had several personalities, and he also knew how to turn them on and off at will.

My youngest sister whom I portrayed as 'Beth' in this account never died from when I stabbed her with a screwdriver. In reality the screwdriver just scraped her skin; my mother's scream stopped what could have happened. In the story I needed to find a way to remove 'Beth' early on to avoid issues that may arise with her. She continues to dispute some of the facts in this account. But I would like to point out that she spent most of her childhood with my mother. Very little of her childhood was spent living with my dad, and when she did he treated her as a princess. While I lived in Texas with my dad and during the time of the events fictionalized in this account she lived with my mother and never saw that side of my dad.

My oldest sister whom I portrayed as 'Holly' is still struggling with surviving day to day, I hope that she is somehow able to pull free from the life she has put herself in. I did interview two 'agents' and one reported to me that the route along Avenue J is believed to have as many as 3,000 cold case dumps, most from the decade of the 1970's. Many are cataloged as suicides, runaway's, accidental deaths or overdoses. Keep in mind that many of those 'miscataloged' were boys under thirteen years of age, and some under ten. In the decade of the 1970's many independent businesses in and around Houston Texas saw the profit in selling boys to visiting politicians, traveling business men and many other powerful men. There was no structure or organized crime, just some very smart and powerful business men that saw an opportunity to make money. That time period is dubbed 'The Houston Boys – Boy's for Sale' era.

When I moved to Texas at the age of 8 in 1975 for the first time, my dad was married to his second wife. She survived his attempted murder and later entered a protection program; she exited that program after his death. She reported to me in an interview that it was not because of my dad that she entered the protection program, but she only came out of it after he died. For a short period of time I returned to live with my mother, and then in 1976 at age 9 I moved back to Texas to live with my dad, alone. John was indeed real, but he was never dumped in the marshes, I added that because I can't forget when he raped me. He still resides in Texas; his son is a registered sex offender. 'Clifford' is a fictitious name for the person my dad worked for after breaking his leg, I can't use the man's real name. As of the copyright date of this book he is still living in Texas as a free man.

So you may be wondering just how fictionalized is this account? Of course names of people have been changed, and nearly every town name altered, but I made other changes as well. In every account given it reflects a combination of several accounts from my life. For example in Chapter 7 "I held my breathing steady", that account is the combination of many accounts. My mother did get stabbed at a bar, my step-dad was 'murdered' by a family member to protect my mother, I was hunted in the darkness of my home by my step-dad, and at one time I did get drenched in human blood from head to toe and not by choice. All those events however happened at different times, ages and places in my life. In the book "David's mark" I combined them into a single account. There's only one account in this entire novel that was not fictionalized, except for name changes and the omission of some details, and that account is the title of the book. I have been carrying the account of David around since I was 9 years old, and after the death of my dad I felt it was time to tell the story.

The last two chapters and portions toward the end are metaphorical. For example, Brain and Scott never in reality fought a battle in the wilderness as is portrayed in the novel. That battle was what the two of them had to endure throughout the rest of their childhood. I as the author am of course Brian. If you look at the profile on my book's you will notice I found some stability in my life, through my beliefs and my wife and friends. 'Scott' remained in Texas in the same area and took on work locally. To this day he still struggles; I shall not expound any further on 'Scott'. For many years, each October, I would give 'Scott' a call, but I realized there was nothing productive for him or me in continuing to do so, so I no longer call him.

As to a few other accounts in the novel, some are pure fiction to help move the story along, but only very mundane items. As an example; Scott and I never enter David's house to find his family members murdered. In the 1990's, in a private conversation, my dad told me what he did to David's sister and mother. As to his father, my dad never told me anything. So in the story I had me and Scott enter the house and find his family. The death of his sister and mother is as my dad told me; I had to create the death of David's dad. My dad also told me that he had to 'clean up the mess' after the job was done. There are few other minor details that were added, some were based on information that I was unable to confirm, but was reported to have happened. My life did not get better after 1977; but I don't believe it ever was as bad as it was that year of 1976. Although I was still abused in every manner one could think of after 1977, what happened in 1976 was the worse it ever got, from my point of view. It was the death of David that released me from being a 'Houston Boy', for that reason alone my life got a small fraction better, but I still carry the memories of that event. Some of the events depicted in this account happened after 1977 and I combined them into the account. So you can now understand why I call this 'fiction'.

I had an excellent editor on this project, although his advice was painful, it was advice that had to be adapted to make the book something that could be published. I had spent seven years collecting data and information about my life, and with that information I wrote my autobiography, something that will never be published in anyone's lifetime. Some things are just not fit to be read. The accounts in this novel are adaptations of that autobiography, and in my first draft I had thought I did a good job of scrubbing. But I was incorrect. My editor suggested that two entire events be pulled completely, they were just too graphic. I emailed him back letting him know that I felt they were needed for the story to be developed properly, he countered that it would not alter the story at all. Both of his suggestions were taken. Later I had discussed the scrubbed accounts with a third professional and he agreed it was the correct choice to remove them as my editor suggested. My editor also suggested scrubbing some of the accounts that were left in even more than I did, which I did. One account that I really did not want to scrub was when John raped me. In the first draft I had just copied the account from my autobiography and then scrubbed it. My editor suggested scrubbing it more. In the end I saw the need to remove most of the account and what I have left is sufficient to help tell what lead up to the account with David. My mother in reality was never as cruel as she is depicted in this account, but the 'mother' in this account is a compilation of several people I encountered growing up.

I did study physics and time travel hoping to find a way to beat the odds and travel back in time, and I also would lie in bed many nights begging God to let me go back and save myself. But as I mentioned in the novel, we are the sum total of our life's events. I would love to believe that if my life had been cookie cutter perfect that I would still end up where I am today. Although I suffer from flashbacks, nightmares, and still have a very hard time loving myself, I'm pleased with where I ended up.

I never did get my Ken doll. In reality I called my mother nearly every year asking her about it, for decades in fact. But it was not until I was 46 that I stopped asking her. The last time I asked her she told me that she could not afford a Ken doll from 1973, I told her I understood. She is after all 70 years of age at time of copyright and living on a fixed budget. It was just the 6 year old boy that was still holding on to hope, the adult in me had to let go.

I by no means survived unscathed, as one might expect. I think of it in this manner. If one gets a deep gash or is cut by a knife or stabbed, the wound heals, but leaves behind a scar. In some cases those scars are on the face and visible to all, in others clothing can cover them up. I have the former, scars all over my face. I can't hide or disguise what happened, it's just always there. Sometimes people ask, sometimes I share, and I'm reminded every time I look at myself in a mirror.

There are of course many years of my life not covered in this account, as I said this is just an excerpt from my autobiography, and most of what happened to me after age 9 simply can't be published.

So there it is. Accept it as it is or just set it aside and try to forget it. Either way it was what happened to one little boy in the

1960's and 1970's. And until I die or this world ends, I will carry the scar of guilt because of David's mark.

Kathy had a choice; suffer the shame of embarrassment & disgrace or save her pride. She chose her pride. The cost to her family was dark. For 6 years the evil of that choice stalked the family; only to be exposed by "The Wood".

"The Boy in The Wood" takes a dark look at the lengths a person will go to save themselves & their lifestyle. How far would you go? Read "The Boy in The Wood".

"The Boy in The Wood"
A Psychological Thriller by
~DeWayne Watts~

Available at Amazon.com

The 1st 6 years of Brian's life was perfect. But on his 6th birthday a storm of evil was unleashed. For the next 2 years his life grew darker. At age 8 he made 3 new friends. But the evil resurfaced. 4 boys, 1 would betray; 1 would die; 2 would fight for their lives. Why? The mark of David. Read "David's mark" To learn the truth about life in Houston Texas during the 1970's

"David's mark"
A Psychological Thriller by
~ DeWayne Watts ~

Livingston author pens psychological thriller

Follow DeWayne on Twitter:
@DeWayne_Watts &
Facebook:
dewayne.watts.758

Keep up to date via the Official Blog:
www.dewaynewatts.com

Check out my other books on amazon.com under DeWayne Watts

Visit and leave feedback on my Blog at www.dewaynewatts.com
Or
Twitter: DeWayne_Watts
Or
Facebook: www.facebook.com/dewayne.watts.758

Made in the USA
Charleston, SC
18 May 2014